MOTHERS, FATHERS & LOVERS

RUBY SOAMES

First published in 2024 by Bloodhound Books.

www.bloodhoundbooks.com

Print ISBN: 978-1-916978-64-5

To Jon, Bluebell, Edison
and in memory of Elvis (1999–2014)

The Mating Game is a never-ending arms race of romantic scepticism and excess.
— Geoffrey Miller, *Mating Intelligence*

What's past is prologue.
— William Shakespeare, *The Tempest*

If love is the answer, could you please rephrase the question?
— Lily Tomlin

PART ONE

LIFEWRECKED

Stop. Right there. Stop right there. There – that's the restore point. The time and place before it all happened: Wednesday, 12th September 2013, at 7.56am on the Central Line, London.

That was me. The girl standing on the Tube on my way to work in a peacock-blue dress with orange-painted toenails because it was still warm enough to wear bare legs with sandals. Me, hugging the designer handbag my boyfriend had given me for Christmas. Employed, in love, running late, busy, perfumed, so *stressed*. Before I had any idea what stress meant. Everything was right then. I just didn't know it.

'California has dolphins, hot water springs, deserts, open-all-night cupcake bars,' Joseph had said the weekend before when he was trying to convince me to move to Hollywood with him. We'd been lying on our makeshift roof terrace in Stoke Newington with Elvis, our dog, curled up between us. Elvis had just licked our plates clean from that day's barbecued lunch – Joseph: pork spare ribs; me, grilled tofu – when Joe's agent, Rebecca Hobson, called saying she'd found him a beautiful five-bedroomed house in Westwood with a pool, gym and landscaped garden.

'Move to LA? We live *here* – we've only just finished doing up the flat.'

'Babe, I know, but it's where the film business is. This is it for me – it's *now*… and it's *there*. Rebecca says we have to capitalise on this moment if we really want to make it big.'

'Make what *big*?' I sat up, put my hand on his shoulder so he'd look at me. 'Joe?' He'd closed his eyes earlier because of the sun's glare but he kept them shut because he didn't want his plan derailed. 'You always said you didn't need to "make it big", you just wanted "to act" – did you change your mind or did Rebecca?'

Joseph took my hand. 'Sparkles, for some bizarre reason people are fighting to give me ridiculous amounts of money to do what I love – I'm not going back to washing dishes.'

His acting wasn't that good he could hide the fact he'd already made up his mind.

'I don't want to look back on my life and have regrets. Sweetheart, all I'm saying is that we could go and live there. For a bit. For an adventure? Just to see. If we don't like it, we come back.'

Playback. Of course I'd have gone anywhere with Joseph, I'd even told my best friend, Kamilla, that I was getting excited about a new life in the US but I wanted Joseph to appreciate the sacrifices I'd make, and, honestly, I was starting to resent how much his agent was becoming the puppet master of our lives.

'But there's a chance I might be offered a partnership, Joe. What about all our friends? Elvis? The campaign for rescue animals? My mother? Kamilla? *My* dreams?'

Joseph, who'd recently been voted that year's 'World's Sexiest Man', lifted himself up to sitting position in one move – just one of the benefits of his personal trainer's fitness regime. He drew me against him.

'I know it's a risk, but…' He brushed his lips with my fingers. 'Stella, there's something I want to ask–'

'Your car's here – let's get you packed.'

A few days later, on that muggy Wednesday morning in rush hour on the Tube, passengers crammed up against each other, methane-morning breath, doing little two-steps around each other wondering whether we were crushing someone's toe or if it were safe to raise an arm to clutch the handrail and expose blooming sweat patches, I admit it, a life in California had some plus points. A lot, actually.

The girl next to me tapped out text messages as if she'd only a few seconds left to live. Tourists puzzled out ads for language schools while the rest of us gazed at the offers for faraway holiday destinations. And I was already missing Joseph.

He'd left that Sunday afternoon for Delhi. After we'd said our goodbyes, his driver had squared his cap onto his head and closed the Bentley's doors between us. Joseph's last words to me were, '*Please* – just *think* about it.'

So I was 'thinking about' starting a new chapter with Joseph in LA.

That was when there was a 'Joseph and I', at around 7.47 that morning.

Although Joseph was over 4,000 miles away, I caught his face on the second page of a newspaper one of the passengers was reading.

My Joe... and *Sylvia.*

Sylvia Amery was Joseph's current co-star. He'd already told me what a nightmare she was – how her food had to be prepared by a Brahmin dietician, how her dog had a designer wardrobe and his own masseuse, how she had a permanent suite in America's most expensive rehabilitation centre. What *now*? I wondered, waiting for the man across from me to lift his paper up so I could carry on reading.

The train doors were closing on the passengers getting off at Tottenham Court Road when I saw the headline:

Joe West Meets Hot Love in the East!

The train jigged through a tunnel. Lights flickered. A couple who hadn't spoken or looked at each other moved to the doors to make a quick getaway. So now there were four people between the headline and me. Nuzzling up to someone's crotch, I strained to read more:

> Joseph West took Sylvia to the Taj Mahal at sunrise to propose. 'My love is even bigger than this,' he'd said before pulling out an enormous diamond and sapphire engagement ring and asking the 24-year-old 'Rear of the Year' to marry him. The couple have been–

Joseph? Engagement ring? To the yappy-little-dog woman? Out of the tunnel again.

I elbowed a push-chair mum out of the way so I could hold the newspaper steady. I trained my eyes over the next paragraph despite the man trying to shake the paper loose.

> ...enough to make any princess swoon! Sylvia's mother spoke from her ranch in Wyoming: 'They have so much respect for each other as artists and as human beings. I'm thrilled we're going to have a Brit in the family!'

I blinked over the words, willing the story to change. It didn't.

There was an aerial shot of the home Joseph and Sylvia were buying in Beverly Hills. Valued at $2.5 million.

The train stopped. The reader jerked the paper out of my fingers, folded it and pardoned his way off the Tube.

At 8.03am I staggered out of St Paul's station with my phone listing *22 Missed Calls* while a *Pop-Alert!* announced Joseph West's engagement to Sylvia Amery. I didn't recognise any of the numbers apart from my mother's. I shot off the same message to Joseph on every media platform I had access to with the same question:

Engaged? WTF?

At the newspaper stand I tore through a selection of tabloids and learnt that they'd fallen in love on the film set and her chihuahua saw him as a positive male role model. In one magazine there was a picture of them holding hands at an elephant sanctuary where she'd named an orphan elephant 'Ellie'. Another showed a photo of Joseph with his arm around Sylvia at a spice market. I could argue with the words, but not the pictures.

2

Scrolling through my phone to find any word from Joseph, I was just about to cross the road to my law firm when I saw a group of people jostling each other outside the main doors. It looked like the end of a fire drill, when we have to congregate awkwardly on the pavement looking as if we're desperate to get back to something very important – but then I saw the cameras, sound booms, notepads and heard phones chiming – they were journalists and it was likely I had something to do with it.

The last I'd heard from Joseph was a text from India to say he'd arrived, filming was starting earlier than expected and they'd be moving around, he ended it saying he'd be in touch in a few days with details of his hotel because his SIM card wouldn't work out there. I had to speak to Joseph and if anyone knew where he was, it would be Rebecca Hobson. His agent was only a few years older than me but her reputation for killer ruthlessness was already legendary. Joseph was her hottest client and her chance to break into the American market.

I crouched in a shop doorway, found her telephone number on her website and put a call through. A chain of PAs connected me.

'Hi, Rebecca? It's Stella – I need to speak to Joseph, I–'

'Who?'

'Stella. Joseph's girlfriend…? We met at that award dinner last month? I'm just calling because I can't seem to reach him. I need to–'

'Right. Stella. Yup. Sorry, why are you calling?'

'I need to speak to–'

Click. Speakerphone off and Rebecca's voice went from a spacy echo to a sound which came across very sharp and clear.

'He's in India. He's filming. He's very busy.'

'I know, but this is kind of an emergency. The press seem to think he's engaged to someone on the set, and,' I threw in a little laugh to illustrate the ludicrousness of such a story, 'there are reporters outside my work – I don't know what to do.'

'What do you mean, you "don't know what to do"?'

'I need him – or you – or whoever – to stop this story. You have to tell them–'

'Listen, Stella. I shouldn't be the one to tell you this but, when it's over, it's over. What you "do" is *move on* – I've another call waiting.'

'But we–'

Click.

I shook my phone, banged it against my palms, my thighs, anything to release a parachute out of this freefall of hurt. But still, nothing from Joseph.

I plodded towards the main doors of Forrester Levine's until someone shouted my name from the other side of the road and a mob holding up cameras ran – and I mean *ran* – towards me. In seconds I was being swallowed up by flashing lights, shouts, elbows, phones, fingers. At one point my feet weren't even touching the ground until Carl, our doorman, yanked me through the doors.

'You all right?' he asked when I got my breath back.

'No,' I answered, avoiding the faces pressed up to the glass doors.

'I hope your man's worth it, Miss Tyler,' said Carl, shaking his head at the racket going on outside.

Forrester Levine were no strangers to the media, dealing regularly as they did with high-profile cases. Having said that, I doubt many of its lawyers had been personally ambushed by journalists. Walking down the corridor to my office, my colleagues seemed particularly occupied as we exchanged 'Hellos', 'Mornings!'.

I hadn't been at my desk long when Angie, the secretary I shared with two others, stood in front of me. I could tell she was about to give me bad news because she drew out the word 'Hi' for as long as she could without passing out. It was even accompanied by a little wave. I said 'Hi' in return, but she didn't move from the doorway.

'Ange, if it's about Joe… whatever you read, it's a load of… you know that, right?'

'It's not about Joseph.'

'So, what's "it" about?'

'Yeah…' she said, looking around the room for support.

'Ange?' Getting information out of her was like prizing a sock from the jaw of a playful puppy.

'Mr Forrester wants to see you.' She looked around for thunder to strike. 'As soon as possible.' And she fled the room.

3

Whenever I heard the name Angus Forrester I saw the first three seconds of an MGM film where the lion roars out of the gold frame. Angus stood at six foot six with a wild blond mane and booming voice – everyone, apart from his partner, Daniel Levine, was terrified of him. So as soon as I'd been summoned, I was in his office overlooking the Thames, sitting in the same chair I'd been hired from.

'Stella, I'm sure you've not encouraged the media attention in any way but you've got it. And so, now, *we've* got it,' he growled. 'And for us it's an untenable situation. Of course, at Forrester Levine we're used to the buzz and we know it'll all blow over, but it's a problem, young lady. I appreciate it's not a lark for you either, but we can't have clients afraid to enter the building, staff being called up by journalists or the firm's name linked with a public figure and his red-carpet shenanigans.'

He'd not complained when I'd got his niece tickets to Joseph's last premiere.

'The partners and I suggest you spend some time away. The terms will be more than generous if you agree to take a short leave of absence – no contact with any other law firm, of course, no discussion of cases, clients, you know the patter – this has nothing to do with how much we value your dedication, productivity and–'

'Suggest? Doesn't sound like I've a choice.'

Angus Forrester stretched his fingers flat against the table and aligned his hands together as though assuring me the claws were in. There was a short silence while my fury gathered into a black cloud ready to break over his flaming halo.

'No, in *this* you don't have much choice.'

I'd been meticulous in keeping my private life out of my

11

professional world and couldn't believe that, on the morning when every indication pointed to Joseph and me splitting up, I was being sacked for his alleged infidelity. Wasn't Angus supposed to be on the side of justice?

'I see.'

He picked up his weighty Mont Blanc pen and signed his side of the contract. He pushed the pages over for me. I pretended to read it, but the figures and terms meant nothing. *Stella Tyler*, I wrote and dated.

'There,' I said.

'As I said, it's only a temporary solution to distance ourselves from the dramas surrounding your personal life.'

It was then that I wondered what I was doing in his office. Although Joseph West's career was the most important matter in my life, it wasn't of such national importance as to interest Mr Forrester who, just a few weeks before, had been to dinner with the Obamas.

'Right! With that out of the way, let's open some new doors!' he roared. 'Stella.' He lowered his spectacles down his nose and looked over them at me. 'We'd be very proud if, after you take off a little time, you would accept a partnership at Forrester Levine.'

I was stunned.

'Oh, don't look too surprised. Your work over the last two years has been outstanding.'

'But Claire. Claire's going to be the next...' Angus shook his head from side to side as I stammered. 'I just thought, because...'

He nodded left and right and back and forth limbering up for his next pounce.

'The lawyers we have chosen to work at Forrester Levine are all of the highest quality, but we've been particularly impressed by your work on some of the mobile technology cases – deals that aren't as "sexy" as others, but intricate and demanding and, let's be real here, lucrative. We need you to keep cutting us a path forward through the wires, the fibres and the waves into our future here at Forrester Levine.' On this note, Angus Forrester rose up and extended his paw towards me.

When I didn't move, he sat down again.

'Not the time for congratulations?'

'I'm *surprised.*'

He glanced at his Omega. 'I heard you were a savvy negotiator. Lincoln's office not big enough for you, eh? Even with a view of the Barbican? HR will run you through how the share options work and there's a little bit of paperwork to tidy up. Let me know when's a good time to make the formal announcement, I know you've got a lot on your plate, but,' he stood up again, 'congratulations.'

'The partnership should go to Claire.'

'Maybe. The obvious choice, yes. Oxford debating team, billing hours and client profile, length of service…'

'You'd risk losing her to give me the partnership?' A Thames riverboat chugged through the roiling waters behind him. 'Why?'

He leant back in his chair to view me from a wider perspective.

'I have five children,' he said, looking at the picture of his wife and their pile of cubs on an Aspen slope. 'When we were considering hiring you, we checked your background – your provenance. Fatherless, raised in difficult circumstances on a council estate, top at university and law school – *I* know what that takes.' I'd already heard this from him, but not what he was going to say next: 'It was recently brought to my attention that your mother made a paternity claim against a Henry Hardwick, QC.' He stopped to acknowledge my discomfort. 'Maybe you've never had contact with the man, but our blood drives us, Ms Tyler. Claire Myers has peaked, but I'm pretty sure that you, Stella, you haven't even started. I'm willing to gamble that with a little more rocket fuel under you–'

'I'll just take a severance contract. I've never met Henry Hardwick but I'm pretty sure we're nothing alike.' The more stunned he looked, the more I went on. 'I've more to give, yes, but not to this firm. I want to work with animals, and grow things, and engender kindness and love. I want to get out of this world of celebrity, disposable culture, status worship and wasteful, hateful greed. We are not evolving in the right direction. I don't want a future in information technology – it's just all… *lies*.'

Angus chuckled. 'I've touched a nerve with the father thing. Apologies. It was a little bit of a fight getting everyone to agree to take you on in the beginning: your atypical background, the rabbit in your office, thespian paramour and your *mother*… but I still believe we need you just as much as the planet does.' He stood up again to shake my hand. 'Okay. Take the time off. Think about our offer. Don't make any rash decisions.'

'You once said that you admired my "decision making". I've decided. This is my last day here.'

4

Carl held open a black plastic sack for me to throw in the last five years of my life while colleagues made regretful, emoticon faces and murmured, 'G'luck, Stella.' No time for a whip-round and 'Sad You're Leaving Us' card.

Dragging my box of belongings down the corridor one last time, Claire rushed towards me.

'I just don't get–'

One finger to my lips, the other pointed to the toilets.

Once inside, we inspected each cubicle like secret agents before nodding the all-clear.

'I quit.'

'Because of Joseph and–?'

'No! No, that's just fake news. Because I want to set up an animal protection association and–'

'But this is a *job* – you planning on living off dog food? Seriously? And Joseph – have you been following him on Twitter?'

'He doesn't write any of that. It's the publicity department.'

'But the photos, they don't–'

Helen Mallard, Mergers & Acquisitions, came in talking to someone.

'...could hardly have expected Joseph West to keep his trousers up with all that temptation. She must be... Stella! How *are* you, darling?'

'Just wondering how you cope with the temptation to put your nose into everyone's business and broadcast your cheap, received opinions. Oh, and next time you blabber to the tabloids about me, don't call yourself a "close" friend, because neither of us even like you.'

I tried to slam the door but with the fire-safety mechanism there was just a slow wheeze shutting after Helen's stunned face.

Claire followed me to the lifts where the receptionists were huddled around a screen before snapping back to life and smiling far too sweetly at me.

'Could you let Carl know I'll need help getting all this into a taxi?'

Claire waited with me, wringing at her already wrinkled shirt.

'Fancy staying at my place? I'll take the day off, we can get drunk and watch slushy films?'

'Thanks, hon, but I've got to get Joseph to refute this stupid story. He warned me the publicity for this film would be crazy but this is just too much.'

'Yeah, you guys are tight,' she said without conviction. 'Let me know if there's anything I can do.'

The lift pinged open and I started sliding my boxes in, including a forty-litre packet of premium soft-straw bedding.

Happy.

'There is something.'

'What?'

'Would you look after Happy?'

'The rabbit? Oh, Stella… when people ask if there's anything they can do, they don't *mean* it.'

'Just a little while?'

Claire scratched her head. 'I guess. Just a little while…'

'You'll be the first partner with a rabbit hutch in her office.'

'Partner?'

'Just keep him away from predators.'

Claire touched my arm, gently, unsteadily, as you might a body in a coffin, and I took my last flight down to the ground floor of Forrester Levine.

Carl loaded my stuff into a taxi which was waiting for us at the rear entrance and soon I was inching through the city traffic. I gripped my phone tight, begging Joseph to call. I tried not to look at anything about Joseph and Sylvia online but couldn't help seeing on his 'official' website:

A close friend revealed that Joseph had been unhappy in his relationship with long-term university pal, Stella Tyler, 26, a corporate lawyer with whom he shared a bedsit in north London.

I didn't know we had so many close friends.

Outside the 'bedsit in north London', there was another frenzy of journalists and the familiar collection of teenagers who'd been camping there for the last year.

The cabbie pointed to my door.

'Must have some pretty fancy neighbours.'

'Could you just drive around the block again?'

I didn't want the *fancy* boyfriend everyone was looking for, I wanted the Joseph I'd met and fallen in love with five years ago, the one I had a direct line to and who'd always been there for me, the man I'd planned to spend my life with – and hadn't he said something about an important question he wanted to ask me?

We drove around the block three times. The taxi driver whistled as he asked if we were to go around yet again. As the journalists and fans surrounded the taxi I took out my wallet, it was empty.

'Could you take me to the nearest bank?'

He grunted as we detoured to a cashpoint where I stood for several minutes trying to remember my PIN number.

Back in the cab, he asked, 'So what're all those photographers doing outside your building then?'

'They're waiting for Joseph West's girlfriend.'

'Oh!' He smiled into the rear-view mirror. 'She's that Sylvia Amery, ain't she?'

'Go round one more time.'

'Right-e-oh.'

5

Home. 11.03am.

I'd only left the flat a few hours ago yet nothing felt the same. It could've been a stage set, the props of our lives arranged around the rooms we called home: Joe's jacket on the back of the chair, photos of us on the shelves and the little notes we'd written to each other trapped under cheery fridge magnets from places we'd been together.

I'd ignored the rumours at first. When the Helen Mallards of this world would say, *He seems to get on so well with his leading ladies, doesn't he?* And I'd go through the lines that Joseph had drilled into me: everyone involved in a film project was sealed in a passionate, soul-searching other dimension for weeks, often months, – of course they'd get close – it's essential for the best performance. I'd seen it over and over again, ever since university productions when he'd be intensely intimate with his drama friends, all those days rehearsing, the trust games, the after-hours drinking sessions, intimate revelations, and then the first-night parties, the second-night parties, reading the reviews together hungover at breakfast, and the last-night party – but by the final curtain call, Joseph was onto the next play and could barely remember their names. I was always there though: the constant, the devoted, his number-one fan.

And I'd read about him and various women too – I'd saved everything written about Joseph for our children and their children. It was part of the collage of his life and made sense that sometimes he went to first-night openings with co-stars: I often worked late and wanted him to get the best exposure he could. Rebecca Hobson was quite persistent about how important it was to keep his *name out there* and being seen out with other beautiful stars did that. Despite what people read into our relationship, Joseph had always insisted I was the light of his life, his *Sparkles*.

If only I'd said yes when he asked me to go to America with him. If only I'd let him ask that question. *If only* – no one wants to hear those useless words.

The door buzzer went every few minutes and an image of the reporters' throng repeatedly lit up the intercom monitor. Every time, there were more of them. If I could get through to Joseph and have him refute the rumour, I could go out there, set the record straight and have my life back.

I found the piece of paper on which Joe had scribbled the name of the hotel he was staying at in Delhi. I tapped in the number and asked for Elvis East, his latest code name. I checked my watch: it would be late afternoon. Most likely he'd be on set but it was worth a try.

'I'm afraid there's no answer, Madame. Please try again later.'

'I have a very important message for Elvis East – could I try him in Ms Amery's room?'

The man hesitated. I heard the flicking of pages and him tapping the phone. 'It's *really* urgent…'

A click and I heard Joseph's voice answer, 'Hello?'

'Joe! Finally, it's–'

Then I heard a woman in the background. 'Who is it?'

End Call.

If I needed evidence, that was it.

I texted:

> Congratulations on your engagement. Stella.
> And Elvis.

I'd sworn never to let a man break my heart and end up the way my mother had. But there I was. It had been impossible not to love Joseph and so easy to let our lives merge; Joseph and

Stella, and then three, Joseph, Stella and Elvis, our dog. Now it was just me and the dog.

Rebecca was right: it was over.

Wednesday, 12th September 2013, 2.19pm.

Before things got even worse.

Kamilla jumped down from a ladder then stamped clumps of plaster from her steel-capped boots.

'Why aren't you at work?'

'I quit.'

'You're gonna move to LA! Fantastic!'

'Not quite.'

'Okay, so what are they saying about Joseph *today*? He's gay? He's an alien? He's–'

'Getting married.'

'That's a new one.'

'It's true.'

Kamilla curled her weighty black hair around a stubby HB pencil, pinning it off her face.

'I'll be out front, guys. Come on, Zorro,' she called to her dog who'd once belonged to a crack dealer who'd beaten it half to death.

Outside the building, I shivered despite the T-shirt weather as Kamilla lit up a pre-prepared rollie which had been waiting behind her ear. Two guys in a red sports car drove by and whistled at us.

'A few days ago he wanted to marry you, you really believe he's shagging someone else?'

'Sylvia Amery.'

'That why you packed in your job? Don't tell me – they offered you a partnership?' she joked. 'Man, you serious?' Kamilla blew on the tip of her cigarette.

'Angus Forrester wanted to give me the promotion because he saw the link to that guy, Henry Hardwick, the one my mum thinks is my dad and–'

'And you freaked. What a surprise! Someone touches on *The*

Big Secret and you're out. Know what? Joe was asking you to marry him but you dodged the question, was it because you can't face the idea of a wedding? I bet it is. Then your work want to promote you, so you leave. I love you – you know that – but all this self-sabotage, it's just so frustrating!'

'Fuck off!'

'You can't stay a kid forever. Life is out there. Nothing's gonna change till you face what you're running from. I get that–'

'You don't *get* anything, you're just like everyone else: so star-struck with Joe's success – even *you*!'

'What?' Kamilla threw down her half-smoked cigarette to the ground. 'You really think…?'

'So why are you taking Joseph's side? He bought Sylvia an engagement ring! They're house-hunting! They adopted an elephant together! And I'm the mad one because my dad fucked off before I was born?'

'Wait, what–'

'Don't pretend to care anything about me when you're just trying to find excuses to get closer to Joe. You're no different from all those paparazzis, tabloid readers and gossip-mongers.'

'Stella, it's *you*! You more than anyone who's been affected by the fame thing, and you're letting it destroy you, can't you see–'

But I was already walking quickly down the street, hating Kamilla more than I had at seven years old.

Kamilla, up until 3.22pm that day, had been my best friend, but before that, my worst enemy. Growing up in Tennyson Tower, Chelsea, Kamilla and her friend, Aisha, had been co-leaders of a gang of pre-schoolers who'd made my life a misery with their name-calling and pelting me with whatever she could find on the stairwell.

'Where's your dad, Snow Whitey?' her friend Aisha would snarl, or give the more effective, 'They locked your looney mum up yet?'

And then came the day of the pigeon.

Aisha and her little gang had got hold of one of her brother's BB guns and were shooting at birds, cats, homeless people or cyclists. I could see them from my window but was too late to stop a young pigeon being struck. It collapsed to the ground. While they were whooping at their hit and looking for the next target, I ran down to save its life. I knew what it was like to be hounded by those girls and had accepted what I had to go through but couldn't stand by to see it happen to a bird that'd just been cooing in the sun.

Holding its limp, warm body in my hands, Kamilla stood over me.

'Maybe we can take it to the hospital?'

Kamilla and I carried the pigeon to accident and emergency at Chelsea and Westminster Hospital. When the receptionist saw that we'd brought a bird into the building she didn't waste time ushering us out into the car park where she told us to wait until someone called Kamilla's dad to come and collect us. One of the nurses had overheard what was going on, got in touch with a friend of hers, Maeve, a trainee vet from Limerick and volunteer at an animal rescue centre. She arrived at the same time as

Kamilla's dad, winding down her car window and letting the air blow through her mass of orange hair. 'You the two girls with a sick pigeon?' She got out of her car with a large black medical bag. 'Right.' She took the bird in her hands. 'He's in a bad way.'

'We think someone might have hit it with something… like a BB gun.'

'We'll get to that. But what worries me is this foot – can you see his toes are all bound up – probably why he couldn't get away when he was attacked. See that toe? He might lose that one.'

The long plastic string that's often attached to bin liners was tightly bound around his claw. Maeve opened her bag and took out some tweezers, a metal implement, and a small pair of scissors.

We were so absorbed in the operation we hadn't noticed Marek parking his van.

'Who's sick?'

'*He* is, Tata,' said Kamilla, her eyes still glistening with tears.

'That's a fuckin' pigeon.'

'I am aware of that, yes,' said Maeve, not looking up.

'I've been called from work cos of a bloody bird?' No one answered him, too riveted by Maeve's medical intervention. Marek slouched over to us. He was – and still is – a big man: blond, green-eyed and intensely muscular. He wasn't used to being ignored.

'They said, *Hospital. Emergency.* You tellin' me this is the emergency?'

'He's almost paralysed,' Maeve explained, tugging at the claw.

'It's a pigeon, lady! Just another dirty, diseased and shitting London pigeon.' He moved over to us, his arms folded across his chest.

'Do you realise,' said Maeve, pausing from the bird to address Marek, 'that a great proportion of London pigeons are in agonising pain because their feet have got caught in human hair? String? Plastic? Rubbish we leave lying in the streets?' Kamilla looked back at her incredulously. 'They pull at it to get free and the problem gets worse. All it takes is…' Maeve cut and tweezed and gradually the bird started to bounce towards Marek's van, where it released a long, verdigris-coloured shit.

'Oh, great. Thanks, lady – you gonna clean that? Kids, get in.'

'You know before we had telephones, a postal service and fax machines we relied on pigeons? Do you know that battles were won, families kept in touch, information was spread because pigeons can use magnetic fields that we still can't even begin to understand?'

'They taste good too.'

'And pigeon parents mate for life. And they would *never* leave their babies unattended.' Maeve handed us her card as Marek started to drive away. 'Call me if you ever see an animal being abused, neglected or hurt.'

Later, curled up in pyjamas on Kamilla's bed after her mum had run us a bath and made dinner, she said, 'I know about your mum and that. You can always come here. Maybe we could be, like, best friends?'

Still stomping through London, not able to go home but not able to keep still, my phone went again. Another *Unknown Caller ID*.

'Why can't you leave me alone? Why–'

'Stella? It's Zoe Preston. Bad news, I'm afraid.' I held the phone from my ear and wondered what could, at this point, be considered *bad* news.

'My mum's had a stroke. She's in the IC ward.'

'Sorry, but who is–'

'My mum's Dot – Dot Preston – she looks after your dog. You

need to come pick him up before six tonight cos I'm in a darts tournament in Toxteth.'

'Dot! I'm so sorry. Yes, I'll be–'

'There are quite a few other dogs here too, ones that she walks – I don't know who they all belong to. Two small ones, a Pekinese wearing a nappy, and a Dalmatian on a lot of tranquillisers, but they're starting to wear off and he's getting a bit... lively.' From the racket I could hear in the background, *lively* was a heavy understatement. 'Mum might be in hospital for a while... Ouch! When can you get here?'

PART TWO

MOTHERS

8

Four months later, I wake up every day hoping I'll be back there, on the rooftop with Joseph trying to persuade me to go dolphin spotting off the Pacific coast. Instead, I'm outside the park toilets pulling Elvis away from sniffing Cha-Cha's bum. She's a long-haired Pekinese with a black melanistic mask. Elvis has fancied her ever since she joined the party of dogs I walk. I don't know what she did in a previous incarnation but it must have been exceptional for she lives a very splendid life gazing from velvet cushions in her Holland Park home where she sleeps in a miniature brass bed. She's way out of Elvis' league. I've read that males are hardwired to overestimate their attractiveness to women but still, it pains me to watch him pawing at her while she looks over his ears for a prospective mate with better fitness indicators. Cha-Cha's molestation only comes to an end when her owner skittles out adjusting his belt.

'Can you believe it? Middle of January – I've got bollocks on the rocks but at least, some sun!' Simon waves his hands in the air as if they're solar pads. Then he stops, shakes his head, I know he's going to say something. Simon's been aware that something's seriously wrong with his dog walker, aka me. I've not washed my hair for so long it's moved into a self-cleaning phase, same principle as drinking yourself sober. I'm wearing the old coat that used to line the dogs' basket in the back of my van and my cuticles are peeling away from the flesh. There are slivers of nail around the edges which catch on to everything like fishhooks. This is what's causing Simon distress. I can say that because I know how much he spends on manicures. Hands matter to Simon. He even greases his left thumb with Vaseline so the dog's lead doesn't chafe.

Graciously, humbly, and very cautiously, he picks up my gnawed sleeves.

'I saw Joseph on the Portobello Road on… let's see, Tuesday and,' he breathes in before bursting out, 'he told me all about it.'

A sword of icy air cuts into the back of my throat. I feel like some unwitting guest of a talk show waiting behind the split screen while the audience hears all about me.

'You poor, poor little lamb! Oh, why can't loving someone be enough? It should be, but we get in all these muddles, don't we?'

'Guess so.'

He squeezes my raw hand.

'And you just can't go anywhere without seeing his face plastered on all the buses or on our screens – those soulful eyes. I saw a picture of them both skiing in Val d'Isère, made me sick! It was the first *Heat* magazine I didn't buy. Out of respect. Must be horrendous, pet.'

'No, no.' I look at Elvis because I can't lie and look someone in the eye at the same time. 'It was a mutual thing.'

A man strides after his Great Dane and gives me a wave. 'All right, Zeus?' I call to the dog.

Simon sighs. 'Thing is, it's the dogs that suffer most.'

We both look down at Elvis, the most recent addition to single-parent quadrupeds. Cha-Cha dodges Elvis' relentless adoration. She can probably smell from his anal glands that his mum's a loser without having to read what Joseph's fans said about me in their chat rooms.

'Joseph and I, we've been moving in different directions and he's got so much on – with LA, the BAFTA, promoting the film and – and I need a little air, too, y'know.'

'Oh I know. We all need air… but what you really need, pumpkin, is a holiday. A few weeks away to get your life into perspective – get away from all this stuff about Joseph West and… and *her*.'

'A holiday. Yeah.'

Simon lowers his sunglasses over his nose. 'Here's what we'll do: Donny's model agency brings out a monthly catalogue of all the boys on their books, we can scroll through it and any man you like the look of, we'll invite for dim sum, hmm, would you like that?' He tugs Cha-Cha away from an empty crisp packet. 'But you'll have to do something about your hair, doll.'

I thank him, trying to rally a hearty tone.

'You'll be round the usual time Tuesday then, for the little princess?' He looks at me uncertainly.

9

A cold, steely lid closes over this morning's little tease of blue sky. The ground is hard and muddied, the squirrels look mean and skinny and the peacocks bedraggled. It's all very clear: I want to be with Joseph. He doesn't want to be with me, and that's all there is to it.

This time last year I wouldn't have been sitting in a park on my own, I'd have been putting deals together at work, recovering from nights out with friends and getting in treats for the brief moments when Joseph returned home, exhausted and elated from filming. I'd meet him at the airport if I could or he'd be delivered by a private chauffeur, and we'd stay in, making cups of tea, watching films, ordering take-outs or getting the best table at the latest hyped-up restaurant. Anything but this.

On New Year's Eve he called to wish me a Happy New Year. Tash, my flatmate, was in Courchevel and I was on my own with Elvis and three other dogs whose owners were out celebrating. I'd sat in bed watching the clock, waiting until it had gone nine thirty so it didn't feel too pathetically early to turn out my light. A few hours after I nodded off, my phone rang with a message from a *Blocked Number*, but it was Joseph's voice.

'Happy New Year, Sparkles!' he slurred as a crowd burst into applause and bells chimed in the background.

'Happy New Year.' I was already out of bed, pacing the room. 'Where are you?'

'New York…? I think. I just want to say… what? I'm on–' I could hear loud music, girls laughing. 'Just want to say… I hope you're happy now. I'm not…' A champagne cork popped. 'What happened, Stella? What happened?' Then the connection was lost.

I tried all the numbers I had for him but with his constant

changing of time-zones and SIM cards to deter stalkers and press, he was gone again. *What happened?*

Breaking up is hard to do, but it's also very expensive. After leaving my job, I couldn't cover the mortgage or the loans I'd taken out for legal training, my mum's care and to support Joseph's early career; on top of that, my dog-walking enterprise involved a surprising amount of outlay: publicity, website, insurance, buying a van then modifying it to accommodate my canine clients. So I put the flat on the market and hid around the corner every time estate agents walked couples through my home pointing out all the reasons why they would have a euphorious future there, and just letting it slip that it also belonged to Joseph West who'd regretfully exchanged it for a new life in Hollywood. After an aggressive bidding war, it sold.

I wish I were a rodent who could dig my way back through time. But I'm not and I can't. So I keep going for Elvis' sake and because it tickles me to see my posse wag their tails as they charge into the back of my van in the mornings, sniffing and licking each other while they vie for who sits on which patch of rug before I close the grille. But things have been quiet since a fortnight ago when a whippet caught my phone as he tore off after a goose at the Serpentine and, instead of replacing it, I invested in peace of mind – probably not the most entrepreneurial move, but if anyone needs to get in touch, I'm here, in the park, same time every day. It's surprising how few people do.

I need to get away, have some time to think without a wet nose nuzzling my palms.

The sun's gone in and we're back to a corrugated iron sky. Kamilla and I used to walk through this park almost every day while at school, my backpack heavy with books, essays and dreams of going to university to become a lawyer and make a life that would be everything mine wasn't – and I'd been so close to the finishing line.

I sit at the base of a tree, small and still, allowing the wind to blow through me.

Elvis, having taken Cha-Cha's rejection on the chin, is straining to sniff a Westie outside a glass gallery where a crowd is gathering. There are people wearing hats and carnations. It looks like it might be a wedding – come on, Elvis, why not rub icing sugar into our wounds.

It's too cold to stand still for long and too small a gathering not to feel intrusive, but I stay to avoid a spaniel owner who never fails to tell me the ongoing saga of her dog's eczema.

The nuptials are an impressive show. Champagne in ice buckets and dollops of Russian caviar piled onto blinis, but most of the guests wave away the food offered them on silver platters. There are no older people, no children and no teenagers. Whoever the couple are, they've clearly dispensed with any notions of family. Most of the women are dressed in dark colours, autumnal velvets and fake fur hats, there are one or two veils and long gloves while a few of the men grapple with torpedo-sized Cuban cigars. The atmosphere is strained, as if they are all under house arrest.

There's one man in a morning coat with a large white carnation in his lapel which droops down to his chest. That's our man, the groom: the dazed, time-pressed look, his thumb and forefinger spinning the brand-new gold band on his left hand. He shows signs of someone who's been indulged, like he can't close his jacket over his paunch and his collar seems to be digging into his second chin. He's almost bald but for ribbons of grey hair stretched over the top of his head. He stands in one place, ill at ease. He waits for people to come to him but appears surprised when they do. Definitely a professional man and this celebration looks a little like the closing of a frantic business merger. I make a silent bet to Elvis that this is not his first marriage.

Every few seconds, he checks his watch and looks at the door as though preparing to detonate the building at a specific time.

I'm about to move away when a string quartet appears. There's a commotion and faces turn to the entrance.

Here comes the bride.

She could be the groom's daughter but only a bride would wear that obscene mass of lace, fat pearls and gold brocade. The train takes up much of the floor and shambolic bustles shoot out from all directions. It could have been knocked up by a six-year-old let loose on some *papier-crêpe* and too many E-additives.

Someone heckles the bride, she answers by cupping her enormous immobile breasts, dropping her head back and twirling around in front of them. There are mock gasps from the audience as she fights the billowing folds of her skirt with her long, white fingernails like overgrown teeth. Another call from the guests and she turns, lifts up the back of her skirt and bends over, showing a light-blue thong and bare buttocks. A few people laugh but most don't. The show goes on – she swivels, kicks her leg up in the air, high enough to level with her nose and show more than just the tops of her suspenders.

The groom parts the crowds to join her as men thump his back and say things to make him blush, one can always rely on the English tradition of embarrassing the happy couple.

The bride could be thirty years his junior and certainly acting like a little filly around an old carthorse as she tosses her mass of black hair in the air like a flamenco dancer with castanets. She has so much hair it's only later that I notice the dislodged tiara trailing behind her.

Nose to the window, I watch her thanking everyone in turn and asking their names, even the waiters as they fill her glass. Every once in a while, when she loses the groom, she'll launch herself up in the air and flag him down with her bouquet. Strands of her hair are now on the shoulders of most of the guests, some are pinching it out of their mouths. This is someone who knows how to leave her mark. As does Elvis, who looks up at me while chewing on his lead, impatient to renew his walk. A few faces turn in my direction but I'm not the only observer. A young man is lurking behind a pillar pretending to be on the phone, but he's actually taking photos of the wedding couple – and of me. Even though it's been a few months since I was Joseph's girlfriend, the press are still hungry for a story. I can imagine it now: *Stella Tyler: Never the Bride.*

Numb fingers and a rumbling tummy, I see the café's now open and that Sergei and Owen are playing chess outside. I buy a hot chocolate and sit down next to them.

'If you don't unblock that knight, he's got you in three moves,' I warn Sergei. He looks at the board, then at me. I raise my eyebrows, sip my drink. 'Just saying.'

'Bloody right you are.' He moves his piece. 'But if you don't unblock that boulder across your heart, you're gonna throw your life away. Just saying.'

10

A bullying wind barges past every living thing in the park leaving the trees in convulsions and people moving fast, shielding their faces from the onslaught of twigs and pointy leaves. Elvis and I make for the exit. In the car park, I overtake the newly-weds rushing to a waiting Bentley, the pink plastic bow on the emblem struggling to escape. A lethargic splutter of confetti is stolen by another gust.

A shivering woman in a short polka-dot blue dress calls out, 'Enjoy the Caribbean, you lucky devils!' Her friends sing into her ear, 'And good laaaaa-uck!' Another chips in, 'He'll nee-ee-eed it!' They have a hard time masking their laughter as they continue waving.

'Shit! The tickets!' Polka Dress pulls out some printed papers in a plastic sheath from her handbag. 'Mr Hardwick! Mr Hardwick!' She taps on his door as the groom searches for the button to open the window. 'The travel documents!'

The window lowers just enough for Mr Hardwick's fingers to root for the documents.

'Heathrow, 6pm tomorrow.'

'Got it. Thanks, Susan.'

'*Samantha*. Sorry.' She presses up to the car door trying to stop her skirt from lifting over her as she feeds another paper through. 'And this is for the Paradise Beach Club Hotel. Enjoy the Caribbean, Mr Hardwick, *Mrs* Hardwick.'

The bride is digging confetti out from her cleavage as the groom peers through his wife's hair to give his last wave goodbye. The Bentley rolls out of the park gates.

The PA looks back at her friend. 'Oops! That was a close one – imagine if they hadn't gone!'

Samantha's friend looks absently at the disappearing car. 'Barbados. Lucky for some, eh… *Susan*!'

'It's all over!' Samantha punches the air. 'I'm taking Monday off if that's all right.'

'Oh yeah, we all need a mega rest. God, I'm freezing my tits off!' She turns to her friends. 'Hey, who's this?' She messes up her hair and pouts: 'Oh 'Enrrry… my big, sexy, teddy bearrrrr, I want a big Harrrry Winston diamond… Henry, give it to me. Not your old cock, your PIN number!'

The girls laugh into their goodbye hugs as Samantha and her friend turn towards Kensington High Street. I'm right behind them when one of them drops an invitation card on the pavement:

Miss McVey,
Henry Hardwick QC and Miss Yuleka Malthuzian
would be delighted to celebrate their marriage with you at the
Orangery, Holland Park.
Sunday, January 19, 2014, 11 o'clock.
RSVP.

I run my fingers over the raised print.
Mr Henry Hardwick.
My father's name.

11

Baseball cap pulled down low over my eyes, I side-shuffle through a few hopeful reporters. I close the door into my building and wait for the thumping in my heart to slow down. Someone shouts my name through the letterbox.

Elvis drags me up the three flights of stairs where I rest my head on the door, praying for the strength to face Tash, my flatmate and landlady.

As soon as I open the door, Elvis bounds in pulling the lead from my hands and Tash shrieks while swiping a dishcloth over his head. Elvis grabs the end of it in his mouth and tugs at it. Tash yelps, lets go of the cloth while he continues pogoing in front of her.

Tash yells, 'For God's sake! Stellarrrrh!'

Finally, I'm able to haul him back where he wriggles in my arms.

The table is set for twelve, and I remember she has friends coming for lunch. Every day for the last week I'd been warned by the little Post-it notes she leaves around the flat to make myself scarce on Sunday. Tash is entertaining. And 'entertaining' is something she takes very seriously indeed. In fact, she takes everything very seriously.

'Those *men* are still out there,' I mumble, leaning over my knees and stretching my back.

'It's getting kind of annoying. They knocked Marcus off his bike yesterday.'

'Sorry.'

'It's not your fault. To be honest, it doesn't do my business any harm.'

'But you don't talk to them, do you?'

'Why not?' she asks. 'Actually, I invited a few of them in for an espresso yesterday – they were so cold, poor sausages. They were really interested in Yukusha's – y'know, I told you about it; the restaurant I'm doing publicity for – and they promised to donate to that appeal for the flood victims. Oh, come on, I still don't see why you don't make some money out of them, what've you got to lose? Give them the story they want and they'll go away.'

'I can't believe you sometimes.'

'Stella! He's still…' She stands frozen, hands held out. Elvis has now pawed open the black bin bag and is dragging chicken giblets across the floor.

'It's okay. I've got him.' Elvis is reeled in, held down and struggling against my lap. Both hands tight around the dog, I wonder if I could quickly make a cup of tea. The signs aren't good.

'I didn't hear you go out this morning, must have been at the gym. Did you get my messages?'

'I told you. I haven't got a phone.'

'But how is it possible to run a business without a phone?'

'I work with dogs, remember?'

'Whatever. I've got people coming over.'

'I know. I got the Post-it note on my pillow. And the one on the toilet seat and stuck to my coffee mug. Don't worry, I'm on my way out.'

'Stella, don't you owe me rent? I hate to have to ask, but we had a deal.'

'But it's due on Wednesday.'

'Yes, but there's a pair of vintage YSL sunglasses on eBay I've made a bid for.'

'Every month you ask for money earlier and earlier.'

'Fine. If it's such a problem.'

'Course not.'

I drag Elvis into my bedroom where we curl up under the

mountain of old clothes, musty towels and dog chews. 'Duvet therapy', Joseph and I used to call it when he'd been rejected for acting gigs and the strain of contract law was getting me down. Except this time, it's just me. And Elvis. And his breath smells. And the aroma of Tash's Sunday lunch is driving him crazy and reminds me it's been a long time since I've eaten.

12

Tash is in PR. When she's not jogging up to traffic lights, buzzing in and out of private clubs, first-night restaurant openings and single-syllabled delicatessens, she rebrands anything from breakfast cereals, perfumes, ex-soap stars to internet millionaires – her only failure to date has been her flatmate.

I'd met Tash when Kamilla did up her place last year and remembered she'd been looking for someone to rent a room in it, so after finding Mum unbearable, I got in touch – I should have wondered why no one else had taken her up on the offer. Tash had jumped at having front-row seats at that moment's crisis, she'd even reduced the rent because she admired my 'authenticity'. What she meant was that I hadn't been to public school and needed to work rather than living off family trust funds. Her world was, of course, always her own, but she was more than happy to muscle in on mine. At first, she seemed caring and gave me refuge, took Elvis to dog yoga classes – *Doga* – to calm him and introduced me to her eyebrow consultant; she insisted I was a 'hat person' and restyled my wardrobe. We sat up at night drinking homemade mint teas while she confided things about herself I'd rather not have known, but it was only a matter of time before she and Marcus heard I'd refused a slot on a morning TV show about famous partners and that I wasn't going to sell photos of Joseph and I for kiss 'n' tell articles. So now there's a plot to get me out.

———

I claw my way up to the surface of my bed gasping: Henry Hardwick?

I meant to go online to my bank but found myself staring at the last email Joseph had written me.

> I'm an actor, not a therapist but it's clear you think I'm going to turn out like your biological dad. Your mum's great but it was wrong of her to bring you up thinking all men are like him and that you have to protect yourself.
>
> Rebecca is arranging for my stuff to be removed from the flat. Forward her any bills or admin. You let me down, Stella Sparkles, not the other way around.

I'd replied:

> Just to be clear, it's all because of my crazy childhood that I'm hallucinating all the pictures of you and Sylvia on vacation in Hawaii? On the radio yesterday there was a competition where contestants had to list all the beautiful women you've dated in under a minute — no one managed it — needless to say, I didn't feature in any of them!
>
> BTW you have enough dogs in your life already, I'm keeping Elvis.

That man today, in the park, getting married – he's the reason I lost Joseph?

13

Whenever I meet someone, there's the point I dread – the bit where we fill each other in on our family histories. 'I never met my father,' I say. That kind of information never ends the conversation, only incites increasing interest as I fight off the same questions again and again.

I knew that my 'alleged' father lived in London with his family and was head of a barristers' chambers in London. He had once been on the cover of the *Law Review* when I was at university. I went through every word of that article hoping he'd say something about me. He didn't, of course, and I didn't learn anything about his private life there either. I'd never seen him in the flesh, until today. And never wanted to. Henry Hardwick had been cruel and hurtful to my mother and shown no interest in their baby. I had no reason to seek him out – until now.

The man in the park could easily have been him, but there's only one person who could confirm it and that same person could also give me a bed for the night.

I huddle over the antiquated landline and dial my mum's number. It rings three times. I put it down. Call for another two rings. Hang up. Call again, leave two rings. That's our code.

'Mum?'

'Agnes.'

'Oh, hi, Agnes. All right?'

'Whatever. Your mama is not he-ah. Prison. Then the psychic ward.'

'The psychiatric ward?'

'Saturday. Police no find you. Police send her to crazy hospital. Same as last time. You collect Monday morning. Is no problem. Can't talk now – I am hurry up.'

14

I need to find enough money to get me out of this flat but all I've got is my van and the 'limited collection' handbag that Joseph brought back for me after his first trip to LA. I put anything of worth in the middle of the floor and stare at it, nauseous from the smells emanating from the kitchen.

Tash peers around my door holding a table plan, she wants to know when I was thinking of leaving. I tell her 'In a minute' and go to the bathroom to stall her. Sitting on the toilet I pick up a notebook in which Tash has scribbled:

GOALS and VISIONS Feb 15–22: Find cheaper car ins./Bk villa St Trop 4 Aug/Lotus position by May/Read @ least 2 bks from O.P. shortlist/Buy Cara D bag, Vogue, p110/No desserts, just a bit of others/Invite JW and SA for dinner Thursday Night (?)/Look down more when talking to boys/Vlog?/Change nutritionist/Stella rent!!!

I flush. Return to my room to pack up all I can.

Back in her open-plan kitchen, Tash is trying hard to ignore me but at the same time, she needs to act normal in case I make a scene in front of her imminent guests. She's seen the case and the plastic bags so now just wants this behind her.

She touches a colourful display of flowers.

'Every room must have a centrepiece,' she tells me. 'I got these arum lilies on the Portobello Road yesterday. If you go as they're closing the stalls they practically give them away.'

'About the rent... I'm still waiting for the flat sale to come through and–'

'Those guys outside are ready to offer you at least £20,000 just for a chat.'

'Tash! I'm not selling my integrity.'

'Where's the integrity in being skint?'

'I said, I'm waiting for the flat sale to come through.'

She perks up with an idea. 'What about your handbag?'

'My bag? Joseph gave it to me. It's all I have left of him.'

'Er… and whose fault is that?'

I let the comment go in favour of an uncomplicated exit. 'Maybe you could take the van instead?'

'Don't be silly, Stella, why would I want your silly van? Look, I've got people coming.'

'Take the van.'

'Stella, it's not worth the fucking rent and it's covered in dog hair!' She presses her hand against her heart to stop it blowing up.

'The van works well when it's not raining and you can easily fit twelve large dogs in the back.'

Tash taps her fingers on the table. 'Well, it might cover *some* of the rent owed. But how would you pick up the dogs?'

'Well, it's all a bit hush-hush at the moment but I've been offered something. It's a pretty exciting work opportunity.'

'Dog walking?'

'No. In the media.'

Inventing an upturn in the nosediving trajectory of my life was yet another low point, but I just want to get out without owing her money or pity.

'A reality TV show? It is, isn't it? Yes!' She springs up and down on the balls of her feet twirling a wooden spoon. 'I knew it! I'm thrilled you're getting yourself out there, hey, if you need a PR person–'

'I know where you live.'

Tash shuffles over to me, arms outstretched.

'You've been through so much, and I–'

'So, you'll take the van?' I ask, ducking past her.

'No, well, maybe. In lieu of next month's rent, and when you hit the big time you can buy it back off me, fair? Is it with Channel 4 or the Beeb?'

15

I'm ready with Elvis, a large suitcase, a holdall, the handbag and a black sack with all my sellable goods. As I heave them to the door, Tash calls out, 'You know a lot of people are *really* worried about you.'

Elvis and I look at each other. 'That's sweet,' I concede, hoping to be spared the lecture.

'You just don't see it do you? You have so much going for you.' And she's off. 'You've got really *good* friends, they really *care* about you, God knows why, the way you treat them.' She moves closer to make sure she's in my line of vision. 'I know it's hard for you not having a family, I mean, a *father*, and then your–'

'Back off.'

'Sorry.' She surrenders her hands above her head. 'I know, I know, "taboo" area. All I'm saying is Joseph's pretty confused at the moment and–'

'Who've you been talking to?'

She dips her fingers in the salad dressing. 'More lemon.' From the fridge she calls back, 'Just Kamilla, Boo, Claire, Anna... Joseph, a *little*–'

'Joseph? You've been talking to *Joseph*?'

'So? He's really worried about you.'

'You've called him, haven't you?' But I can tell by the jumping pulse points in her neck.

'It's not like that. I just wondered if he'd participate in a campaign we were doing for–' The buzzer sounds. 'They're here!' She answers, cheery and breathless, buzzing her guests in.

'You used *me* as an excuse to call Joseph?'

'Oh! You're so dramatic!'

'Go ahead – *Invite JW and SA to dinner Thursday.* Take my room, and the van, and my ex!'

I toss the house keys to her but she's not fast enough to catch them so they knock over the flowers. Water cascades from the vase over her table decorations. Elvis lurches towards the cataract manically licking the puddle until I drag him out the door.

'I said I don't want the van!'

'Just as well – it's been clamped!'

I hear Tash's gaggle of guests in the hall as I slam the door.

I pound down the stairs, struggling to keep hold of my belongings. I pass them, my bags scraping against their legs as Elvis sniffs at their ankles. They avert their eyes though one of the girls sings out, 'Bye, Stella!' while the others giggle.

16

At Camden Market I find a stall selling winter coats where I unload a leather jacket and a pair of boots.

'It's a nice jacket, sure?' asks a trucker checking it over for his girlfriend.

'I'm not comfortable wearing leather anymore.'

'Right,' he says, rubbing his large, round, front-loading washing machine of a belly.

'You sellin' that bag, love?' the stall-keeper butts in.

'It was a present.'

With the cash I made, I buy two baked potatoes, one for me with grated cheese, and one for Elvis with bolognese sauce. He eats his lunch as we watch the tourists pass by and run through my memories of Joseph because this is somewhere we came to on Sunday afternoons looking for stuff to furnish our flat.

I'd seen Joseph around at uni where he was the college heart-throb, studying English and drama, tipped to be a star, and I'd heard all about him from my friend Boo who was besotted with him and determined to penetrate his inner circle of gorgeous, brilliant, Olympian females who made it their business to protect him from mere mortal adulation. Then in our last term, Boo invited us to her family's country house in Devon for the weekend hoping that this would be 'the weekend' for her and Joseph.

As I had a car and Joseph didn't, Boo suggested we travelled together from London where we were both working. Me, in the City entering data for a merchant bank while Joseph was a waiter in a Cuban restaurant in Covent Garden.

'When Boo told me she'd asked her friend to give me a lift, I hoped it was you,' he said, pointing a red rose at me. He was wearing a sombrero, white shirt gone grey from overwashing and a black waistcoat two sizes too small for him.

'Why's that?' I asked, pulling the stem of the rose through my buttonhole.

'I always thought you looked...' his dark eyes looked into mine, 'like a girl who could map-read.'

'And you look like a boy who should be doing this trip on a donkey,' I said, eyeing him up from his hat to his stirrups.

'Okay if we eat first?'

A warm, sunny evening in spring. We sat outside the restaurant with a plate of black fried beans and tacos. He'd laughed at my jokes, agreed with my ideas and even tapped the names of books I recommended into his phone under the heading, *To Read ASAP!* I wanted to get up and stop passers-by, boasting, 'This is Joseph, Joseph West! Look, he's talking to me! Line up to take photos!'

We left later than planned, shared the driving and, as the suburban rooftops became stone walls and sleepy sheep past our windows, we let tractors and horse trailers overtake us to stall the eventual end of that time, encapsulated and enthralled in the discovery of each other. As the evening got darker, so did the subjects: perhaps it was not being able to see each other's faces but we shifted from banter to revealing intimacies about ourselves that maybe a therapist would have waited a long time to hear. I told him about my mother, the council estate I was brought up on, the father I'd never met and how our struggles had directed me towards studying law. Joseph had come from a stable, happy family although when he was doing his GCSEs his mother had been diagnosed with breast cancer and his dad had started an affair with one of her friends. At that time, Joseph was in conflict with his father who was adamant that he took a steady job once he graduated, however, he was secretly investigating drama colleges and dreaming of working as an actor. From there, we went on to love. Joseph ran through his romance CV but said that apart from a ski monitor on a school trip, no one had really got to him.

17

We arrived at the weekend party just in time for Joseph to unload the tequila bottles and set up a bar for shots. A few hours later, after dinner, karaoke and port, Joseph suggested we play 'The Bottom Game'.

'The Bottom Game?' Joe was dumbfounded no one had heard of it but not all of us went to house parties every weekend.

He asked the girls to line up in a dark room with their bums bared. The boys then came in and had to feel each bottom and say who they thought it belonged to. When it was Joseph's turn to fumble around each of us, no one could keep quiet through the giggling.

'It's so obvious he'll just go for Stella!' lamented Boo.

And that's what happened. He found me within seconds, circled the tops of my thighs and touched my bum tenderly for as long as he could get away with.

'Hmmm, I'm not sure about this one… could it be…'

When we changed roles, the girls lined up to feel the boys' bums in the lightless room. I did the same, leaning into his back, closing my eyes and letting my lips brush against the back of his neck. Joseph turned around, took my wrists and kissed me. All the intimacy built up on the journey, the tension, the attraction, all of it went into that kiss. We had a few minutes in the dark before Boo announced the game was 'sexist'. The lights went on, we jumped back from each other and eventually all made our way to bed at around dawn.

The Sunday afternoon as Ali and I washed up after the lunch Joseph and the boys had put together, we watched him in the garden carrying logs back into the house.

Ali followed my gaze and said, 'He's doing all this caveman stuff to impress you, y'know? He's hoping you'll realise that although he acts like a flirt, he's actually capable of looking after someone, but he isn't.' We continued watching him through the window cutting off branches with a penknife. 'Be careful, Stella. Joe likes a laugh and playing characters, he's never serious.'

We watched him lugging a tree trunk over to the house. He looked up at me and smiled 'the smile'. It got me every time.

'Why would I need warning?'

'He told me he thinks you're "intriguing" and "cool". You intimidate him. I've never known anyone be able to do that to him before – but in a few days there'll be another weekend party, another round of bottom games and…' She drained the washing bowl down the sink.

———

Driving back the following Monday morning, we were silent, hungover and in a fog of uncertain emotions. On the way, I stopped at a motorway station and bought some Danish pastries and coffees in Styrofoam cups for breakfast. As Joseph was driving, he let me drop little bits of chocolate into his mouth while I allowed him to lick my fingers. Soon we were stopping at every traffic light to kiss, once even pulling into a lay-by. When we approached London, he took my hand and said, 'Don't go to work. Stay with me.'

'Until Friday and the next weekend party?'

'No! Until I'm a film star and drop you for a gorgeous young starlet.' He grinned. I punched his arm. I'd thought he was so funny.

18

The bags of clothes are too heavy to carry around anymore so I go into a dry cleaners and try to convince them I'm just someone who likes all my clothes in plastic covers. The woman fixes a stern, suspicious look on me in between itemising each piece: work suits, jeans, underwear, hats, tights… She points at the cost of each one, waits for me to nod, goes on. The list covers three pages. It's easily more than an entire designer collection.

'I'll pay when I collect.'

She rolls her eyes. 'You got ninety days.'

As I come out of the dry cleaners, a grey Aston Martin that has been sitting on the other side of the street moves slowly away and into the crowd of tourists. I'm sure I've seen that car several times already – being stalked by the press or any of Joseph's fans would not be unusual, but in such a car?

Passing a stall selling old trinkets, I catch sight of a Victorian brass compass. The dealer lets me look at it and the next thing, we strike a deal, with my watch as a sweetener. He throws in a chain as well. It fits snug and warm in my palm. I examine the magnified N, S, W, E half scratched on the yellow face. As I walk from the stand, I realise the needle is stuck between south and west. The streetlights come on and the air turns icy. With Mum in hospital, Kamilla and I still not talking, my distrust that unburdening myself to friends might end up being a sensational story, I wander to the nearest ATM machine to see if I can afford a cheap hotel that allows dogs.

The machine not only gives me notes but shows that I'm over two hundred thousand pounds in credit.

The flat sold and for some reason I've got Joseph's *and* my share.

Enough for another baked potato. Enough for a holiday.

Enjoy the Caribbean, you lucky devils!

Enough to go find my dad.

'Elvis, I'm going to the Caribbean to confront Henry Hardwick. I'll send you a postcard and you can sniff the picture.'

I take out the compass, look at it again, the needle hasn't moved but I can see the direction ahead of me: I need to find my oldest friend and let her know that finally, I understand what she was trying to tell me all those months ago.

19

It's been years since Kamilla and I pulled an all-nighter but settling on the sofa in front the fire, our dogs licking our plates clean of the pierogi, my favourite Polish dish that Kamilla makes, I tell her why I'm booking flights for the Caribbean.

'I saw my dad today.'

'What?'

'I saw my dad. In the park. I was walking Elvis and there was this wedding going on and then someone said the groom's name – Henry Hardwick. It was my dad, getting married to a kind of obnoxious woman.'

'You sure? Could you have wanted it to be him and…'

'Maybe. That's why I'm gatecrashing his honeymoon.'

'What are you going to do there?'

'I don't know yet, but you were right that day I packed in my job. I should have listened: what you said about trust and commitment, running away from success – I get it now. I messed up. I have to meet him, ask those questions – for *me*, not for him or Mum or anyone else – it's time I face the past and get things straight in my head, and, hey, I need a holiday.'

We are still up talking when Monday morning rolls in and we hug one last time.

'Stella, don't freak, but before you leave, you've got to see Joseph. He's been desperately trying to get in touch with you. Just hear him out. Here's his new address. You've got time and, of course I could look after Elvis, but Joe misses him too.'

She brushes specks of snow from her hair before sliding on her woolly hat.

'I'll let Joseph know you're on your way over. Barbados, eh?' She smiles, then shivers. 'Okay, Henry Hardwick, this is going to be a honeymoon you'll never forget!'

20

When I press the buzzer to Joe's building, a bald, burly guy in black leather opens the door but blocks the entrance. He asks for my name and waits for identification. While he brings a phone to his ear, I see him clenching his buttocks in the mirror's reflection behind him. Then I hear Joe's voice down the handset say, 'Yeah, let her up.' The guy steps back, calls the lift for me.

'Mr West. Penthouse.'

When the lift doors open, I'm standing in Joseph's new flat which is nothing like the one we shared. A picture of us decorating flashes up in my mind: Joseph and I jousting each other on stepladders, singing along to our joint playlist and racing oversized trolleys down the aisles of DIY stores. I assume his new pad was done up by Rebecca's interior decorator who must like the idea of living in an airport hangar. Space, windows and skylights; exposed metal pipes and radiators. It would be empty apart from a so-dark-purple-it's-nearly-black velvet five-seater sofa, a chrome standing light with a bulb as big as the moon and a floor-to-ceiling painting of a man on a motorbike.

'Stella?' Joe calls from the kitchen.

He is by his state-of-the-art coffee maker in grey jogging bottoms and a black sweatshirt with the logo from his last film, *Preternaturally Yours* across his chest. He looks so cute I want to crawl over and grovel at his pedicured feet. He must have just come out of the shower as his dark hair is still a little damp and looking like shredded black silk. Elvis flies across the room and Joseph bends down to let the dog jump up into his arms. I have to stop myself from leaping in too.

'Mr Kong didn't give you any trouble, did he?'

'Mr Kong?'

'He's the–' Joseph tries to say something but Elvis is still

60

perched around theback of his neck. 'Security detail.' He nibbles playfully at Elvis' ears. 'Ah! I've missed him.' He scratches under the dog's chin. 'Missed you too, Sparkles.'

He takes a swig from a bottle of water, blinks a little with those long lashes.

'Want a coffee, tea…?'

'No, I… have to… er… see Mum, and then… I'm going away so if you want to look after Elvis for a few weeks you can. I've other people I could ask, just thought you… might… want to. And you know the flat sold but all the money seems to have been transferred into my account, so can you give me your–'

'No, Stella. Keep it. It's yours.'

'Joe, that's–'

'Hey, I'm just paying you back what I owe you. You made it possible for me to go to drama college, covered everything. If it hadn't been for you I'd still be living off enchilada scraps and washing up till three in the morning. And I heard that you might have lost your job because Forrester and Levine weren't too happy with the publicity, and is it true, you were going to be made a partner? I feel terrible about that. So please. Have it.'

'I'll put it aside. For the moment.'

We sit on bar-stools at his kitchen island sipping our freshly ground Italian coffee. 'Good plan.' Joseph scoots closer to me, and as much as I try to immunise myself from wanting to hold him and never let go, an element inside me starts burning with light, and heat, and a blistering pain. 'Kamilla said you'd had a bust-up? And you're dog walking now? And apparently you rent a room from Tash, she keeps calling me?' Joe hasn't been in the US that long, but already, all his sentences go up at the end like life is just one mind-blowing surprise after another. Although his probably is. 'I tried reaching you soon as I got back from India and then I had to go to LA – but for fuck's sake, you could have at least talked to me.'

'What for? So you could tell me one thing and I find out another? It hurt me every time I read about you, so I gave up my phone, social media, the internet. You.' He blinks several times, trying to imagine how this could be possible. 'Yup, I pulled the plug, disconnected. You should try it, it's liberating.' As if on cue, the Samsung nearest his coffee cup starts having seizures on the work surface. 'But somehow you seem to know everything about me. Why have you been following my misery like one of your salacious stalkers?'

'The last thing I ever wanted was you to be sad. It's just I had to find you, to explain. You think you know about me but you've got it so wrong and we need to talk.'

'So talk.'

His desktop computer pings and the screens on his three telephones flash.

'I'm guilty of letting a situation get out of control, but it's not what you think.'

'Wait–' I jump down from the bar-stool and fumble around in the holdall. 'I got you this.' I hand him the brass compass. It hadn't occurred to me to give it to him until that moment, but it seems the perfect gift. He rotates it through his fingers, smiling. I take the chain out of my pocket and thread it through the top. He lets me put the compass around his neck, looks at it. 'You might need to get it fixed; I think it's stuck.'

'And you will always be stuck until you make a decision about me based on reality, not lies and paranoia.'

'That a line from one of your films?'

'The soppy romanticism, all mine. I'm saying that I never stopped loving you. I totally get what you must have thought but you were so wrong.'

Joe flinches when the phone goes again, this ringtone makes the sound of a whistle.

'Take the calls.'

'Later.' He kisses the compass. 'Thank you for his.' He clasps his legs around mine so I can't move away, not that I want to. And we are us again. His hands run through my hair, touching my face, neck. I kiss the little dimples that punctuate the curl of his lips at each side of his cheeks – until the phone starts thrashing around again. Locked in together, my longing for him moves deep inside me as we open our mouths – now music plays from the phone. Joe reaches over to turn it off but he can't resist looking at the screen. He waits a few beats before saying, 'I've just been nominated for an Oscar.'

I actually scream as we bounce together, pulling each other close as tightly as possible, both our hearts racing in time, our lips press against each other's and just as I'm about to close my eyes, I hear the musical ringtone and see the phone screen light up with the unmistakable face of Sylvia Amery.

'No wait!' Joe calls out, reaching for my wrist. 'Stella!'

I don't even stop to give Elvis a goodbye kiss.

21

My flight for Barbados leaves this evening, but first I need to collect Mum.

It's not the first time I've had to collect Florence from the psychiatric wing of the Chelsea and Westminster Hospital so I know the drill, even recognise a few faces.

Inside the hospital, I lounge against a wall the colour of overwashed pants waiting for the senior staff nurse to sign my mother over. The receptionist looks at me, flicks over my mum's notes and chuckles. 'She makes me laugh that one, Mrs Florence.'

It's always the same thing: big houses speak to Florence.

For as long as she's lived, grand homes are all she's ever had a passion for. All her life, she's wanted to be surrounded by lawns with sculpted hedges leading to giant-sized doors. Not doors to council houses, bungalows or even glossy house-sized doors, but doors to homes too big to be numbered. Doors protecting a multitude of rooms. Rooms, vast and light, like unexplored glaciers.

My mum can stand and stare at people's houses like others do shoes in a shop window or paintings in a gallery. When I was a child, I used to have to stand with her as she pointed out architectural features and the owners' bad taste. I can see her now, looking through the windows while the sprinklers pirouetted, chucking out diamonds onto budding roses. Florence probably nodded to the chauffeur rinsing away the soap-suds on one of the cars and pushed open the gate. The large maple door was already open so that the maid could rush in and out, beating the smaller carpets. She had left the Persian rugs abandoned while engaging in animated conversation with the two gardeners. Florence felt the wetness of the path under her feet but couldn't hear the details of their chattering – all she heard was the glorious concerto of people doing their best to dress and pamper a very spoilt residence.

The nurse shows me the part in her notes about her having a bath. They'd written down how she described the events of last Friday, and I can imagine it all. Inside the bathroom suite, Florence running her hands through the hot water as it gushed out, how she apparently added in an entire bottle of bath oil. The glowing pools hovering on the water before disappearing into the steam. Her placing her foot inside the bath, seeing it dislocate and expand in the mirror's reflection. How she unfurled as the heat wrapped around her when she came eye to eye with the maid calling to, 'Mrs Metcalfe! Mrs Metcalfe!'

Florence rested back in the water.

'Tell her I'm in the bath. I'll call her later.'

When Florence next opened her eyes. A large woman was standing over her, her tongue wildly slapping against orange lips. Necklaces swung close to her nose; Florence's heart jolted. The tepid water turned her cold.

'What in God's name are you doing here?'

'Having a bath.'

The woman called to the maid peeping from behind the door. 'Donna, get the police! Tell them there is a woman in my bathtub.' She turned to Florence and ordered, 'You! Up and dressed and out in twenty seconds.'

Mrs Metcalfe turned her back on the now shivering Florence and thudded down the stairs.

All eyes were fixed on the main staircase. The crowd waited for the trespasser to emerge.

'She doesn't look dangerous, but I mean, how would I know?' Veronica Metcalfe declared to her troops. No one answered, too absorbed by the space at the top of the stairs gradually filling with the slight silhouette of the intruder lowering herself down, stair by stair, walking as if asleep, unaware of the pools of water she was leaving on the parquet flooring.

A police car arrived and two men pushed through the gates, past Mrs Metcalfe and into the hall. They stopped to watch the naked woman reach the bottom stairs.

'Well, aren't you going to arrest her?' asked Mrs Metcalfe.

'It's all right, madam, we know who she is,' they answered, filling their lips with air like tired baboons.

'Is she wanted? Is she a known criminal?'

The older officer stepped forward, ignoring Mrs Metcalfe. 'Come along, Florence. Where are your clothes?'

Florence muttered something under her breath.

Donna stepped up to the officer handing over the trespasser's clothes and covering her with a large towel.

Mrs Metcalfe turned to the officer. 'Excuse me! Can you tell me what's going on here? This is *my* house, my bathwater!'

The policeman opened the police-car door for the dripping woman, with an encouraging, 'Put these on. Mind your head.'

Florence turned to the man, her eyes wide and imploring. 'I've done a poo,' she whimpered.

The policeman looked at her.

'In the bath.'

'Never mind, love, hop in the car,' he added, somewhat distracted by the sight of her bare, shrivelled feet as she curled up on the back seat.

'Could someone please…?' enquired the lady of the house.

'No need to be alarmed, madam. We know her, she's just a bit…' He tapped his forehead. 'She does this a lot. Turns up in houses all round Holland Park, Knightsbridge, Chelsea – mainly the W1 area. She usually just goes to bed or watches TV… some places she stays for days, weeks even, before anyone notices. She don't do no harm. Check to see if anything's missing and if so, give us a call. It's unlikely though.' He passed her a leaflet on Victim Support and circled the helpline number.

'Have I seen her on the telly?' asked a passing traffic warden who'd given herself a break from ticketing to watch the action.

'It's possible. She does a lot of them game shows and quizzes, phone-ins. She won a Ford Fiesta once, apparently.'

'But d'you think she'll be all right?' croaked Mrs Metcalfe.

'If you don't file a complaint, we'll just take her down to the station. Her daughter usually comes to pick her up. She goes out with Joseph West, you know the...?'

22

Mum can be found arranging the plastic flowers in the hospital's day lounge. Florence doesn't acknowledge me; just stands a few feet behind as I flag down a taxi.

'A taxi? You're not going to bounce a cheque on him are you?'

'The money from the flat came through.'

'Won't last long if you're taking black cabs across London.'

'Next time they're throwing away the key.'

We go back to the red tower block in World's End where she's lived all my life. It's in Chelsea, which makes Mum proud. The lift's out of order so we take the stairs all the way up and I notice as we get to the top that she's barefoot. I take her keys, lead her in. She sits in the chair by the door, not moving. I make some tea though Mum's not a tea person, but it's my closest approximation to first aid.

I smoke one of her cigarettes. I don't usually smoke but there's something about being in my mother's presence that draws me to self-harm. We have more in common than she realises.

Apart from these sporadic excursions into other people's homes, Mum rarely leaves her flat, thanks to home deliveries and Agnes' weekly visits.

The place looks like Versailles compressed into two bedrooms. Brass doorknobs shine, cold to the touch, and the bed is made, always, with the pillows rounded and welcoming. The towels, curtains and tablecloths wait, pressed, starched. There are no tell-tale signs that anyone actually inhabits the place, apart from a small radio that she leaves on at all times, often between stations so that there's a constant sizzle of voice in the background. All the old people in her building seem to have their radios blaring, I guess it must make them feel like they've got company.

In the corner of the room there's her 'work lab' – an antique writing desk she hauled back from the rubbish dump. It's where she keeps a large ring-binder documenting all upcoming competitions and another for her relentless correspondences. There's also a microscope, shelves of plastic tubs filled with syringes, rotting fruit, food coupons, loyalty vouchers, lottery tickets, scratch cards and bingo slips. That's what Mum does: complains for a living. And she's very good at it. Green mould on the edge of a crisp. A dead ant in a biscuit box. Hair dye that turns blonde hair a shade of khaki. A black baked bean in a tin. Deodorant that doesn't last twenty-four hours as promised. And there's a box for all the free samples she collects: testers, trials and give-away products. 'Freebie Florence' she's known as on the estate.

She waves away the tea I put in front of her.

'There's wine in the fridge.' As I'm about to fetch it, she takes my wrist. 'It's not surprising he left you for Sylvia Amery.'

'And how's your love life going?'

'Better than yours, my dear. Where's the dog?' she asks in a baby voice, as though she expected him to collect her.

'With Joseph.'

'I saw him on the telly the other night.'

'Elvis?'

'Don't be stupid. *Joseph*. Some costume drama with that woman, you know, the one with the mole, married to whatshisname. He's been nominated for the Oscar, y'know. Heard it while I was in the hospital waiting room. I told the dribbling fool next to me, "He was nearly my son-in-law," and she said,

"Oh yes, mine too." Of course, she was delusional. Just think, we could have been sitting next to him at the award ceremony when he wins it. But no, you're too independent. Too tough. You put men off.' When I finish pouring the wine that she really shouldn't drink with her meds, she adds, 'I miss him, so much... so much.' Her cries are heart-wrenching.

'I know. You and Robert were really special.' I put my hand on her quivering arm. Robert Atkins had been my mother's boss for many years and I always suspected he'd been secretly in love with her.

'Not *him*! Not *Robert*,' she snaps, withdrawing from my touch. 'Henry. *Henry Hardwick*. Your father.'

'My father?'

The man I saw in the park yesterday getting married to the woman flashing her buttocks at the waiters? The one with the diamond on her hand the size of a golf ball? The one going to Barbados on holiday while Mum is struggling to pay her heating bill? The one who'll be on my flight tonight?

'You miss my father?'

'Every day.'

'Right. I'm taking you back to the Jellinek Unit. Get your bag.'

'But listen, Stella, he's coming back to me – he is. I read he was getting divorced – divorced! It was in the *Mail*. Now! After all these years. Our time is coming!' she wails as if hitting the bridge of a love ballad.

I have no doubt hearing about Henry is what triggered her last escapade. It's happened before, but not for a long time.

'Mum – *hypothetically* – if I were to find my father... what would you like me to say to him?'

She moves with surprising gusto to her desk. I assume she's about to treat herself to her stash of barbiturates or food from her stockpile of bulk-bought crisps and biscuits, but her hand falls on a pile of papers. She takes out an A4 manila envelope and drops it in my lap.

While she pours another wine, I look at my birth certificate. I can still feel the sting from the first time I ever saw this piece of paper. It confirmed what Kamilla and her little gang used to call me in the girls' toilets in Year 5. '*Bastard kid.*'

Originally, Mum had said that my 'father' was away on business but when this work trip started going into years, I had more questions. Then one night I asked Mum: 'What's a "bastard kid"?'

It was the prompt for her to know I was old enough to hear the truth, but I'd got her on a bad day. She thrust my birth certificate in front of me.

'Bastard means "Father: Unknown".'

Dad wasn't away on business, he was away making another family, one he *did* want. What stung, what stigmatised, was that it had been an anomaly in my class or on the estate for any of the children to have two parents around, and yet, I was singled out and marked by this lack.

Twenty years later, I was looking at that paper again.

'That's what you should do,' she says, pointing at *Father*. 'If you were to see him. Make him accountable. Course, when DNA testing came in, I could've done it. Remember Abigail, the social worker we had? She was always on about it. The DSS wanted him for paternity payments, I mean, why should the taxpayer pay when he earned a fortune? But that's not my way. Courts. Lawyers. The shame. Ours was a love affair, not something for paperwork… And then after the incident–'

'That restraining order?'

'Ummm, that. I had to drop it all. But Stella, you could do it, you could make him responsible… if you saw him, couldn't you?'

She rocks her head from side to side: the drugs and alcohol are kicking in.

I stare at the paper, it seems too silly, old-fashioned. A crumpled-up birth certificate, what does it matter unless you're a character out of Dickens?

But it matters to her.

With one hand around her frail shoulder I look down nine floors below where the council recently planted a flower bed and put in a bench. An old man sits on it with his two shopping bags collapsed by his side, he watches a grey Aston Martin cruising by.

'Mum, listen. I'm going to Barbados.' But she's lolling into unconsciousness. I open my wallet and hand her a large roll of fifty-pound notes. 'Here's a little money. I'll be back but I don't know when. Okay?'

She nods, not really listening, mumbles, 'Our time is coming. I'm going to get my turn, Stella, I'm going to…'

23

'Welcome to the high flyers' lounge, Ms Tyler.'

The hush is reverent. My feet bounce across the carpet to one of the soft, wide armchairs. I pass the counters serving fresh coffee, Danish pastries, gleaming fluorescent bowls of fruit on one side and on the other, a line of silver platters of hot foods.

I haven't eaten since this morning so pour myself a coffee and pile three mini chocolate croissants.

Just as I open a paperback and start reading, I hear a shriek.

All heads turn towards the other side of the room. A couple are laughing loudly from inside a large wingback armchair. Thick strands of black hair bounce over the top of the chair, then a black-stockinged leg. An empty champagne bottle falls over. As it rolls across the carpet, the woman whoops while clapping. 'Oh well done, my man. And now… for your next trick!' She laughs so hard she snorts.

The woman straddles herself across the man's lap, then I see the top of his bald patch as she gnaws at his ears and pulls on his tie making sloppy, lapping noises.

The man strains under her weight, tries to look around to see the other passengers, the few hairs on the top of his head are askew and his glasses are at an angle. One business exec, no longer able to tolerate the distraction, closes his laptop and moves away.

'Bye bye!' she sings after him with a little wave.

'Whoops,' says the man while his wife dips one of his fingers in champagne, sucks it off with a pop.

Before I can make out their faces, they disappear behind the back of the chair again. But I don't need confirmation – this is yesterday's wedding couple.

'Baby – watch this!' she calls out as she leaps up, heaves all her hair behind her and picks a champagne bottle out of its bucket. Henry Hardwick covers his eyes as she shakes the bottle, pushes it between her bare legs. She thrusts at him, pushing the bottle in and out, causing him to laugh out loud – the woman from the front desk walks as fast as her tight pencil skirt will allow.

'Excuse me, sir, madam, could I please ask you to quieten down?'

The bride juts her hips forward and backwards. 'We're celebrating! We just got marrrrried!'

'Congratulations. But if you wouldn't mind keeping the noise down. Thank you.'

'Shut up, everybody!' says the bride.

'I'd also like to remind you we have regulations about alcohol consumption prior to boarding, which we'd appreciate you respect.'

'I do apologise.' The bride falls into her new husband's lap. 'I promise, this is only our *first* bottle today!' she says, fighting against laughter. She spins around. 'Want some?'

The airport assistant fails to hold up the professional smile. 'Your flight to Georgetown boards in twenty minutes. We'll call you as soon as it's announced.'

The groom turns theatrically to the few remaining people around him.

'Jolly good. I'm very sorry… for my very noisy wife… she's a terribly naughty girl.'

This is the first time I've ever heard his voice.

'Hey! Thank you! Thank you verrrry much!' says the "noisy wife". 'It was him! He's a bad influence! A bad boy! Rrrright! That's it! I wanna divorce – but first, spanking!'

'Please…?' Another woman from the reception desk scowls. This one more senior with a line of badges stuck to her royal-blue lapel.

'It wasn't *me*; it was him!' says the bride, pointing at an elderly man asleep in front with his *Daily Telegraph*.

'I said–' Henry puts his hand to his forehead and salutes her.

'Ab-so-*lute*-ly.'

The bride slides her bottom lip out, 'Sowwwy.' As soon as the woman turns, the bride sticks the end of the champagne bottle back between her legs into the tight leather band of her skirt and rocks back and forth.

'Do you wanna see how high I can get my leg?' she asks Henry. 'Seriously, watch this, darling, you'll be so impressed!' While she goes through a dance routine, Henry drinks and occasionally shushes her when she knocks into furniture.

I watch over the top of my coffee cup as she spins into his chair and falls on him.

'Where's my prrrrresent?'

Over the next twenty minutes they unwrap the latest iPad and take photos of themselves until the flight is called.

'Enjoy your flight, Mr Hardwick,' says the steward.

'Enjoy your flight, Mr *Hard Dick*!' The bride cackles, looping her arms around him.

My father turns to me, raises his eyebrows and says, 'Do excuse her,' before joining his new wife.

PART THREE

FATHERS

24

Hi Daddy – Stella here!

How are you? I hope you are fine. I am too. It's hot today. I went to school. Borrring apart from double English. I hope you like this picture. It's of a dog. And me and Mummy. And you. Please write to me. My address is at the top. It's a hotel. Mummy and I are pretending that it's the Ritz in Paris and we're royals on holiday until the council give us accomodation but only if Mummy doesn't do it again and then maybe we will get a dog. Do you have any animals?

Lots of love,
Stella XXX

25

My seat has nine different settings – ten if you include 'zero gravity'. I go with the shiatsu massage option and sit back listening to Michael Bublé. I eat all of my meal, as well as the one donated by the person nearest me, he's 'bulking' – Neil, three children, accountant from Ohio on a trial separation from his wife. I watch a movie until Joseph comes on, riding a motorbike with a half-naked Latina clasped to his torso, then I read the in-flight magazine, three times, especially the page where their astrologer analyses Joseph's character. She says he's very passionate in bed but predisposed towards moodiness. Forget Joseph, focus on my mission.

Henry Hardwick. The name on the boarding card read 'Henry Hardwick'. The man I saw must have been the same age as my father and he's a lawyer – is that enough of a connection?

'Mum, what was my dad like?' I'd ask my mother after gauging a safe mood for her to talk about the past.

'A marsupial.'

'A what?'

'Hairy hands and his nose twitched. I used to call him *Mr Wombat*. Mr Wombat! And he called me Mrs Wombat. Come here, Mr Wombat. Mr Wombat wants a–'

Is that Mr Wombat sitting a few seats behind me?

———

Pop! goes another champagne cork. Laughter.

Henry Hardwick separated by a curtain, but close enough to hear her laughter, calls for drinks and food and blankets as I see the constant flow of air crew coming back and forth with chocolates and canapés, and disinfected cloths to wipe up their mess.

This isn't the first time I've been convinced I've seen my father. At school I would stand at the gates looking out onto the busy road, watching the men pass, waiting for one of them to stop and recognise me as his daughter. I regaled my peers with stories of my dad – the underworld spy, the explorer lost in a jungle with only a crumpled photograph of me to keep him going, a world champion boxer and raconteur. When home, I'd sit watching TV, replacing the hero of every programme with my father.

Of course I looked for him. He could have been anyone in a crowd. Anyone being served in a queue, the homeless man outside the Tube station I'd pass every day, the father of a friend of mine, anyone of the besuited men in the City.

Henry Hardwick.

I'd come up with several scenarios about what I'd do if ever I saw him, me receiving the Nobel Peace Prize, waiting for the applause to die down before getting out my thank-you speech, but one person at the back keeps clapping. As the audience turned to him, he'd be weeping. 'That's my daughter! That's my Stella.' Perhaps one morning he would turn up on my doorstep. I'd make him tea and he'd fix my leaking radiator and later stand over a sizzling barbecue on a hot Sunday afternoon serving veggie sausages to my friends who'd say, 'Oh, he's so cool your dad, wish mine were like him.'

Henry Hardwick. Maybe he'd be poor and old, unable to die without the forgiveness of his long-lost daughter. I'm sent for. We come face to face in the hospital room. I bring my ear to his dry mouth and listen for his last croaky words... The script finishes there.

Another few episodes of *The Sopranos*, Henry and his wife have now passed out, their seats transformed into beds. I stand outside the toilets with a cup of tepid water, peering through the curtain at them. The newly-weds lie with their arms around each other, mummified in airline blankets, a hillside of pillows, crisp wrappers and magazines flanking them. His mouth is open like an upturned drain, a nest of her hair hovers above it. He's grey around the temples and wears long socks. I try to understand why the intensity of my mother's love for him never changed despite what he did. When a father and his young son come out of the toilet and the boy slams the door behind him, Henry shudders and half wakes. Turning away from the galley light – or perhaps conscious of being observed – he opens his eyes, squints into the distance, bleary, half-asleep and intoxicated. It seems that without his glasses, he isn't able to focus on more than shapes. But then he lifts himself and looks straight at me. His new wife stirs, pats him and he settles himself again, his fingers curling around the edge of the blanket. He goes back to sleep.

Henry Hardwick. Well, here he is. What do I do now?

26

Warm air scented like a favourite shower gel eases me down from the plane onto the new tarmac in front of the airport. For the last six months, I've only been able to see in shades of grey, but now I'm blasted with the full spectrum of colour as the chill of winter evaporates from my skin.

A man in a chauffeur's uniform holds up a card with the name of the hotel. Six of us are led into a white SUV. The door slides closed and our driver tilts his hat over his eyes and bounces into his seat ready to point out little villages of pastel-coloured houses and hoot behind rusting blue and yellow buses packed with people, animals and crates and thudding with music. We spot white Palladian-style homes set behind immaculate lawns as we pass the electric-blue sea lined with uninterrupted stretches of sand.

'Mahogany Grove,' says the driver, explaining why the light has been temporarily obscured by huge trees. Someone points out a green monkey. Then another. Through the forest we come to a bridge bordered by blue lotus flowers floating on the water and arrive at the sea again and the main entrance to the Paradise Beach Club.

My heart beats like a Motown tune when we stop at the glass doors of the hotel. Inside, a receptionist says my name as if she's been waiting for me all her life. A tall man with superb posture, who can't be more than thirty years old, stands by my side in what looks like an admiral's uniform. This is Ferdinand, I'm told, my 'personal butler'. He smiles when I go to shake his hand and asks me to follow him.

There's a heady silence in the air, broken only by the faint clicking of expensive shoes over marble and colourful little birds chasing each other through the front of the lobby. I stop at a flower display the size of my room at Tash's place.

'Wow!'

'Splendid, aren't they? They are known as The Pride of Barbados flowers.'

I look down at Joe's T-shirt and my worn-out Converse trainers and reassure myself that in a place like this, you could only be exceptionally rich to dress like me.

At two enormous wooden doors, Ferdinand swipes his magnetic card which opens to a vast white room softened by the billowing mosquito net over the bed.

'Ma'am.' Ferdinand places the key card on a dresser and looks back at me. 'The Walter Raleigh Suite.'

A large four-poster bed populated with pillows, a fireplace, a large white armchair. There's a cinema-sized plasma screen which spells out my name, the room number and a letter written in ink to me explaining in depth how dedicated the hotel are to making my stay as pleasant and luxurious as possible.

'Here is the dressing room, the safe is in this cupboard.' I nod as he opens the teak shutters wider. 'Your terrace leads to the sea. I'll have the maid unpack your belongings while you visit our gardens.'

'No, I'll–' I rugby tackle him for the bag. 'I'll do it.'

'Is everything to your satisfaction?' he asks, bewildered.

'It's perfect, thank you.'

'When you want a tour of the hotel, or if you need me for anything, I shall be outside your door, if not, dial zero for reception and ask for me. Ferdinand.'

'Thank you, Ferdinand.'

'Or Ferdi. Everyone calls me Ferdi, ma'am.'

'Ferdi. Call me Stella, not ma'am…'

'Is there anything you require? A rum punch, daiquiri, club sandwich, coconut, papaya cocktail…?'

'Maybe later.'

He bows. 'Ma'am.' After he closes the doors, I fall back onto the Chesterfield sofa and squeeze a cushion to my chest.

27

Outside my room is a terrace with a hammock the size of a small rowing boat, a table, chairs and sun lounger. Next door is another suite with matching terrace but the shutters are closed and chairs are folded. All clear. No Tash, no journalists, no mother. No dogs nipping at my ankles. Just space – and two whole weeks of it.

Sand crunches under my feet until I stand at the edge of the sea, feeling my feet tingle in the frothy water. Two men are tugging out a red-and-green fishing boat, they wave, I wave back. Ambling back to my room, I wonder what kind of swimming costume I'll buy before snuggling into my white waffle-cotton bathrobe. I lie on my bed drawing in the honeyed breeze rolling in and out of the open windows.

Someone knocks on the hotel door, and I hear the shuffling of shoes and a low cough. Another tap. I turn the handle to see Ferdi.

'I apologise if I've disturbed you, ma'am, but I thought you might like something special to drink before you rest.'

'That would be lovely. "Stella", please.'

'Yes. Miss *Stella*. I would like to offer you this.' He hands me a tall green drink dressed with mint, rosemary leaves, bits of pineapple and shavings of what looks like tree bark.

'Does it have a name?'

'I call it, Mother's Special Drink. It's a wonder for jet lag. For *anything* really. A few sips and you'll feel refreshed.'

'Thank you, Ferdi, it looks delicious. What's in it?'

'I can't say, ma'am. It's a secret passed down through the female line of my family.'

He places the drink on a table, then waits for me to try it, which is a little embarrassing as I was hoping to flush it down the toilet.

I take a sip. It tastes strange – creamy, spicy with a few woody lumps that catch on my tongue.

'You have to finish it all to experience the full benefits.'

I pick up the drink again and wonder if this is standard procedure at the Paradise Beach Club Hotel.

'You're from London, aren't you?' He rolls onto his toes which turn up under his light canvas shoes, then drops back on his heels.

'Yes, I am.'

'Very cold country.'

'You've been there? Ferdi, do sit down.'

He doesn't, choosing to smooth out my bedclothes instead. 'Yes. 2009 to 2011. They were difficult years for me.'

In *2009* Joseph and I had left university and were renting a flat together in London. We used to have all our friends over on Sunday afternoon to play parlour games – I see him now, *one word, two syllables…* When will I stop converting every date into what I was doing with Joseph at that time?

Ferdi shifts his weight, looks at me as if he expects another question.

'Where did you stay?'

'All around, but I did my hotel training in Hyde Park. Do you know it?'

'Sure. Did you like it?'

'No, ma'am. I hadn't planned to work in the catering profession. I went in the hope of making it in the film business. That's my dream, you see, to make films. I believed Britain would offer more opportunities than America and went laden with my scripts and a showreel, but alas, doors did not open for me. It was very cold, ma'am. Everyone talked of cutbacks and redundancies, but what I saw was not merely a shortage of money but a recession of the heart.'

'I'm sorry to hear that.' I look up at a fleet of white sails scudding across the ocean. 'Maybe it wasn't the right time for you.'

'That's what my mother said.'

'The film business, it's never easy, but don't give up if that's what you really want.'

'No, ma'am – *Stella* – I haven't. I love working here and I meet very interesting people, like yourself, and of course, many people who come here are in the film industry, so, who knows? One day, maybe.' He opens his palm for the empty glass. 'It's in the lap of the gods.'

My mouth is now burning.

'Now I shall leave you to rest. And you'll have the most healing and restorative of sleeps. If you wish for anything…'

'I'll call you,' I manage to say through my scorched vocal cords. 'Thank you.'

'It's a long flight, I know. Such travel, for us, is not a natural state; we aren't birds. The body, mind and soul need to recover. Enjoy your sleep.'

Ferdi leaves me with the fragments of his life and very sore lips as blades of the fan spin me back in time.

28

'Tell me about my dad?' I'd ask my mother as we lay in her bed, me bridged over her legs, her tray of coffee perched on her knees. She'd plump up her pillows and stretch.

'Pass the codeine; here, open it. Bloody thing's childproof.'

I twisted the top open. 'About my dad?'

'Ugh! What *more* do you want to know?' she'd ask, pouring her pot of black coffee into a mug half filled with whisky.

'You know, how you met, stuff–'

'It's *Beat the Intro* in seven minutes – start phoning the radio station.'

'Okay – it's dialling now. Which name shall I use?'

'Yours. I'll tell you because you're bright and you're going to make something of yourself. I'll tell you so you *never* think you've met "the one", and then get pregnant, and think he'll stick by you – they never do, never do. Got that?'

———

I spent much of my childhood on Mum's bed. Until I started secondary, I'd miss school in three-day sequences – enough time until a doctor's note was requested. She'd make herself a strong black coffee and a small glass of Fernet-Branca to steady her shaking hands before she could lift her first whisky. After that, drink after drink, pill after pill, the days went by. Mum only left the house during the day if she really needed to, otherwise it was my job to buy her the cigarettes and alcohol. Our place was cramped and airless and we were high up in a building whose lift rarely worked. By night things at home could get rowdy, usually with Mum trying to go out and me trying to keep her in. The days would end with me dragging her heavy, jerking body near enough to her bed when she passed out. I'd stay awake, listening in case she got up again or choked. Twice she miscalculated the dose of barbiturates and went into a fit. I taught myself CPR from watching medical TV series.

'Henry Hardwick – *your* father – was *crème de la crème* my mother would've called him. She was such a snob – she came from the north, Lancashire; her dad was a brigadier, whatever that meant, distantly related to some squire – and she thought she'd struck lucky marrying my dad because he worked for a bank and was a member of Lloyds and been to a private school. So I was brought up posh – you wouldn't know it looking at this dump.' We looked around the overflowing bins, broken curtains and damp walls of the said dump, imagining it through the horrified eyes of the granny I'd never met because I was illegitimate.

'But I was brought up in a big house in an old village. Church. Pub. Post office. All old stone and timber. We had our own garden, garage, a hall with a fireplace, hollyhocks and a small rose garden, a few trees. A view. It wasn't grand, but so pretty. And spoiling. We had a cleaner, a gardener – I thought everyone lived like us. Didn't I come down with a bump! That's why, Stella, I love beautiful houses – I once lived like that and believe me, it's a much, much better way to live.'

'Can we go there?'

'They had to sell it when my dad lost everything in the market crash. After that, anything they could scrape together went towards my private-school education because up until twelve years old I was top in everything. Then came boys, drink, clubbing… eventually I got expelled. My parents didn't know what to do with me so I was sent away to secretarial college in London. Anyway, my dad didn't think women could do any better than being a secretary – apart from marrying the boss! So I went to stay with his sister in a little flat off the Fulham Broadway. She had all these curfews and laminated rules posted up all over the flat. We argued constantly but I did the course and got a job as a legal secretary in the city. And that's where I met Henry. Roll me a spliff would you, love?'

She sipped her drink, lolled her head around a bit.

'And...? And?'

She'd gone on standby for a little bit until I pinched her toes, never tiring of hearing about my father although her memories dragged her down.

'It was a very old-fashioned chambers, in Temple, it was like something out of a Trollope novel, but I loved it. The routine, earning money, getting to know London, I was really, really happy, and good at it. One of the bosses suggested I do night school with a view to a law conversion course and training contract. So that's what I started doing. And my parents were proud of me, finally! And then...'

'Henry.'

'And as soon as I'd heard the name – Henry Hardwick – I thought, that's the one for me. I don't know why, it just sounded... strong, important... smart, gentlemanly. I wanted to impress my parents, stop them worrying all the time.' She looked into her drink as if she could find that silly teenager whose impulse had led us to temporary accommodation. 'He wasn't dashing or handsome – no muscles on his chest or funny stories – in fact, he hardly spoke. He wore glasses and seemed sort of... vulnerable, in a way. He'd been to Balliol College, Oxford. He was arrogant yet shy and older, twenty-six at the time. There was always a hoo-hah about him – his dad was an important lawyer and Henry used to go to all the toff parties around London. The girls used to pick out pictures of him in *Tatler* and the Nigel Dempster column in the *Daily Mail* in our lunch hour.'

'And what did he think of you?'

'He was the only man who paid no attention to me at all. None! The joke is, I thought he'd be easy – I thought I was doing him a favour picking him when no one else fancied him. But I'd been there a year before he even knew my name!'

'What did you do? You know, to make him fancy you?'

'I used to spray his brief ribbons with perfume! I'd stay late in the evenings working on this access course for university hoping he'd say, "Let's have a drink" – that's what the others did – but he'd just say, "Goodnight, Florence" and walk out. And I'd be left thinking… what…? My friend Jessie, she used to shag all the lawyers – when I went into work she'd have been there all night, she just went right into the day without even changing her clothes. And there was Sally as well, I told you about her, didn't I? The one who invested in a small flat in–'

'But what did you feel about *Henry*?'

'Oh. Well, I guess you could say I'd fallen in love – romantic idiot that I was. Had I been like Sally–'

'Then what happened?' Mum's digressions were as inevitable and frustrating as the adverts on TV.

'I've told you this a million times!'

'*Again.*'

'Really,' she huffed, sipped. 'So it was a Friday and I'd finished work with no plans that weekend. Remember I didn't know London and hadn't really made that many friends. It was evening but felt like midnight. Cold, windy and raining hard, and I was waiting outside for the bus. And then I saw Henry dashing out the door and trying to flag down a taxi. He was wearing a long black coat and carried an umbrella, which the wind was pulling away from his face. As he struggled with it, he saw me and waved goodnight. When a taxi pulled up, he gestured at me to get in. As I trotted up to him to say I was fine, he said my name, and,' she laughed, 'then he went all funny. Boss-eyed and mumbling and tapping at my shoulders. What had happened was that the rain had drenched my white shirt right through and he could see my bra. It was black. Lacy. He could see everything! So much for perfume and roses, all he wanted was to see some tit! So he goes, "Jump in, Lancashire hot pot!" All very posh like. I started talking about a big case they were working on but he just carried on staring at my breasts through the shirt. He couldn't even speak! When we arrived at Onslow Gardens, South Kensington, where he shared a flat, the cab stopped and he just grabbed me, put his mouth on mine and just pressed it, hard as possible. It's a wonder my lungs didn't explode.'

I put my hands over my face in embarrassment. 'Gross.'

'No, amazing! It felt like something really important had begun. Like I'd actually arrived on the planet and could finally see what all the fuss about being alive was about. But then he pulled away, grappled around for his wallet. I remember insisting that I paid for the taxi ride. He said, "Are you sure?" But I made out it was nothing – it wasn't at all; it was a fortune for me but I so wanted him to like me, be impressed by me, all that stupid people-pleasing started then.'

'And then?'

'I spent the whole weekend planning what to wear and running stories in my head about how it would be when we next met. But when we did the following week, he didn't even seem to recognise me. Weeks went by and he acted like it had never happened. I began to wonder if it had. If anything, he was a little sharper with me, but it was difficult to tell.'

'And?'

'Quite a while later I stepped into the lift at work and he was already in it. We said our "Hellos", I expected the same old glacial nod, but as we went down, he turned me towards him and kissed me – a real passionate snog. When the doors opened on the ground floor, he wished me a good day and let me walk ahead. I was stunned, imagine, I was just a young northern lass…'

'Then what happened?'

'The big moment came when there was a work function –

cocktails to celebrate a case or a partnership – Mummy even came down to London to help me pick out a dress beforehand. Of course, I'd told her all about Henry, maybe made out things were a little more mutual between us. Go and get the dress I wore, the blue dress in the cupboard.'

I knew exactly which blue dress it was. I took it out and we both looked at it lying on the bed as if all my mother's expectations still clung to it.

'He didn't talk to me all night until right at the end and he said, "You are the most beautiful woman I have ever seen".'

'That night, was it perfect?'

'Yes, I suppose it was. We kissed, we talked, we cuddled and naturally he wanted to go further – they always do. I knew I shouldn't but he was strong, forceful. He told me he was crazy about me... he talked about restaurants he wanted to take me to, places he wanted me to see and weekends away. I knew I should have resisted, protected myself but I didn't want to lose him.'

29

Henry and Florence would meet every Sunday after he came back from his family estate in Norfolk and he'd lure her into a bed that stank of his father's labradors. It never occurred to her that Henry's father's flat existed so he could also do exactly the same with girls who weren't his wife.

'Didn't you want him to meet your friends, parents?'

'Of course! But he said weekends were difficult.'

'Did he ever say he loved you?'

'Not exactly… but… after… y'know… *doing it*, he'd play with my hair and we'd talk. I got to know the *real* him… the *Wombat*.'

'*Wombat*?'

'Oh you ask so many questions – you're going to be lawyer, not just a *secretary* to a lawyer – the real wig and gown, you!'

'And?'

'I called him *Mr Wombat*,' she laughed at the thought, 'because without his glasses he couldn't see a thing. And Mr Wombat would…'

Curious as I was, I didn't want *all* the details.

Mum chose to interpret his secrecy for serious commitment, imagining that their great love had to remain undiscovered only to be disclosed at the right time. So while her friends collected oversized crucifixes and back-combed their hair, Mum doodled pictures of wedding dresses and practised what she hoped would be her future signature, *Mrs Florence Hardwick.*

One Saturday, when she was wandering through the Great Gear Market on the King's Road with her friend Sally, she felt sick. She gulped back the saline waters filling her mouth until the nausea passed, but not the fear of what it meant. When she saw

Henry the following Sunday night, she bathed him and he splashed like a baby. She rubbed him dry with a towel and they laughed and heated up a meal for two in front of the TV. Instead of ordering a cab and going their separate ways as usual, Henry asked her, quietly, almost nervously, if she would stay the night, all night.

The next morning, waiting for the taxi to take them into work, his fingers grappled for hers and intertwined in her hand. She nearly told him then that they were going to have a baby together.

'And then a few weeks went by and he didn't call. But that was his *modus operandi* – Latin, Stella, you'll need it for your law studies. He'd let his guard down, be tender and gentle with me, and then pretend I didn't exist. But there was this moment I went a little wrong – you know how I can get – you were just developing your little ears at the time – I found his parents' home phone number through directory inquiries and called Henry. I told him that I had to see him immediately. I'd had one or two drinks… not too much…'

I know Mum after one or two drinks; it's always too much.

'We met at the office because his father was using the *love warren*, as he called the Barbican flat, to "prepare for a case". When he saw me he was pretty over-excited – well, Mr Wombat was pleased to see me! He said he'd always wanted to "do it" on his desk – sorry, close your ears. He even offered to drive me home afterwards as he'd brought the car down to London. I accepted. It was magic, sitting next to him, a Sunday night, being a couple when I'd missed him so much… and I told him I was pregnant.'

'And?'

She blows out smoke and her eyes dim.

'The way he looked at me. It was a face I didn't recognise. He had these bloodhound eyes and no words seemed to come out of his lips. He was anything but my Mr Wombat. I started crying, saying things like, "I know it's come a little earlier than we wanted, we can still marry before it comes, I'm sure our parents will be delighted..." And then he shouted at me: "What are you on about, you stupid woman?" He was so angry. I said, "Wombat, what difference does it make, now or later and–" Then he said, "But Florence, you know I'm engaged".'

I heard the drains of Mum's oesophagus clearing, alcohol down, tears back, pills in.

'The next day, Henry was in Manchester working on a case. I was called up by the employment agency who'd found me my job, they said they were placing me somewhere more *appropriate*. The promises of a future training contract, all the work I'd done, all gone.'

That's when her obsession with Caroline Baxter started. Apparently Caroline was pretty and popular and everyone adored her. Henry was 'mad about her' – so said one of his colleagues who Mum went out with a few times to make Henry jealous.

'A few weeks after I'd lost my job and was still temping around London, he met me in Green Park. Of course, I thought it was to make up and plan our future but it was to make sure I would do exactly what he wanted. At first he was kind and patient, told me if things were different, that we were right for each other. He said he regretted he'd not been clear about his situation but he'd thought I knew all about Caroline; it hadn't been a secret. But he was adamant that there was no way he could back out of this "arrangement" unless he wanted to lose his inheritance. The Baxters had a long-standing relationship with his family. He and Caroline had been going out for three years, she was the reason he went home most weekends and they had plans to marry in the next year.'

Henry promised that after Mum terminated the pregnancy, let him get married and waited a decent period – two or so years –

he'd divorce Caroline and they would be reunited and of course he'd help her with her legal training.

'But I had to abort. That was his condition. So I said, "No. I'm having the baby, come find us when you're ready to marry for love and not money".'

30

At six months pregnant, Florence returned to see her parents in their 30s semi-detached in Croston. Her mother asked one question on opening the door, 'Where is he, your husband?' Florence's father lowered his newspaper and said, 'There appears to be a tart in the house. Please see it leaves by the back door.' His daughter's pregnancy embodied all they loathed about London and the new world, everything they'd read about in the *Daily Mail* and all that their heroine, Margaret Thatcher, despised. If she was doing this just to get a council house, well, she was free to live in one.

Florence knew it was unlikely that she would ever see her parents again – unless, of course, Henry stood by his responsibilities.

Florence went back to London and joined the end of the line at her local DHSS office. She was placed in a room at a boarding house in Ealing until a council house was ready. She became good friends with the main booker at her temp agency, Shelley, my godmother. Shelley gave Mum any work that could be done at home. In her spare time, she stayed up late at night writing letters to Henry, they were returned to her, unopened. When the last of her savings dried up, she gave birth to me on St Clement's Day as the weather turned icy cold.

Florence had been assured by girlfriends that the moment Henry laid eyes on his baby, he'd be bowled over with love and wanting to protect his child. I was a few weeks old when Henry came to see me.

'What happened when he saw me?'

'He was *horrified* by where we lived – it was terrible. Odd types spitting in the corridors, shuffling around in their bedroom slippers, blocked toilet and cockroaches. I shared a bathroom with the six other families. I made him tea, which he didn't drink. I'd spent the last of my money on a cake which he didn't eat. He was in a hurry to get out. It was raining, of course, and there was water running down the walls.'

'But what did he say when he saw *me*?'

'He didn't really look at you, darling: he had a taxi waiting.'

Florence knew then he was never coming back; however, a significant amount of cash in white, typed envelopes would appear every month, with no note or signature. It fired her hopes that the *postponement* plan was on. Years later, after her father died, she learnt the money wasn't from Henry but from her mother. 'Denial makes the world go round, darling.'

She heard all about Henry's marriage from Sally, her spy on the inside. It had been the traditional country church wedding, marquee, multi-tiered white cake and honeymoon in Tuscany – Florence's dreams all went to Caroline Hardwick *née* Baxter. A few years later, she read that they'd had two sons.

Ferdi's mother sure knows what to put in a health drink, after drinking her potion I went to the beauty salon to get my hair cut and coloured, a facial, mani-pedi and replace the brushed-chrome skin with a St Tropez tan. Now I'm swishing down the glossy corridors of the Paradise Beach Club Hotel like a frisky palomino.

Now I need to think about what I'm going to wear this week so head for the golden palm-tree arches of the Paradise Beach Club's shopping arcade.

This is a new shopping experience: rows and rows of glass fronts, no other customers, and open throughout the night. I walk into a shoe shop having spotted a great pair of sandals.

'Hey! Hey! Bring me this in a four and a half!' The tone is harsh, more than supercilious, it's vindictive. From the corner of my eye, I see another shopper drop a pair of black thigh-length boots into the salesgirl's hands and wonder how these would work on a beach holiday, when I turn to look, there's the woman from the park, the departure lounge. My father's new wife. My *stepmother*.

In the mirror's reflection I watch her lying across the banquette, checking off the many gold bangles on her wrist as she rotates her naked foot in the air and hums. She plays with her hair, scrunching it up, bringing it down, massaging the vast slippery strands and encouraging the coils to spring up of their own accord. She's a strange combination of petite and doll-like, but also makes me think of a hirsute squid in dominatrix boots. She reaches out to pick up a red thong off the shelf in her kitchen-scissor fingers, humming, 'Whoa, I'm going to Barbados!'

I take a few tentative steps in the sandals.

The Medusa purrs in an affected drawl, 'Hot.'

'Think so?'

'I know so. I'm going to try those too but I'm still waiting for the Louboutins…' she juts out her chin in the direction of the shop till, 'but that stupid girl can't even remember one type of shoe.' She laughs. 'When d'you get here?'

'Today.'

'Me too. Where from?'

'London.'

'Same.' She claps her hands together and throws her legs in the air. 'London!

'I thought that as soon as I saw you.'

'*That* pale?'

'Know how I knew?' She jangles her bracelets in the air. 'London people have a *look*.' She raises an eyebrow to make sure I'm giving her hypothesis full attention. 'They look like they could fit in anywhere – it's unique. See? The Germans are always aggressive, the French are killer bitches – not just the women – the Italians – talking, talking rubbish and their mamas; the Americans, so loud and obvious – *no class* at all – but the English? These people are *subtle*; they're like those universal keys: fit in everywhere. Am I right or am I right?'

'I try to take people on their individual merit–'

'Bravo!' She points a long, manicured finger at me. 'You're smart. I can tell that too. Me? I'm like, from *every*where… and *no*where. I love people, people *love* me.' She picks up a stiletto and starts skewering the heel into her palm. 'I don't need to be labelled. Y'know, I spent time in LA, Qatar, Paris, Stockwell. I'm a nomad of the soul – I say to Henry, my man, "Darling, as long I have a Platinum American Express card I'm at home!" But listen, I'll tell you a secret,' she bends so that her mouth comes close to my ear but not before a brush of wiry hair, 'I have a gypsy heart.'

The salesgirl hovers with the boots until the 'gypsy heart' strikes out and snatches them into her lap.

'And guess what, you two?' She wiggles her fingers at me and the shop assistant. 'I just got married!'

'Wow! And who's the lucky man?'

'Henry Hardwick. He's a lawyer. Went to Oxford. English, of course. We have an estate in North... Norf... somewhere in England. An "estate" – not like *council* estate but like garden-open-to-the-public *estate*. Get this – *fifteen* bedrooms.' The girl and I nod to each other. 'I went there once: walked in and straight out again. I said I won't go back until they put in more heating and a stripper pole in the basement. But that's not a problem because we also have an apartment in Knightbridge. Doorman and everything. Hey, you, how am I supposed to get these boots on with these nails?'

When the assistant kneels on the floor ready with the boot for her to step into, she waves her away.

'Hey, we must hang out, you and me and Henry, huh? We need people around us otherwise, well, he can get a bit, y'know... *old*. I can tell you're cool, otherwise I wouldn't be talking to you.' She takes me by the wrist and pulls me closer to her. 'And go blonder.'

'Enjoy your–'

'Henry will be wondering where I am, he can't bear it when I shop without him.' She rests her handbag over her shoulder. 'He just loves to watch me getting in and out of clothes, and me? I just love to watch him pay! Ha! But I couldn't resist those boots when I walked by. Don't you think I'll look just like Julia Roberts in *Pretty Woman* – imagine, little French knickers, this bra–' She lifts her top over her balloon-like breasts, barely covering each one is a shiny, yellow triangle. 'Yah, *real* gold-plated!' She snaps her top down and shouts, 'Girl! Have those sent up to the Marco Polo honeymoon suite. In red *and* black.'

The shop assistant comes out, flustered by the pile-up of requests.

'Mrs Henry Hardwick.' She turns once again to me. 'Darling, if you see us, you must come up and say hi, huh? I'm Yuleka. And you're...?'

'Stella.'

She puts out her hand for mine. I take it, carefully, to make sure the nails don't slice through a main artery. She looks at the sandals I'd tried on. 'Get them in pink.'

33

I'm sitting on my terrace watching the last light edge over the slick, still sea and munching on the roasted cashew nuts left by Ferdi. After meeting Yuleka, I need to work on a strategy for what to do when I meet my father. Surely, he'd recognise my name. And if not, at what point in the two-week holiday do I tell him I'm his daughter? And from there, how do I make him add his name to my birth certificate?

The door in the next villa opens. Lights go on and I see a shadow lengthen along the teak planks. Footsteps. A man walks to the end of his terrace, looks out to the sea. He's well-built and, as he smiles at the coming night, I see good, healthy teeth. Late twenties, handsome, like something out of a men's 'weekend wear' catalogue.

He drinks from a bottle of water before taking off his T-shirt then he lets his coral-coloured linen trousers slide to his ankles. He stands naked on the terrace with his buttocks to me. I'm staring at his firm backside, not daring to breathe. To make matters worse, he starts swaying his arms and kicking out in long graceful steps. I've seen people do this in Holland Park, capoeira.

I let my head loll onto my shoulder feigning sleep in case he looks over. When his sequence finishes with a climactic double kick lifting him high above the fence that separates us, he puts his hands together and bows low – a bit too low.

After staring out at the ocean for a few moments, airing his extremities, he saunters over to a nearby bush to pick up a pair of swimming trunks left to dry. My neighbour pulls up his trunks, ties a knot in the waistband and sees me.

'Oh hi!' he says.

'Hmm?' Mid-yawn.

He sweeps his lips over a set of perfect white teeth and challenges me with a facetious smile.

'Enjoy the floor show?'

'This isn't just the intermission?'

He chuckles to himself. 'You must have arrived this afternoon.'

'Yeah, from London. The snow was settling when I left.'

'Time to take a vacation. I'm Peter.' The firm handshake continues over the terrace wall.

'Stella. And you're from…?'

He raises an eyebrow and inclines his head to one side. 'New York. You here on your own?' He sneaks a look into my villa.

'I am.'

'Like me. I always prefer travelling alone, that way you get to meet pretty

peeping Toms.'

'It's how I find all my naked men.'

'I would have used a fig leaf or a coconut shell if I'd known.'

'I didn't see much… only enough for a short YouTube clip.'

'I'm in your power forever now. Hey, been on the beach yet?'

'Not properly.'

'Not "properly" – love your accent.' He puts his hands on his hips and looks out to sea. 'This is the best time. The sand's cooled down and the water's warm; it's going to be a full moon tonight. I'm just going to have a last dip now.' We watch the seagulls cutting into the sky like blades. 'Say, want to join me?'

I hesitate. The birds cackle. A strange man who goes around naked… in a strange place. 'I'll just get my things.'

It takes me a minute to dash in and remove the price tag from my new swimsuit, put my hair up before dabbing a little lip gloss on my lips – and I stop. Something's different. I feel like I've left something behind. That gnawing pain which has been with me for so long – it's gone.

'No need to guess why they call this the Platinum Coast,' Peter says, as we stroll over the powdery shoreline, sifting the sand between our toes. There's something homely about Peter that puts me at ease. He's friendly, relaxed and fine with the occasional silences that swirl between us.

We pass the restaurants as they start switching on their strings of coloured light bulbs and the volume on their sound systems, walking along the coast, over rocks and through mango groves until we're clear of the hotels and bars. And I'm smiling because it's kind of erotic, the moonlight, my feet being massaged by the soft sand and the warm air.

'Is it your first time in Barbados?' Peter asks.

'Yes. And you?'

'I've come here every year since I was a kid. My folks used to have a house over the other side but now they take vacations on some of the other islands – they say the social life's better. But I still love it here. Feel the water.'

I let the ripples tickle my feet while Peter loosens his shorts.

'I like to feel the water against my skin. You okay if I…?'

'Sure. There's nothing I haven't seen already,' I answer, before peeling off my clothes and wading in behind him.

34

We swim, naked, at first together, then separately, and then side by side. I lie on my back, letting the water hold me. He's right; there really is a full moon above us, throwing silver flakes onto the water. I watch Peter doing little dives up and down over the waves before we float, weightless, our toes occasionally poking up over the horizon. We wade onto the beach and he turns away to let me dress.

'Come on,' he whispers and pulls me up by the hand. 'Let's drink.'

'This is bliss!' I sigh, seeing the black outline of our villas in the distance.

'Sure is, you picked a perfect night to arrive. Oh my God!' He laughs, staring at my legs. 'Stella, are you a mermaid?'

'What?'

'Look!'

'What?'

He's laughing so much I have to wait for him to get the words out. 'You've got scales! Look, up and down your legs.'

We both look down at my skin, which is streaked orange and white from my toes to my thighs. There's a dark-brown V shape on one knee and on my other ankle speckles of yellow, like I've got trench foot.

'It's the St Tropez tan,' I say.

'I've been to St Tropez, honey, and I've never seen a tan like that!'

'Now I remember, she said don't go in the water for four hours.'

'I love it! You look like a giraffe! And I love giraffes – except for their black tongues, that kind of lets them down. You don't have a black tongue, do you?'

I stick my tongue out at him. He laughs, then goes to kiss my cheek. 'You know, you don't need that stuff. Why'd you want to look like everybody else? You're skin's like, yoghurt, creamy, smooth…' He puts an arm around me.

'And you're pretty smooth too,' I say, taking his arm from my waist.

'Touché.'

A few yards away, his room butler is placing what looks like a large warmed brandy on his table.

'Nightcap?'

'Sure.'

'Asari, wait,' he calls out to his butler. He looks to me. 'What would you like?'

'Whatever you're having.'

'Make that two Armagnacs,' he calls over. 'You like Armagnac?'

'The book of prophesies?'

'Better make them doubles.'

Sitting on his terrace, we sip our drinks while I comb out my hair and despair over the remains of my tan. Every time he sees my stripey legs he chuckles.

'Whatcha lookin' at?' Peter asks.

'Sirius, the Dog Star.'

'Huh. Sure is bright.'

'See around it – the shape of a dog. And, fun fact, it marks every new year by reaching its highest point in the sky around the stroke of midnight.'

'Good to know if I forget to charge my Apple watch. You seem to know a lot of stuff, I mean, like–'

'Useless trivia?'

'Yeah. You pick it up in jail or dated Stephen Hawking or something?'

'My mother got money off her bar tab when she won the pub quiz at our local. So we'd cram for competitions, radio phone-ins, anything that paid. Surprising how much has stuck. What colour is Sonic the Hedgehog? How many time zones does Russia have, and why are you looking at me so strangely?'

'It's a long time since someone surprised me, that's all.'

We look out onto the beach where I see a couple holding hands with a little boy walking between them. I notice that the parents have matching tattoos on their arms.

'Hi, Peter,' the woman calls out. He waves back. She smiles to me as the trio disappear into the night and Peter's butler rests another two drinks on the table.

'Isn't she that model? Audrey something…'

'Yeah. She's cool but I'm not into that beautiful-people-Tribeca-junkie scene.'

'Me neither.'

'Having said that, I'm pretty partial to a little Bajan grass…' He goes to his room and returns with a little bag. 'Want some? I got the best the island grows. Hey! Maybe I could put it in a tree and you could stretch your neck up and nibble at it?'

35

A few hours later, I drift back to my room where the maids have closed the shutters, turned down the bed and sprinkled rose petals over the covers.

I flick on the TV from my wall of pillows and go through the channels, stopping when I catch Joseph's face, unshaven and brown, talking to a woman about his early life. The camera pans down to his shoe. His foot twitches in the air as he talks. The camera zooms in over his hand. He scratches his knee. I can hardly bear to watch. His soft, intelligent voice sounds dry and tired. Then there's a clip from a movie. Joseph is crawling through a paddy field with water droplets on his forehead and a rifle in his hand. A building blows up behind him. We return to the interview. He's congratulated and gives the interviewer one of his smiles, one of those long, heartfelt beams he's pulled from his catalogue of devastating expressions that turn women's brains to helium. She stumbles over the next question, he helps her out by suggesting words, but that makes her worse. That's my Joseph.

I turn the TV off and watch the fan above my head. I can still hear Joseph's voice in my mind. I tell him that I'm here and I'm going to meet my father and that maybe when I do that, I'll be able to let someone love me.

36

Ferdi brings me breakfast at nine o'clock. 'Did you find the drink I gave you yesterday reviving, ma'am?'

'I felt great. And this morning, no jet lag.'

'Excellent.'

I sit up in bed as he opens the shutters.

'Oh look, the sea!'

'Yes, ma'am. It's still there.'

'Stella,' I corrected.

'Yes, Miss Stella.' Okay. We're getting somewhere. 'You certainly are feeling better.'

'Yes, I am. You must thank your mother for me.'

'I wish I could, ma'am, but sadly she expired two years ago.'

Then I see the grief on his face. 'Oh, Ferdi, I'm sorry.'

'Don't be sorry. It was only her physical body that died. Our relationship is still as strong as ever and I'm sure she's delighted you benefited from her cure. Some people on the island used to think of her as a witch, a white witch. She was a good woman.'

'She sounds very special.'

'She was.' He closes his eyes for a moment before they spring open. 'Miss Stella,' he puts out his hand to present the tray, 'I thought, being English, you would want eggs. I don't know how you like them so I asked chef to give you a little bit of everything.' He begins lifting the top of each salver in turn. 'Fried, scrambled, poached, boiled – and, my favourite, eggs Benedict.'

'That's a lot of... thanks. And I'm sorry but I forgot to say I don't eat meat.'

'This I had anticipated.' He serves the scrambled eggs on to a plate, adds some toast. 'This is vegetarian sausage. Do you have any plans for the day?'

'Not yet. I'll just see what comes along.'

'Who was it that said, "Adventure is just bad planning"?'

'Amundsen. Ferdi, this fruit salad looks delicious.'

'The first time I ever went abroad was to Paris, I was eighteen and was accompanying an uncle who was on business. The morning we woke up he said we were going to have a continental breakfast – I was so excited! Continental – I had visions of yachts sailing into Antibes, the roulette tables of Monte Carlo, the sparkling snow on the Alps, milkmaids ambling along the Rhine, bullfights in Seville and cathedral bells ringing out over the traffic of Rome – and all I got was a stale croissant, shop-bought orange juice and a hot chocolate. The disappointment! Ever since that day, I always try to make sure my guests have a breakfast that lives up to their expectations.'

'Well, you've won me over!'

'Excellent.' He smiles widely and leaves the room. Something tells me he already knows about my evening with Peter.

I chew on a slice of fresh coconut. The sweetness of its flesh reminds me of Peter's skin under that cool shirt he was wearing. I'm starving.

'Stella, I want to know all about you,' Peter had said after I'd managed to evade most of his questions.

'I'm an open book.'

'But what *kind* of book? I'm curious. See, I know you English girls, underneath all that "proper" and "golly gosh" are just plain *filthy*.'

'You first.'

'Thirty-two years old. My family originated from Virginia but I was brought up in a brownstone apartment on Fifth Avenue, with weekends in the Hamptons. I studied law at Princeton, then a stint at the Sorbonne in pursuit of a model who was also a princess and *cum laude* student. Huge heartbreak. This was cut short by 9/11 – I won't go into why and how but I found myself in

Afghanistan when the Americans invaded. And that's where I found my true love: war reporting.'

We'd finished our drinks and were rocking in his hammock while looking up at the stars.

'I'm a danger junkie, Stella. That's my vice. I can never marry, never have a home and I'll die before I'm forty. But it's the best life I could ever wish for. Now, when I'm not on the front line, I'm bored out of my mind. I'll probably head back to Syria but I wanted some time off to work on a book, so part of this holiday is to kick back and let ideas turn over in neutral while I get my body into shape.' We both admired the contours of his biceps as he flexed them in the moonlight.

37

After a shower, walk along the coast and re-reading the first five pages of my paperback, it's time to have a snack by the pool. The hotel's gardens include waterfalls, an orchid house, lines of gazebos, a heated pool that curls around the Paradise Sunset Bar, two freshwater lagoons and a saltwater infinity pool. If guests don't want to venture out for water sports or tours around the island, there are numerous enclaves around the grounds for tennis, golf, archery, yoga classes, volleyball or billiards.

But the Paradise Beach Club's social focal point is around the pool where a steel band plays easy-listening classics. So far we've had 'Feelings', 'Raindrops Keep Falling on my Head' and now Jay-Z and Alicia Keys's 'Empire State of Mind'. After watching the 'clubbers' a while, I notice there are some who are regulars who acknowledge one another with either cursory nods or somewhat vaudevillian repartee: 'What are they laying on for us tonight, eh? Naked dancing girls jumping out of the turtle soup? Watch where he's putting that sun cream, Barbara!'

Once the guests have staked their territories with towels, books or hats, we relax knowing that the other bathers will leave us wrapped in the smell of coconut tanning lotion and rum punches. Even lifting one's head in order to attract a passing waiter is too aerobic, so many of the personal butlers will dip their ears to the sunbathers' lips to take the next commands.

One corner by the bar, however, is not behaving like the rest. There's a lot of moving the pool furniture around, popping champagne corks, loud conversations and eruptions of laughter. An occasional 'tut-tut' marks the other bathers' disapproval, though few can resist looking over the tops of their magazines to see where the noise is coming from. Even though some disgruntled individuals pad off to their rooms shaking their heads, the fun goes on.

Every time I try to engross myself in reading, the laughter breaks my concentration. While my sunglasses slip down my nose, I try to see what's going on through the slats in my sun lounger, but I can't actually make out the faces hidden by the shade. I can, however, hear the clinking of glasses and the bubble of good humour fizzing above the hotel's band. I keep to myself, dipping in and out of the pool and reapplying sun lotion but just before I'm about to order a sandwich, I hear my name being called.

I look up to see Yuleka standing on the other side of the pool in an orange wraparound with white flowers in her hair and several large gold chains around her neck which, when she moves, throw off the sun's reflection like laser lights.

'Yo!' She waves, standing with one hand forming a sunshade over her eyes. The group turns to see the object of her summons.

I wave back but it's clear she isn't *asking* me to join them, she's *telling* me.

Tucking my wraparound into my waist, I take in a deep breath and walk over to them.

This is it: this is the moment I meet my father.

'Stella my dear, *there* you are!' Yuleka throws a slippery arm over my shoulders and kisses my cheek. I hold my breath, afraid of choking on a mouthful of hair.

'Please, girlfriend, save me from all these geriatrics!' she says while shepherding me into their tropical hut. 'It *is* Stella, isn't it? Didn't you hear me calling you?' Once in the shade, I'm only a few feet away from my father. 'This is Stella. She arrived yesterday on the same flight as us.'

Like little birds they all open their mouths and turn to me, starving for a morsel of intrigue. 'We met in the lobby, didn't we?' She whispers to me, 'You know, that stupid girl sent up the wrong boots!' Then she announces back to the crowd, 'Let me introduce you to everyone. This is Roy, *Lord* Templeton-Crest.'

The aristocrat raises a small, childlike hand. I take it while noticing two white, waxy legs in a wheelchair.

'Remember Roy means k-k-k-king.' He keeps my hand in his. 'Hello, you beautiful young thing. Thank you for cheering up a crippled old f-f-fart like me.'

The gang behind him laugh.

Yuleka points to a tall woman with an exquisite bone structure, though her skin is deeply lined with either worry or years of sunbathing. She is thin, dressed in fuchsia from her shoes to her turban. 'Roy's wife, Bunny,' Yuleka says.

Bunny lifts a hand absently to acknowledge my existence while lighting a cigarette in a long holder.

'This is Michael Hammond – from South Africa, Elizabeth, and… Oh yes, Basil,' Yuleka turns me around, 'and *this* is Peter Lyle.'

'Hello. *Again.*' Peter smiles lazily as he chews off the tail of a large prawn.

'Oh you know each other already!' Everyone laughs. A little too much.

'Sure,' he says with his mouth full, 'it was a full moon last night so we went swimming,' he winks at me, 'naked.'

The crowd rumble with laughter.

'Good heavens!' exclaims Roy.

'Fast work, Lyle,' says Bunny.

Yuleka laughs. 'Now, Stella, the reason I got you over here was to warn you about some people like *this* one!' She throws a flip-flop at Peter. 'But I'm too late! Oh, Peter! You!' She swipes his knees with her hand. 'So, darling, I was going to tell you – woman to woman – about who to watch out for at the club. This one – *this* one!' she shouts out dramatically, pointing at Peter, 'he is *such* a *bad* boy!' She makes an elaborate pretence of smacking him. 'He seduces women at lightning speed. You know he's a war reporter?'

'Skinny dipping? My, my,' Lord Templeton-Crest splutters to Peter. 'Suppose you never thought of asking me along, you selfish c-c-c-cunt!'

Peter grins boyishly, helping himself to more champagne from the ice bucket.

'I get it, 'fraid of the competition, eh?'

'Don't,' drawls Bunny, 'you're making the poor girl blush.' She stubs out her cigarette on a pineapple slice.

Her husband shouts above us, 'So, Lyle, that's where you were when you didn't join us for d-d-d-dinner last night!' Then he addresses me in a concerned voice, 'You must watch out for him, Stella, he's our young Lothario.' I feel Bunny's eyes on me, like a boxer's before a fight. She brushes past Peter, tipping over a champagne flute. 'And I thought you were losing your touch.'

'And you must meet, darrrrrling Stella,' Yuleka leads me into the nucleus of the hut to make the final introduction, 'my *husband*, Henry Hardwick.'

38

Henry Hardwick raises a colourful drink that looks like a pot plant to his mouth.

Yuleka steers a cocktail sausage in and out of her swollen lips.

'Henry, Henry! Look what I'm doing! Look, Henry!' She then bites the end of it off and doubles up laughing. She holds on to my arm to steady herself and says, 'Darling, this is my new BFF.'

Henry looks to me and smiles.

'G'morning,' he says all in one syllable.

'Henry! Morning? It's not *morning,* you randy old man, it's the bloody *afternoon* already – I'm starved! Doesn't sex make you hungrrry, eh?' She throws an olive at his crotch and stretches out her arms. 'I could eat a house!'

I force myself to look directly at Henry.

His forehead glistens as he brings it down towards his drink, the plastic umbrella in the cocktail pokes up his nose.

'Bugger!' He chuckles.

'Baby, you're supposed to drink it not snort it!' She spins around. 'Henry! Let's do cocaine! Wouldn't that be fun? Peter? Can you buy us some cocaine?'

'Sure,' says Peter, standing up, 'but I'm going to swim first.'

'Last time I checked, cocaine was illegal,' mutters Henry, studying his drink.

'Or mushrooms! Henry, I gotta see you on 'shrooms.'

Yuleka takes hold of my arm. 'Henry has had the most borrrrring life you can imagine. All work and frigid women – we got married in London last week and it was so borrrring that I said "No! Henry, we're going to do it *again*, Yuleeeeeka style!"' She applauds herself, falling back against a totem pole which has a laminated sign on it thanking 'Dear Gusts' for not smoking.

Peter picks up his towel and gestures at me to join him in the pool.

There's a surge of metallic taste in my mouth and I can't catch my breath. I move my hands back to reach for something solid.

'Sorry, I didn't catch your name,' says a voice coming from my father's direction. For an instant I refocus and see him drawing an olive from a cocktail stick.

'*Stella*, darling, she's called *Stella*,' says Yuleka, tugging me tight against her. 'I told you already, she's the English rose I met on my late-night shopping trip. You got Alzheimer's or something?'

'You slovenly, slutty sloths!' calls out a lithe, blonde American woman in a pale-pink tracksuit jogging towards us. She dries her hair saying, 'Really! I can't believe not even one of you made it to the Zumba class – it was wild!'

'Perish the thought of it,' groans Bunny Templeton-Crest, inserting another cigarette into the end of the cigarette holder.

'Four o'clock is the beach volley tournament. Mike, you'll come to that, huh?' The American holds out a hand to me. 'I'm Susie, Susie Barton from Manhattan. I used to write for the *New York Times* but now I'm mainly online. You on Insta, Facebook, Twitter? What's your name and you can follow me back?'

'Stella,' I manage to say. We shake hands.

'Sorry but… Stella…?' She raises an eyebrow, anticipating more. 'Stella…?'

She wants the whole name. All eyes are on me.

'Stella. Stella…' I have to say my last name. Tyler? But do I want him to know who I am right now? He might not even connect the young Florence to my name, but if he does…? The moment I meet my father can't be now, not like this, not in front of all these people and me swooning from the heat. Fear and self-preservation draw me away from saying my real name. I need to choose my moment. 'Stella–'

'Banks! B-B-B-B-Banks, Oh! Course!' Lord Templeton-Crest exclaims. 'You're Teddy Banks' girl! Of course, of course, Bunny, this must be T-T-Teddy's filly – gosh, you've grown up… quite a stunner!' He splashes himself with water while smacking his lips. 'How is the old sod?'

I catch Peter's eye as he shakes out his towel.

'Banks. Right, Stella Banks,' cries a scrawny woman sitting at Bunny's feet rolling a joint.

'I just saw your sister in Marbella, she's such fun!' someone else pipes in.

'Remember Teddy Banks, darling?' Roy's wife doesn't look the least bit interested.

'Oh God! Not another Brit! I feel I'm on the set of *Downton Abbey*!' Susie moans as she adjusts the tassels on her bikini top.

I watch my father perusing the selection of cigars from the wooden box held open by one of the waiters. In 1492 off the coast of Venezuela, Columbus was offered tobacco leaves as gifts – having expected gold and treasures, he was a little disappointed to say the least. Little did he know. Australia is wider than the moon. The sun is burning and my mouth is dry. Wombats do cubed poos. Two women are talking to me but I can't hear them. Mark Twain smoked three hundred cigars a month. When I see the flame of my father's lighter against the glare of the sun coming in through the straw in the walls of the hut, I stumble forward, landing in Peter's arms.

'Peter, stop groping her! Get the girl a seat, for goodness' sake!'

I sit down as someone puts an ice cube into my palm as I catch snippets of different opinions about how to treat me: *Too much sun… It's her first day… From London she said… Peter, give her the kiss of life – the kiss of her life!* Laughter all round. *Who is she…? T-T-Teddy's daughter. Banks. At Wickham with*

Charlotte… She was trying on the pink sandals… Brandy always does the t-t-t-trick.

Peter pats my hand. 'You okay?' He brings a drink to my lips.

Yuleka shouts over: 'Look! Stella my dear! Look what I can do!' And she dives backwards into Henry's lap, tits last. She pats down damp patches on her new husband's shirt. 'Bravo! I told you she'd be fine! She's got Doctor Peter to take care of her!' she cries out, wiggling to a Caribbean version of Adele's 'Rolling in the Deep'.

'Peter?' Henry Hardwick snuffs. 'That's out of the frying pan into the fire.'

39

As the ice cube melts through my fingers, my heart resumes a steady canter. I take this quiet opportunity to study this man, my dad, the one slurping on champagne with a hand sliding inside a woman's skirt. There is something undeniably familiar about him, yet nothing specific to connect us. His mouth makes a large 'O' before he slots the end of his cigar into his face. Both his eyes roll down towards his nose as he draws the smoke in. Henry pops the cigar out of his mouth with a ball of smoke. I breathe it in. He looks to see if the cigar is sufficiently lit. He then moves it up and down to refute what someone's saying and catches my eye. He looks at me for a few seconds then turns to someone else and says, 'Ab-so-*lu*-te-ly.' Yuleka tugs at her bikini bottoms, recharging between performances.

Ferdi's words from this morning come back to me, when he said that his relationship with his mother continued despite her not being there. Although I haven't ever really seen my father before, our relationship has never been broken. It has always been there, linking us over the years, and here, today by the pool having cocktails, the two parts have come together.

I watch Henry and Yuleka twittering to each other in that unintelligible mumble exclusive to lovers. My sneaky glances in their direction must have attracted their attention, as Yuleka looks at me and whispers in Henry's ear. She calls over, 'Stella darling, do I look like a bride today?' She gathers up her hair and heaps it up over her head. 'Do I? Do I look like a *virginal* bride?'

'Steady on, "virginal"? That's pushing it!' gurgles my dad.

'Bet it's been a while since you've c-c-c-come across a virgin eh, Henry! P-p-p-pardon the expression!'

Henry chortles into his drink.

I bring the cold mojito to my lips, chew on the mint leaves.

'Stella,' Yuleka yells. 'Darling! I am going to be a brrrrride. We're getting married... yah, again! Henry and I, tomorrow morning!'

'Congratulations!' I say, lifting my glass to them. She kisses my father.

Then she breaks away so he can inhale more of his cigar.

'It will be our *second* wedding, yes, darling. Last weekend we married in London, just a little registry thing, now we're gonna do it again. Isn't that right, my teddy bear?'

'It is. We're rather enjoying the wedding thing – might have a few more, with the tax breaks and the refundable presents, might break even.'

Yuleka slaps him playfully.

'Well,' sighs Bunny, 'all these ceremonies should ensure that you treat this wife better than your last, Henry, hmm?'

'Bunny!' Yuleka puts on a face of grave seriousness. 'One day I will tell you about Henry's ex-wife. What a bitch! He was so unhappy with that woman, but he stayed, he stayed with her all those years because he was such a gentleman, and for the children. Such a good daddy! Such a great, great man!' She pings his chest hairs.

Daddy. I try to imagine him playing football in the park with his boys or making breakfast in bed for Mummy on Mother's Day. Difficult.

'Uuurgh!' says Yuleka, standing up and shaking herself. 'Just thinking about her makes me sick. The Cockroach we call her. A toast. Freedom from the Cockroach!' cries Yuleka, raising her champagne flute into the air before Bunny interrupts.

'Yuleka darling,' says Bunny, enunciating every syllable either because she's very drunk or she wants to make the point as sharp as possible, or both. 'We only met *you* last night so you might not know this, but some of us here actually went to Henry's first wedding and knew the Cock – Caroline – rather well.'

'So!' snaps Yuleka, 'then you know what I mean.'

'Just be careful – she's still a very old and good friend of mine.'

'Darling,' sings Roy, 'holiday! Let's not f-f-fight on holiday.' Bunny throws him a hard look. Yuleka drops back down against my father, looking up at him to defend her, but he says nothing, just raises his eyebrows at his cigar. The rest of the group have gone quiet. Then Roy thrusts his wheelchair into a spin while singing, 'La Cu- ca-ra-cha! La-Cu-ra-cha, twirrrrrling rrrrrround and rrrrround we g-g-g-go – La Cu-ca-ra-cha.' He does a wheelie and lands with a thud spilling his drink into his lap. 'Olé!'

The crowd applaud; even Bunny can't resist a smirk.

'Everyone deserves a chance, m'dear,' muses Templeton-Crest to Bunny out of Henry and Yuleka's earshot.

'I know,' says Bunny. 'But she doesn't need to be mean about Caroline – isn't it enough that she got the house?'

'Listen up guys!' exclaims Yuleka, spitting out an olive. 'You're all coming to the wedding, it's going to be very hot and steamy!'

'And expensive,' mutters my father under his breath.

40

While the party orders yet another round of drinks and debates the merits of different lunch options, I dive into the pool. When I reach the other end of it, a few people are clapping, including Yuleka who's paddling by the steps.

'You can swim all right, bravo.'

'I only learnt a few years ago. Got lessons at my local sports centre. It was like finding this secret passageway out of space and time, got hooked on it. You not coming in?'

'I can't go in water, my hair,' she says. 'Anyway, I prefer exercises that get my butt firm.'

We dangle our feet in the water while Henry talks to a man about, from what I hear, vineyards in Provence.

'That Bunny, she's a bitch, huh? They just don't want to see Henry happy. Haters. But we'll be friends, won't we?'

'Sure,' I answer, lifting a ladybird from the water's edge to safety.

We walk back to the gazebo where Bunny rolls her eyes and asks, 'Are we going to have lunch or what?'

'Where's the snack menu?' asks Susie.

'I have it!' announces Yuleka. 'Listen up guys. First, starters: grilled scallops, crab cocktail – I always like cock! – lamb lollipops…' Henry looks away at a lone white sail-boat while his bride continues with her litany of food options from his knee like a ventriloquist's dummy.

'Enjoy your lunch. I'm going to go in now,' I say, drying off.

Bunny calls out, 'Peter, why don't you share the seafood platter with me?'

'I had it yesterday. You guys go on without me. I'm gonna escort Stella back.'

'Fine,' she says. It sounds like 'fire'.

When I return to where I was originally sitting for my book and room key, Susie is already there, folding my towel.

'Listen, I just wanted to get a few things straight, that okay?' she asks, raising her thin, drawn-on eyebrows at me. 'You've probably worked out that there are a lot of single girls at the hotel and only a limited supply of men. So, we could work together or, if you want to fly solo, let me know which ones you're interested in so that way we don't tread on each other's toes. Got it?'

It takes me a few moments. 'But I'm not–'

'Shhhh. Peter's coming. Anyway, we should hang out. Strategise.' Susie puts a warning hand on my shoulder before jogging back to the group. 'Enjoy your afternoon, Stella, Peter.'

Yuleka yells from across the pool, 'Stella, Stella! Before you go…'

'Yes?'

Yuleka totters towards us beckoning me over again.

'Henry and I want to invite you to our wedding tomorrow.'

'Oh that's so–'

'We want you to be our bridesmaid.'

'Really?'

'Don't we, Henry? Want her to be our bridesmaid? Henry! This one? She'd look good, huh?' She gestures at me, her bangles rattling .

'By all means, if she'd like to…' he says indifferently.

'Yes, of course she *wants* to! She'd be perfect, wouldn't she? I mean, she's the only young person here! Apart from me.'

'Thanks,' mutters Susie.

'So it's tomorrow?'

'Tomorrow! Whoa!' Yuleka spins on her heels. 'At three. And you'll be our bridesmaid! It's the Wedding of a Thousand Dreams. On the beach. Over there…' She waves her hand in the general direction of the sea. 'Grab yourself an outfit in the arcade, charge it to the Raleigh Suite. And Peter, you must bring her – maybe we'll have a double wedding! Stella, we can be sisters!'

'Catch you later,' says Peter, leading me away.

I wave goodbye without giving myself time to reconsider what I've just agreed to do. Roy waves back to me, glistening like a roasted quail, but the others have already started organising the table for lunch. I hear Roy saying, 'Shame they don't make English roses like that anymore, eh? G-g-g-g-girls who faint in the sun. Splendid, absolutely splendid.'

'Gorgeous skin,' says one of the men. 'Let's just hope she's got enough protection.' To which Susie chips in, 'With Peter Lyle buzzing around her, the sun's the least of her problems.'

'I'll say! He got in there pretty sharpish.' Roy chuckles.

'Does she play bridge?'

Peter puts an arm around me. 'Don't listen to them.'

As we cross to the other side of the pool, I look back to see if my father is watching me but he's too far inside the hut to be seen. All I can make out is the red glow of his cigar.

41

Massaging my toes in the rubbery, recently-sprinkled grass, I hand Peter my key card.

'You've been through war zones and here's me, collapsing from a little sun. You must think I'm–'

'It's not the sun, it's the company. They're awful. Anyone unaccustomed to toxic waste would react.'

'But they're your friends, aren't they?'

'Hell no. I'm only polite to them because they know my parents. Bunny and Roy have a house in the Hamptons and their kids are cool but, but the rest… I'd rather have a live grenade in my pants than spend a day with people like that. That Yuleka, where'd she come from?'

'And yet you told them we'd swum naked together.'

'Ah, I did. I was indiscreet.' We tiptoe over a line of hot tiles.

'Before I got here, I'd been in Peshawar, on the border of Pakistan and Afghanistan – I've got too used to the company of men and travelling around in steel armour-plated vans. I'm not used to such refined – such beautiful – company. Still mad?'

I shake my head. At the door to my room, Peter moves the key card up and down the frame, he puts his ear to the door while lightly touching the handle.

'Just checking no one's been in the room since you left it.'

'Well, housekeeping might have come.'

'Right. It's just… my training.'

———

Ferdi arrives out of nowhere with a pot of tea, thinly sliced cucumber sandwiches and piece of carrot cake.

'Ferdi, that's exactly what I wanted.'

He cocks his head toward Peter. 'Will *sir* be joining Miss Stella?'

Peter smiles. 'Would you like me to stay a while?'

'I think I'm going to just rest – the jet lag, sun…'

'Gotcha. You going to this stupid wedding tomorrow?'

'I'm a bridesmaid!'

'Right! So, tomorrow, unless I see you before. Look after her, Ferdi.'

Peter hops over our communal fence to his terrace, gives me another wave and disappears.

'He's sweet, isn't he?'

Ferdi raises his eyebrows. 'I suppose.'

I sit on the bed, wiping my filmy hands with a tissue while Ferdi sets the speed of my overhead fan.

'You do like him, Ferdi, don't you?'

He adjusts the cushion by my head. 'We don't have too much wildlife in the Caribbean. No safaris or riots, no sharks in the waters or erupting volcanoes, but, ma'am, one must always be on one's guard. Don't you think?' He refills my teacup.

'I guess… every year over one hundred people choke on ballpoint pens.'

'Exactly.' Ferdi walks to the door, then stops. 'Mr Lyle asked to be moved to the room next to yours yesterday. He made his request as soon as he saw you step out of the taxi from the airport. Call if you need anything.'

Daddy,

How are you? I hope you are well. I'm not. Can you please come get me?

The other night Mum left and didn't come back for 2 days. I finished all the Coco Pops and watched TV. I couldn't go to school because I didn't have the keys or money. The phone's still disconnected. A man kept ringing at the door. When she came back she said she didn't know where she'd been and gave me two kittens but she couldn't remember where she'd found them. Everything was OK but then she started drinking again and made new friends from the pub down the road. They are not good friends. All they do is go to raves and sleep all day. If I wake her up she shouts at me. She even said she doesn't want me anymore and I'll have to get rid of the kittens so I think maybe I will come and live with you for a bit.

Please please please please come to my school gates in break and we can talk about telling Mum. I'll be waiting for you like I always do.

Lots of love, Stella xxxxxxxxx

When Ferdi arrives with my breakfast tray, he congratulates me on being a bridesmaid and lays a long pink dress across the armchair. There's a note next to my croissant which reads:

> Darling Stella,
> Our beautiful bridesmaid! Had to get this as Pink is your colour!!! Wedding at 3pm. At the Beachfront Conference Centre!!!!
> Yuleka and Henry xx

Pink is not my colour.

'What do you know about the couple?'

'She's very *lively*,' he offers. 'They were up until five in the morning, dancing in the Billiards Hall.'

'D'you think they're in love?'

'I think she likes dancing. What we say here, "De higha de monkey climb, de more he show he tail".'

'Again?'

He repeats it, explains, 'It mean, give dat skettel time and we'll see more than just her tail bits, ma'am.'

'I think I've seen enough of her tail bits, but him? Do you know if they have people coming to this wedding, like children?'

'I rather doubt it, judging by the nature of the... ahem... *event*.'

I agree, sliding a camellia flower from the tea tray into my hair.

'I believe he has two children,' he replies, setting out my breakfast on the veranda, where two little birds chase each other behind his back.

'Three. He has *three* children.'

'Mum?'

'Stella, where are you? You sound miles away.'

'I am. I'm on holiday.'

'Holiday?'

'Yeah. I told you. Barbados.'

'Are you okay? Hush now!'

'Mum, who are you talking to?' Then I hear the familiar sound of a dog barking. 'What's Elvis doing there?'

'Joseph brought him over. He said I could look after him.'

'Why? Is he okay?'

'He's fine, just needs a wee. Ring me later in the week. Go and get your lead, I said I'm coming.' And she's off the phone.

My mother can never say goodbye. She has issues with endings, which is why I resisted telling her what I'm doing this afternoon. I stab my scalp while trying to pin up my hair. I'm nervous. I'm going to a wedding. I'm going to be a bridesmaid. My father's bridesmaid.

PART FOUR

THE WEDDING OF A THOUSAND DREAMS

44

Printout signs for the *Wedding of a Thousand Dreams* pinned to trees and buildings direct me to the far end of the beach where Henry and Yuleka's tribe stand under the palm shade. The viscount is coiled and wilting in his wheelchair which someone's dressed in colourful flowers and pineapples. His wife chomps on her cigarette holder looking semi-conscious with boredom in large, mirrored sunglasses. Susie is chatting up the chef who's barbecuing squid on a skewer. The bride is in a bright-red gypsy-style dress with matching flowers in her hair; even her stilettos are red. A bleeding-heart clashing with the bougainvillea. My father has tucked a Hawaiian shirt into his Bermuda shorts. They all look like they're in desperate need of a siesta or intravenous saline solution. Even the waitresses seem exhausted; their lemon cocktail dresses are creased and the waiters can't keep up with the demand for more champagne.

There's a loud bang on a drum and a man in a silver-white suit waves his arms to get people's attention.

'Welcome to Barrrrbaaaados!' We jump when there's another thud of the drum. 'My name is Zechariah. I'm the special couple's wedding planner. Thank you all for coming to be a part of Henry and... and Yuletide's beautiful and special day.' He blows kisses at the crowd as the drum is whacked by a man in a tribal headdress. 'Now, before we start, let us prepare by joining hands to unite us on our tunnel of love!' People look awkwardly at each other. 'Come on! Come on! Tunnel of love!' Zechariah moves off the podium and starts physically attaching the congregation hand by hand. 'Yes! Yes! The tunnel of love! Don't be shy!'

Henry and Yuleka take their places at one end, the steel drums roll.

The suited man sings out: 'Please, everybody, open wide! Here comes the bride! Our Bajan pride!'

The drum rolls as Henry and Yuleka push their way through the human arch. 'The tunnel of love'. A few people look confused when Henry gets stuck three-quarters of the way down and Yuleka trips over Roy's wheelchair.

After some random, confused applause we are ushered back to our plastic seats where I'm next to one of the men who was at the bar yesterday, he doesn't look up from his phone.

Henry stands at the altar in his socks, his feet resting over the top of the flip-flops. He doesn't turn my way. He doesn't even know I'm here and probably wouldn't even remember who I was anyway. But nobody seems to know anybody, most of the crowd have stumbled in from the beach or were part of the hotel's poolside bathers.

'Who are the ones getting married?' asks a South African lady behind me. I point at Henry and Yuleka. The spectator squints at them over the top of her Jackie Onassis sunglasses, then picks up the order of ceremony pamphlet from the table and starts fanning herself. 'Oh right. And where's the groom?'

'There. That's the groom.'

'Oh.' She cups her mouth. 'I thought he was the *father*.' She pulls out her phone. 'Hashtag dirty old bugger.'

The man next to me turns to join a conversation behind us about where to eat lobsters caught fresh out of the water cooked in any style you want.

'What are we waiting for?' someone asks.

Henry takes more of an interest when a group of girls wade topless into the sea, his gaze follows them until they intersect with my own. He puts out his hands and pretends to make them tremble, mocking a sign of nerves. Yuleka catches our exchange. She whispers my name tenderly, humbly, as brides do when moved by old friends who've travelled miles to be there for their big day.

Zechariah reads something on his phone, which by his expression and the wiping of sweat from his brow looks like bad news.

'Please accept my humblest apologies. There will be a short delay. Usually we're waiting for the bride, but today it's the best man who is late!'

My father's white knees knock and a garland of flowers wilts around his purple neck. This man, the other half of my story. Patches of sweat spread under his arms and his nose is red, near to blistering. If only my mum could see him now.

'Any minute now,' says Zechariah, tapping his foot. Yuleka scowls back at him.

Henry takes out a crumpled white handkerchief to mop up his steaming glasses. I am the only family member at the wedding. A wedding deliberately designed to preclude anything as pedestrian as blood relatives and yet, their bridesmaid is his illegitimate child.

45

Why didn't you want to see me when I came to your office? Are you cross that I just turned up? Maybe I should've rung first but I thought it would be good to surprise you. Did they tell you I was there? I waited a really long time in that big room reading my book on different dog breeds before the woman said I had to leave or they'd call the police. Did you tell her to say that? I didn't want to do anything bad, just to see you. But you don't want to see me and I don't understand why. Was she your wife or secretary? Why was she so mean? Don't worry. I didn't tell Mum. She's having one of her black attacks and got caught shoplifting the other day. I'm staying with Mrs Olsen downstairs because Mum's friends make lots of noise at night. But she says she can't keep me too long because her grandson is allergic to my cats. Then I'll go to my friend Kamilla when her mum comes back from Bangladesh.

I will keep writing and maybe you'll write back.

When I'm older I'm going to be a lawyer like you. I like the quietness of your offices, and the views, but I'll be nice to people, especially children.

Stella xxx

46

Just as people are losing interest, the steel drums start up again as a large, grinning Caribbean man bounces down the aisle to the altar. Zechariah leaps up, announcing:

'Ladies and gentlemen, may I present the best man, Nelson!' He makes a big show of hugging the best man, slapping him on the back, maybe a little harder than necessary.

Nelson wears the classic black tailcoat, white starched shirt and extra-large yellow bow-tie with a white carnation pinned to the lapel. He spins around, opening his arms wide so we see two dark circles of sweat inside his jacket.

Nelson takes the microphone. 'Thank you all for coming to this very special day! Let's say a loud welcome to the bird – *bride*! – and groom!'

A few people have to put their hands to their ears because his voice is so loud. 'Welcome on this very special day of love!' Zechariah stands beside him, flapping his hands in the air to encourage the crowd to clap. Nelson taps Henry and Yuleka's heads. 'Can I hear you? I said welcome!' He holds the microphone out to the congregation. A few people answer, 'Welcome' to him. He repeats the exercise.

Zechariah snatches the mic out of his hands.

'Thank you, best man Nelson. Now before we start this blessed, blessed ceremony, do the beautiful couple of a thousand dreams have their playlist ready?'

A man nearest Henry fumbles in a rucksack.

'I'm Terry, one of the witnesses. I put this together earlier. Hope you like it…'

Henry looks at the man as though he's never seen him before in his life, probably hasn't.

A small choir break into a gospel verse. As the song reaches a climax the tail-coated man blows kisses at the congregation.

'Beautiful people! What a beautiful day!'

Yuleka beckons me right to her side. I pretend I don't see her but Terry nudges me. 'Hey, lady, I think she wants you up there.' I've no choice but to hop over the scorching sand until I bump into her swaying hips.

As the singing comes to an end, Yuleka catches Zechariah's shirtsleeve and says, 'Hey, this is our bridesmaid, Stella.'

'A very special welcome to our bridesmaid.' He places my hand in his fleshy fingers.

Nelson beside him gestures at an attendant. 'Flowers! The bridesmaid should have flowers.'

'I'm okay.' I hold up the posey that Yuleka had her butler bring in a vase of water.

'*More* flowers! We need many more flowers for our beautiful bridesmaid. Big, big ones on this wonderful big, big day!' Nelson says over the girls' humming, releasing clouds of alcohol from his breath.

A woman drops a heavy armful of gladioli in my arms. I look over at Henry through the petals. He squints straight past me at a latecomer. Yuleka pulls my hair back from my face.

'There, show off your sexy lips, make sure you get laid tonight. You like the dress? It's one hundred per cent silk, eh, not polystyrene.'

The sun's at its highest. The sea is calm, pale blue, almost the same shade as the sky. Three guys carrying surfboards stroll up from the beach, I hear one of them say, 'No, that's the bride... in red... I guess the groom's not shown up yet – not surprised!' They laugh, point, move on.

I wonder how long I can hold up these flowers and feel a bug crawling down my neck. Someone takes a photograph. A small group shuffle out mumbling about being late for the turtle swim experience.

We wait for the music to start. There's a high-pitched squawk as the iPhone is connected to another set of speakers. Then, through the amplifiers comes the twanging of an electric guitar followed by the jaunty introduction to The Carpenters' 'Top of the World'. As members of the wedding party sway to the music, Karen Carpenter begins and Yuleka turns around to her 'friends' to make sure they appreciate the wacky choice. She wiggles her hips and clicks her fingers at the crowd, unable to keep from an impromptu cabaret act.

'The marriage of a thousand dreams!' calls out Zechariah. 'I present to you, Henry and Ukulele.' He gestures for the couple to stand right in front of him. 'And here comes the priest!'

The volume is turned down as a small, round, very old man dressed all in black appears from behind the speakers. He nods his head at me before wringing his hands together. He touches the couple's shoulders in devoted reverence and stands with his eyes closed in front of the altar.

'Father Omanada,' says Zechariah to Yuleka and Henry. 'Very spiritual man. He has an eighty-seven per cent success rate.'

The priest mumbles something about being 'blessed' but no one's listening. There's coughing, chatting and the ping of messages coming through on phones. But I'm attentive. Every few seconds a light wind breathes warm air against my back, urging, 'Go on, *do* something.' Do something. I will. My mother never had the wedding she so desperately craved, but all the same, here I am on her behalf, by my father's side in front of a vicar. And I must do something. When the 'Are there any impediments?' bit comes, I'll say, 'Stop right now! He already promised himself to Florence Tyler twenty-seven years ago – I am the impediment.'

But while I'm thinking about all this, I hear the holy man

stuttering, 'I n-now pronounce you man and wife.' He places his braceleted hands on their heads and bows to them before shuffling away behind the speakers where he came from.

Zechariah leaps forward and announces: 'Thank you, Father! Okay, folks, now the juicy bit, that's right, Henry, you may now have a good "snog" as they say in Britain!'

There's applause, whistling and the two surfers from earlier reappear with beers in their hands. One of them heckles, 'You've done it now, mate!'

Yuleka turns to the crowd and holds up her arms to get everyone's attention – in one move she yanks off the Velcro of her red flamenco skirt. She stands in front of the congregation revealing her red G-string bikini. Henry claps in between wiping the sweat from under his glasses. Yuleka jumps at him, both legs on either side of his stomach. She presses her mouth over his as he staggers back until she releases her grip in case he collapses and brings her down with him. Henry is propped back up by the photographer. He takes Yuleka's hand and the two of them trudge towards the bar.

47

'Welcome to this bountiful marriage of a thousand dreams!' says Zechariah, his silver suit crackling when he moves. 'You make a gorgeous bridesmaid.' He takes my fingers, kisses them and laughs again as if I'd said something incredibly funny. He then brings me into his chest, enclosing me against the strong smell of aftershave with a base note of rum. 'Let me introduce you to Nelson, my colleague.'

When I'm released, the man in tails squeezes in next to me and says in the deepest voice I've ever heard, 'You were an excellent bridesmaid, excellent. I know it's not easy standing still and being serious with such tremendous excitement all around. Congratulations! Let me introduce myself. I'm Nelson, Henry's best man.'

'Stella.'

'Stella.' He grins, taking his time to adjust his focus. 'Stella. Sorry I was a little late – the bus broke down just out of Jamestown, but it was nothing serious.'

'Have you known Henry and Yuleka a long time?'

'Over many lifetimes, yes.'

'How did you meet them?'

'It is not important to ask how and when – those, just numbers, details, facts. No, that doesn't matter when it comes to old souls like us. What matters is that Yucky and her man are both in my heart for ever and ever – the future, that's what matters, not the past.'

'But how do you know them?'

'I was the first person to greet their airplane on Tuesday,' he answers, smiling and smiling, as if he can't find the stop-smiling switch.

'Oh. So not a friend from before last week?'

'Do friends need to be "old"? Does love age?' he asks, as if we're leaning over the gymnasium wall in fifth-century Athens. 'They are beautiful people.'

'It's just that... well, usually a best man–' I stop.

Nelson helps me out with my old-fashioned notions. 'I am included in the "Paradise Beach Club Wedding Package". We provide everything for the Wedding of a Thousand Dreams: the compère, Zech, the priest, the best man – me – the well-wishers, they're over by the drinks, and here is my colleague, Lucille, the maid of honour.' Lucille gives me a tired, I've-been-with-strangers-all-day smile. 'I also do a lot of freelance work. Here's my card, if ever...'

'Funerals?'

'Oh yes. Lucille is a wonderful crier, and she's also Rihanna's second cousin. Hmm? You know Rihanna? Lucille sings even better – ah, she breaks my heart every time. Her daughters are very good too. If ever you have need of our services, give me a call,' he adds casually, while looking over my shoulder at whoever else might benefit from his pitch. 'We can even provide a groom.'

'Really?'

'No.'

Zechariah joins us. 'You have a lovely figure, you shouldn't have a problem finding a suitable man but don't leave it too long. May I just have a word with Nelson?'

The best man and Zechariah hiss at each other about something, from what I catch, it sounds like they are already late for another wedding further down the coast. The priest joins them. 'Bless you, my child,' he says to me while fumbling in his robes for a set of car keys.

'Stella, we have somewhere else to be now,' says Nelson mournfully, 'but will be rejoining you tonight. But first, I have to ask something. As you know, my big role is yet to come. The speech!' He smiles so wide I see that all his back teeth are silver. 'What do you know about the beautiful couple, especially Henry?' He bends down to my ear and whispers in a voice so low he could be talking into a bucket, 'Stories, anything humorous, maybe, or embarrassing tales or anecdotes – we even have a PowerPoint projector if you've videos or photos I could show?'

For a moment I'm tempted to suggest he tell the guests about the abortion he tried to push my mother into, then something else comes to me.

'Nelson, there is just one little thing...' And I tell him something that he seems to like very much.

'Marvellous! Thank you for that golden nugget. It's wonderful to meet you and I look forward to having a dance with you tonight and, hopefully, the occasion to work with you one day. You have my card.'

Over my champagne flute, I watch Henry frequently checking a large gold watch on his wrist. I try to quash any tenderness I might feel for him but his thick glasses, his flat-footed gait and even his astounding choice of wife, evokes an odd instinct to protect him. Perhaps I am just gentling my emotions so that when it comes to the time, I'll be too mushy to exact my revenge.

It's then I see a figure dart behind a palm tree. The man – young and dark-haired – peeps out and stares directly at me before he shoots back behind the tree again. I move fast towards him. If he's a reporter I want to stop him printing anything about me. Joseph and I are no longer together; they have to leave me alone. Seeing me get close, he sprints in the opposite direction.

48

A gong makes everyone jump. Nelson stands on a table and announces in his didgeridoo of a voice that we will soon be saying goodbye to Mr and Mrs Hardwick after we toast their marriage. This will be followed by more champagne and canapés in the hotel tea lounge. He briefs us on the evening's entertainment and passes around a printout with the itinerary and lists of specialist dry cleaners and taxi services provided by the hotel. Lucille, the maid of honour, slops out flower petals for us to throw at the couple as they pass by holding up their multicoloured cocktails.

Nelson finishes, jumps down and leads Yuleka and Henry through the centre of the marquee with Lucille and Zechariah. Occasionally, Nelson breaks off to encourage passers-by to come forward and wave the happy couple goodbye. Most people, however, are picking up their beach bags and finishing off the last of the champagne.

When it comes to my turn to chuck petals, Yuleka draws my face into her bush of hair. 'Our brrrridesmaid. Bravo!' Yuleka squeezes our heads together. 'Wasn't it beautiful?' Her kisses make my cheeks prickle.

'Thank you for being our flower girl,' says Henry. 'You will join us for our little bash tonight?'

'Sure.'

Then Henry looks at me as though he's going to ask me something. My heart swells in my chest, pushing against my lungs. He moves closer to my cheek. 'Do you know where there's a loo?'

'Er, no, there's the hotel lobby,' I suggest.

'That's what I thought.' And he shuffles down to the next colony of well-wishers.

Yuleka and I stand opposite each other.

'You look–' I start, but she interrupts me.

'Do you think they overdid it with the flowers? I keep finding greenflies in my drink.' She looks around the room wearily. 'Oh, I can't wait to get out of here, into our room and have a long cool shower before Henry and I start doing it all night. Between you and me, darling, it takes him all night to do once what a young man can do all night. Thank God for the V-word all's I can say. We really need an *heir* – you know what an "heir" is?' I nod. 'Eh? So it's oysters, champagne and *ne pas déranged* until we get one!' She winks at me and tosses her flowers in the air. 'Hey, Stella darling, catch!'

Before I have a chance to think, I put my arms out and the bouquet lands into them.

'Stella's next! Stella's next!' Yuleka applauds. 'Henry, Henry! Stella caught the bouquet!'

'Jolly good. If you're quick enough you can use our marquee – share the cost.'

'Not a bad idea. They've been ripping us off at every turn,' says Yuleka in a muttered breath. 'I'm demanding a cake upgrade. How late was the best man? And he was drunk! Oh, here he is.'

'To Henry and Yuleka!' announces Nelson.

'To the couple of a thousand dreams!' hollers Zechariah.

The couple stand in front of us, kiss each other on the lips, make a dash through the makeshift chapel while we throw the last of the confetti.

'And now, one last tradition! Attention!' calls Zechariah who's finally taken off his silver jacket and shirt, and is now down to a black string vest. 'Attention, everyone. The bride and groom will jump over the broom.' He places a besom in front of Henry and Yuleka's feet. 'This is an ancient African custom to symbolise the beginning of a new life. The couple jump over this everyday kitchen utensil and the magic of eternal happiness will begin!'

'Cookin', cleanin' and pickin' up after him, eternal drudgery,' calls out a woman with two teenage boys gawping at Yuleka's breasts.

A drum roll starts, the singers hum. Then there's a loud bang, one of the singers cries out something in an African tongue, and Henry and Yuleka are cued to jump over the broom. They hop together, Henry losing his footing and spilling most of his drink.

'A new life!' calls out Nelson, clapping his hands in the air. 'Another toast to the couple's happiness!'

Henry looks embarrassed as someone places a champagne flute in his hand. He dabs his forehead with a serviette.

'And now,' Zechariah bends towards Yuleka and whispers, 'are you absolutely sure you don't want to change your minds about the "releasing of the peace doves" option – we have them here?'

Henry shakes his head. 'Get on with it.'

'Fine. Mr and Mrs Hardwick, you may now depart from this beautiful, magical ceremony of a thousand dreams!'

Henry and Yuleka are pushed out of the arcade by the wedding team. Henry plods forward, his legs bowing to ease the friction of his shorts rubbing against his thighs. Yuleka stumbles in front of him, heels in the sand and her Velcroed skirt dragging behind her. The couple reach the perimeter of the hotel's beach only to find the gate is blocked by the street traders and coconut vendors perched on crates tucking into a late lunch.

'Jeez, we'll never get rid of them,' says a voice next to me.

Henry and Yuleka are then forced to turn around and walk by the side of the hotel past the line of bins. Another wave and they're gone.

'Wedding of a thousand nightmares!' Peter laughs. 'Tell me, what does he see in her?' I can feel his breath against my neck.

'Of all the species, the human female is the only one who has breasts when not lactating – natural selection shows that men like big tits.'

'Of all the species, the human male has the biggest penis.' Peter leans his head to one side. 'I know shit too.' He winks. 'And don't you make the most appetising bridesmaid. I saw you leap up and grab the bride's bouquet – can't wait for your big event.' He kisses my shoulder, puts his hands around my hips.

'I'm a good catch.'

'You certainly are. Hey, I came to your room to collect you but you weren't there.'

'I went for a walk.'

I wave at Susie who's leaving the beach on the back of the hotel's chef. 'See you two at the party tonight! Giddy up!' she calls out before being carried off.

'Fun wedding,' I say mechanically.

'You think so? I make it a rule not to do weddings. But this, I *had* to see!'

'You don't like weddings?'

He's still clamped around my waist, talking in a low voice. 'Oh, you know. The idea of spending a day rejoicing in someone else's happiness is kind of unappealing, don't you think? At least we were spared the tedium of meeting their families, but hey, I don't want to be cynical, I could see you were pretty moved by it all.'

'Hardly! Their best man was on an hourly rate.'

'But I was watching you, Stella, you kinda looked choked up. Don't be embarrassed, I'm sure there's a romantic in me, it just didn't surface seeing that old man slobber all over that little gold-digger.'

'So what do you think he sees in her?'

'Never underestimate the sexual vanity of an ageing man – it's caused empires to fall and the great men of history to act like total assholes. Henry Hardwick is a walking example of the depths it'll take us.' He raises his eyebrows and looks over his sunglasses. 'But on a lighter note, you coming to the dinner?'

'How could I miss the chance to toast the happy couple one more time?'

'Shall we go together or will you be running off beforehand?'

'Together. Why don't you jump over my wall about eight?'

'Try and stay out of trouble until then.'

49

Daddy,

Please don't be angry at Mum. I know I wasn't supposed to but I read why she's in hospital in our social worker's folder. She said that Mum followed you and your wife to a restaurant and attacked you both with a toilet brush. Mummy is bipolar. This is when you are sometimes nice and sometimes a wild thing like a polar bear. She said that her problems weren't recognised before. Still, she did a bad, bad thing and I'm sure she's very sorry. At the moment she's still in the psychiatric ward and on pills which make her dribble, but when she gets better she'll be really embarrassed and I'm sure would say sorry except the police will come if she is near you cos of the order.

We now have a new social worker because the other one burnt out. She's called Abigail and she practises Feng Shui. She said we had to get all the red out of Mum's bedroom and close the toilet seat. She says she won't tell anyone about the cats and she might have a job for Mum at a publisher's but it all depends on you not pressing charges. Please don't press charges!

Sorry this is so rushed but my host mother's calling me for dinner. I'm staying with the Davis family, temporary care people. They're both dentists. Last night we won a quiz at their town hall so they want to take me to another to raise money for a new hospital wing.

I want to go home but they can't say when I'll be allowed to.

Stella xxx

P.S. Please don't press charges!!!

50

Peter and I sit in the hotel lobby – after he's verified all points of access and found a seat with his back to the wall – while someone fetches us a car. Every time he speaks, the scent of his aftershave makes me fizz with desire, does he drink the stuff? I try to focus on his story about the time he was kidnapped on the Côte d'Ivoire but octaves of lust play through my body. I hold his gaze far longer than is self-respecting.

'What do you know about the happy couple?' I ask.

'Never met them before, just heard the dumb gossip.'

'Like...?'

'You're interested?'

'I am the bridesmaid, remember?'

'Apparently,' he lowers his voice, 'Yuleka and her ex-husband worked in a nightclub in Mayfair – I can't remember the name, though I've been there, bet you have too. Yuleka was a "hostess".' He flicks his index fingers in the air to show inverted commas. 'The owner was pressing charges for theft, embezzlement, prostitution and drug dealing and Henry was paid to defend her. He not only won her the case, he counter-sued for sexual harassment, pimping, exploiting workers and selling to under-age customers. That's how the "love affair" started. Bunny told me that once they were together – suffice to say, she dumped her husband pretty damn fast – they launched a ferocious campaign against his ex-wife – Caroline? Catherine? Whatever. When the former Mrs Hardwick found out about his affair and that Henry was gonna clean her out, she went pretty crazy and that played straight into their hands. They arranged, through the kids, to have her sent to a rehab centre. Once she was there, Yuleka moved into the house, changed the locks, had the dogs put down. She turned the boys against their mom and had them testify all kinds of things against her: "incompetent mom", "unstable" and a "prescription-drug addict". Henry had an easy divorce – not only that, but he also came out a hero for having put up with a "terrible woman" for so long.'

'So Henry's children *liked* Yuleka?'

'Seems so but only for a hot moment. They're now in the process of suing him for the Norfolk estate and heirlooms. Gotta feel sorry for 'em. People who knew Henry and his last wife say Yuleka was like a living nerve gas, decimating everything in his life until she was the only thing left.'

'Nasty.'

'This is from Bunny, by the way, who's an old friend of the ex-wife's.'

'But why doesn't Henry speak to his children anymore?'

'Yuleka's not the sharing kind.'

'Hasn't anybody said anything to him about her?'

'What can you say? He's hooked. I mean, she's not subtle – their first night here she tried to make out with Wheelchair Roy, but hey, I'm not one to gossip.'

'But they're all so friendly to her?'

'They're on holiday, she's part of the entertainment. Here's our car, ready?'

51

The place is packed, loud, hot. To the side a man dressed up as Marilyn Monroe is playing a white piano under a mist of aromatic smoke. Sitting next to him is Henry, pressing down on the same note over and over again.

Yuleka sashays up to Peter. 'You can't flirt with me now – I am a married lady!' Then she shouts into the crowd, 'You know, you're not officially married until you've consumed it – well, now we've been married *five* times over!' She claps her hands to her pelvis, juts back and forth.

Henry turns to the pianist with a smug grin. 'She means "consummated". Not exactly *five*, but…'

'Stella, our bridesmaid! Have one of these,' she hands me a drink from the waiter's tray, 'it's punch – don't touch the "champagne", it's fucking Prosecco.' She stops a man wearing nothing but a waistcoat and tight black bathing trunks. 'Welcome! Have a drink!' Then turns back to us. 'Who the fuck are these freaks? Oh, there's Antonio! Catch you guys later.'

Peter is an attentive date, introducing me to people, leaving me to chat before eventually we sit in a dark recess, our knees touching as the DJ announces: 'And now the first dance: Mr and Mrs Henry Hardwick!'

The spotlight searches out the newly-weds only to find Yuleka berating one of the kitchen staff by the toilets.

'*Mr and Mrs Hardwick!*'

The crowd breaks into a chant of, 'Dance! Dance! Dance!'

The DJ has chosen 'When a Man Loves a Woman'. The audience makes the appropriate 'oooh's and 'aaaaah's.

Yuleka tugs at Henry while he knocks back a Martini. They appear reluctant but it's a poorly acted charade to prolong Yuleka's moment in the limelight. She levers her husband out of his chair, stubs out his cigar in a slice of watermelon and tows him under the glitterball. Henry plays up to his audience, acting the victim of this sexually demanding nymphette.

I chat to two hairdressers from Crouch End, 'Da Split-Crouch Endz' who'd saved their tips to come here. It's only been days since I left London but to hear these girls talk about home makes me long for Joseph – just when I thought I was getting better.

'He's a bit of all right,' says one of the girls when Peter calls me over to join him where he's sitting with the hotel crowd. 'That your bloke?'

'More of a Band-Aid, y'know?'

I join Peter in an oversized cane armchair where Bunny is snorting cocaine from what looks like a silver pepper mill. She wipes her nose, keeping her eyes fixed on Peter.

Roy is very drunk, his eyes sad and red. He points towards a Swedish bodybuilder who's writhing lethargically to the music. 'Peter old boy, give her five hundred d-d-d-dollars to sit on my face.'

Peter shakes his head. 'It's okay, man.'

'Go on, old boy, do what you can for us.' Peter tries to laugh the offer away but Roy shouts loudly over the music, 'I'm a fucking c-c-c-c-cripple, P-P-Peter. I've only got two things I can thank our blessed Lord for: a t-t-t-t-title and a c-c-cock!'

Bunny wraps her pashmina around her shoulders and glides to the other side of the room.

Roy eyes up one of the London girls I was talking to earlier as she makes her way to the toilets. He grapples for her arm.

'Do I know you?' she asks.

'I'm your future ex-husband. *Enchanté*!'

She pulls away from him as he tries to wheel himself into the ladies' after her.

Peter puts his hand out for me to take as we head back to the dance floor, Roy calls to him, knocking into the table causing a tumbler of rum to turn over into his lap.

Peter and I dance around each other. I'm aware of Bunny watching as though I'm someone dawdling in a queue in front of her. Keeping her eyes on me, she strides over to Yuleka. I try to ignore them as Peter takes me by the waist and twirls me around. Each time I land into his body, he gives me small kisses on the shoulder. The singer is belting out Madonna's 'Holiday'.

Then Yuleka cuts in, insisting I dance with her husband. 'Henry is the best dancer. Oh, Henry, tell her about that night at Tramp's… Oh, Henry, tell her about the…'

Bunny yells over the music: 'Come on, Henry, the girl wants to dance with you! It's your bloody wedding night.'

She pushes me over to him while yanking Peter for herself.

The tempo slows. Most people leave the dance floor but my father puts his arm around my back as he totters us over to the centre under multicoloured lightbulbs. A saxophone toots and a woman sings the words to 'The Girl from Ipanema' although we hear Yuleka in the background chanting about an 'enema'.

'Apparently this is the most recorded pop song in history after "Yesterday" by the Beatles.'

'Sorry, that your toe?'

'No worries. Enjoy your wedding day?' I ask Henry. It comes out like I'm practising words from a foreign-language phrasebook but I'm concentrating more on keeping him from toppling onto me.

'All came off rather well, eh?'

Henry twirls me around.

'Well done,' he remarks when I return to him in one piece.

'How did it compare to your first wedding?'

'Ah, well, that. I sort of had to go along with all that, family and whatnot.'

Before I can ask any more, the song has segued into 'Let's Groove' as we're halfway through a spin. Henry reaches too far as I twist towards him and he inadvertently touches my breast before plodding off towards the table where Yuleka is sitting with one of the waiters on her lap.

52

Yuleka cheers at us. 'Isn't he something?'

'Yes, he certainly is,' I answer, after a few well-earned gulps from my cocktail.

'You should get Yuleka to show you some moves – she can do that bottom-wiggling thing.' Henry reaches out for her hand.

'Oh, listen to him, "that bottom-wiggling thing"! Y'know, darling, I was a professional dancer?'

Susie looks up from rolling a joint. 'Did I see you in *The Nutcracker*?' People at the table laugh.

'Yeah, well, you know what? I had a podium and my own theme song. You know, darling, even in twelve-inch fuck-me shoes I could do a high kick–'

'Fuck-me 'n' pay-for-it shoes!' a man next to Susie intercepts.

Yuleka ignores him. 'But now I only dance for my big bear! Hmm, private dance for you, you like that, don't you, baby?'

Susie pulls Henry out from under Yuleka. 'Mind if I take this big boy a spin?'

I am left again with Yuleka. She leans into me and takes my arm.

'Susie's very jealous of me. Women always are – they know I can have any man just like that!' and she clicks her fingers. 'Henry is crrrrrrazy for me, devoted, well, see the way he looks at me.' She waves at him.

'Crazy... yes.'

'No woman could ever make him feel like I do. Henry really believed me when I said he was the only man who could make me come. Tsh. Imagine that, darling.' She bites at the cuticle on her little finger. 'You've got a better chance of finding a rich guy here than Susie, don't worry about it.'

'I'm not, I–'

'You don't wear enough perfume. When Henry first smelt me, he was rock hard – smell first, sight later. It's the *endolphins*.' A gulp of her piña colada leaves a white moustache on her upper lip. She stretches out her hand and points at her ring. 'How big are these diamonds?Check it out. I designed this one myself. I'm a gemmologist, you know?' She points at the rock on her fourth finger. 'Henry loves to treat me. See? Diamond. Diamond. Ruby. Diamond. Sapphire. This one's not silver, it's *white* gold. What's the point in white gold for fuck's sake? Point is, I know all the stones, I've got a refractometer.'

'Where d'you study that?'

'I didn't need to study it because I would have known more than the teachers.' She sucks on her straws. 'You know his last wife's in an institution now. They'll never let her out.'

'Really?'

'That's why Henry's so generous with me cos that bitch is after every penny. Speeches!'

While champagne glasses are being refilled in preparation for the speeches, toasts and cutting of the wedding hash cake, I make a rushed exit outside to hold up Kerry, a Kiwi girl I met earlier, who's being sick.

The smell of jasmine floats in the warm air as the sea rasps in and out over the sand. I lean against a dozing palm tree, look up at the stars.

'That poor sod in the chair… is he really, like, royal?' asks Kerry.

'They say so,' I answer over the excitable 'Ssshhhhes' going on inside.

'How can his wife let him make such a fool of himself?'

I shrug and move to the window to see Nelson, the best man, walk onto a makeshift stage wearing a judge's horsehair wig. Everyone laughs. He holds up a judge's gavel and bangs it against the microphone, and again, and again, and then he starts moving his hips and dancing to the beat. As the crowd clap, he stops and shouts: 'Silence in court!' More laughter. 'Even you, Henry QC. Silence in my courtroom!' Henry sniggers. 'Now you are all underdressed! I mean, Sir Henry, you are *under* arrest: I charge you with fatal attraction to your woman!'

Kerry groans while pouring a bottle of cold water over her face. I catch something about Henry's work and more about the Wedding of a Thousand Dreams, their website and discount rates. Just as he starts about Henry and 'Yucky' and how fortunate we are to be gathered here, Kerry pulls on my hand. 'Isn't it exciting about the wedding?'

I move over for a better view and see Yuleka bowing to the audience. Bunny is nowhere to be seen, nor is Peter. Roy, however, talks animatedly to a Bajan girl who fingers the spokes of his wheel. The best man moves on to the groom: 'And Henry – Henry!' People cheer. 'The quintessential Englishman, Oxford graduate, esteemed man of law and letters – and you all thought Henry was only known for being at the "bar" of the Paradise Beach Club – he was called to the bar at the English courts – and not just for vodkas and tonics!' I hear chuckling and mumbling and phones going off. 'But they call him "QC", they call him "sir", they call him "esquire", Your Honour, but *we* should call him… "Mr Wombat!"' The crowd laughs. 'Mr Wombat!' They look to Yuleka. She doesn't laugh. She frowns.

'What?' she asks Henry.

'Mr Wombat! Did you know this, Mrs Hardwick? This is the name his first girlfriend called him! Let's not ask why – Mr *Wombat*!'

Henry jolts upright. He squares his shoulders leaving Yuleka to flop over her drink. He looks at each person accusingly.

Who could have passed on this intimate detail about his private life? Who could have known?

53

Peter steps out of the club holding my bag out to me. 'You ready?'

Kerry rolls her head in his direction, wipes spittle from her chin and grins, 'Howdy, cowboy.' She then falls on her knees, picks up a litre of water and drinks it down.

'There you are!' says her friend who lands on her knees in front of us. 'Man! You stink! Have you pissed yourself as well?'

The two girls knock their heads together laughing.

'You going to be okay now?' I ask.

'Yeah, thanks, mate. You better go join your hot date, lucky bitch.' Kerry nods towards Peter.

'Hey,' says Kerry, using her friend to lift herself up. 'If I hear more 'bout the wedding, I'll let you know.'

'What wedding?'

The girls look at me aghast.

'You haven't heard? Next weekend Sylvia Amery's getting married to Joseph West. Here on the island.'

'What? Where did you hear that?'

'Everyone's talking about it! We're going to crash the party after – it'll be a blast!'

Peter scuffs his feet. 'You girls still "nattering"? Isn't that what you Brits say?'

Kerry's friend offers him some of her beer. He puts a hand up to say no. 'You okay, Stella?'

I start walking back towards the club hoping that getting out of here will be quick.

'Bye!' they call after me. 'And thanks!'

Joseph is getting married, he's coming here, and I'm just about to wish my father a 'happy wedding night'.

'Why don't we hit the casino?' Peter suggests. But I've already turned back into the club and am searching the faces for my father's.

'I need to talk to Henry, tell him something. It's important.'

I weave around the dancers looking for Henry but no one's seen him, no one seems to remember who he is.

Peter tries to take my arm. 'They already left, Stella.'

'I need to…'

Peter catches up with me, points to the car park outside the club. 'They're out there. And then can we lose ridiculous amounts of money at the tables?'

Peter and I stand at the back door watching Henry and Yuleka talking loudly to each other by the bins.

'So why is everybody laughing when he says, "Mr Wombat"!'

Henry holds her by her shoulders. 'How should I know?'

'Who called you a wombat? Who?'

'Can we please just get back to the hotel?'

'Is it the Cockroach? Is it?'

'Can we just… discuss this calmly, like adults.'

'No! They were all laughing at me! And you didn't defend me!'

'Defend you? What are you on about?'

'You should say, *this* is the only woman I've ever loved!'

'Oh for God's sake. That Nelson… he's some sort of a pothead, darling.'

'I bet it was that Bunny who told him! She hates me! They all hate me and I hate them,' she goes to lunge at him, 'and I hate you!'

'Darling! Steady on, please!'

Yuleka yanks an amaryllis flower that has detached itself from her hair and stamps on it until there's nothing left but pink slime.

'Just tell me, do you still love her?'

'Love who?' asks Henry, trying to stop her arms from pounding the parked cars.

'Love *her*!'

'Love *who*?'

Peter's hand squeezes my shoulder. 'Stella, if what you have to say is important, might be better to wait.'

Mesmerised by this argument, I don't answer.

'You do, you love her! That bitch who called you *Mr Wombat*.' Yuleka slaps Henry's back repeatedly as he ducks for cover.

Peter sings out, 'Night, you two. Great party!'

Henry dodges a swipe at his head to wave us goodbye. 'Goodnight and thank you for... thank you for being our – ouch! – bridesmaid!'

'My pleasure,' I whisper as the bride swings a left hook and knocks his glasses off.

'Why don't you call him Mr Wombat? That's his name apparently!'

'Yuleka! Stop this, you're being preposterous and ridiculous!'

'I'm pre... ri-ridiculous? I'm ridiculous! He called me "ridiculous" – there! Two witnesses! Okay, that's it! Ridiculous, am I?'

Peter points in the direction of our patios. 'Shall we?'

'Let's,' I say over the sound of Yuleka crashing two dustbin lids together and calling out to me, 'Let's do lunch!'

'Boat trip, maybe?' says Henry, trying to put his arm around Yuleka.

'Let's talk in the morning,' says Peter, picking up speed.

The next thing I see is Henry diving to the ground to pick up his glasses.

'See my foot? See my foot, here, Henry Hard Dick? I'm

gonna crush your precious spectacles if you don't tell me. Who is she, Henry? Who is the woman who called you Mr Wombat?'

54

We arrive at the white bridge that links the Paradise Beach Club's gardens to the beach. Peter scoops me up by my waist and twirls me around.

'Your face! It's like white satin in the moonlight!'

So here goes – my first kiss since Joseph.

A breeze whispers through the palms. Peter is strong yet tender, it's an expert kiss. He feels for my hand and holds it as we stroll through the hotel's side entrance to our rooms. At the end of the corridor, Ferdi is waiting for me outside Peter's door with his butler, Asari, holding a tray of brandies and two mango sorbets.

'Ma'am.'

Am I so predictable?

My date doesn't blink as he walks ahead of me, throwing his jacket across the bed and opening the doors onto his balcony.

'A good wedding party, Miss Stella?' asks Ferdi, stifling a yawn.

'As we left they were fighting in the car park, so, a great success.'

Peter walks out to the terrace and calls back to Ferdi, 'Could you bring us a BLT sandwich each. We didn't get to eat and I'm starving, you must be too.'

I join him outside where someone has already lit tea lights all around the borders.

Peter flicks away a mosquito, sits back in his chair as we listen to the waves over the shore, snippets of distant conversations as guests walk back from their evenings out, the odd night-time squawk of a bird ripping through the black sky. Peter has changed from the party animal of earlier to someone quiet, pensive, almost moody. Something is on his mind.

Every few seconds the cicadas chirp in chorus and then stop –

all but one, who continues chanting until he realises he's on his own. Then he stops and they all start again then stop, but the soloist cicada continues. Peter and I both notice it and the more we tune our ears to this lone insect, the louder he sings.

'There's a species of cicada near the Mississippi that takes seventeen years to mature – just lives in the ground, eating sap and shit – then when he's mature, he breaks out of his skin, goes to the top of a tree, mates, falls off and dies. Do you think he'd consider his life worth it?'

'Depends how good the fuck was.'

'Peter, we cool? Has something happened? You seem–'

'See, I'm interested in nature too. I like to know what's going on around me.' He stares at me intently. The cicadas start up again. Peter holds up his brandy glass to the candlelight, watching as the reflection sends off amber sparks.

'Why did you lie, Stella?'

'Sorry?'

'You heard me.'

He moves closer so that his blue eyes are level with my face, burning up my thinking time.

'Lie?'

'Why did you lie about who you are? You said you were called Banks. You're not.'

'Oh *that*. When I met you and Bunny and…?'

'Yes. *That*. Then. When you *lied*. You made out you were a friend of the Templeton-Crest's daughter. She's never heard of you.'

'No. I've never met their daughter.' The brandy heats my throat and feels as good as the truth. 'You checked up on me?'

'I liked the look of you when you arrived, I asked reception what your name was. Kinda due diligence. It wasn't Banks. It was *Tyler*. So, before we get to know each other any further, who, *really,* are you and why did you cover it up?'

'I'm Stella, just Stella Tyler.'

Peter raises an eyebrow.

'That first day, when I was introduced and they thought they knew my dad I didn't disagree with them – it seemed less complicated than to explain. The heat... Henry and Yuleka... I didn't want to go into who I was, y'know?'

'How could lying be less complicated?'

'It was just a silly nervous thing. Are you really bothered by it?'

'Not *really*, but Bunny is. She checked you out. After she met you, she had a feeling you weren't "quite right" so she made a few calls. She has some pretty outlandish theories about what you are *really* doing here.'

'I'm sure the reality would disappoint her; shall we just keep her guessing?'

'Unless one of them is true...'

'Who do they think I am, Peter?'

Peter looks out to sea. 'Are we being honest here? Honesty is very important to me – I can't tolerate bullshit and I have a diploma in Advanced Interrogation.'

'Yes, I'm honest. It was silly of me, the other day. I was just shy and put on the spot... I didn't mean it as a *lie* lie.'

'Okay. My concern is that I think you could be–' He stops, grimaces as if he has a mouth full of sand. 'A *journalist*.'

'A journalist?'

'Come on. Some very wealthy and important people stay here, there's always some snoop hanging around in the bushes with a wide-angled lens.'

'No! No, Peter.' I can't help laughing. 'No, I'm not a journalist.' It would be too complicated to say that one of the reasons I'm here is to escape media attention. 'Look, I'm here on holiday! Surely *you* can tell a journalist – you're one yourself!'

'I'm a *war* reporter. No way near the same thing.'

'No, sorry, course not.'

'I was surprised. I was hurt too, that you didn't trust me. I thought we were friends.'

'Oh, we are. I told you last night. I finished with my boyfriend last week, had some time off work and planned a holiday. How could you think that I–'

'You do ask a lot of questions.'

'I like to know what's going on around me too.'

'Cool. That makes two of us,' he says, pouring me another brandy. He sits back, looking as if he's making a long-distance call. He's not as clear-cut as I had imagined and I had underestimated him. The sure trajectory of our alliance has hit dry land. I stand up, walk out towards the end of his terrace to relight one of the candles that a breeze blew out. When I turn, Peter is behind me.

55

'Enjoy tonight?' Peter asks, leaning his head against mine.

'It was *different*.'

'You looked a little uncomfortable dancing with ol' Henry!' He laughs and imitates me on the dance floor, holding out my arms and looking horrified. But I'm not laughing. 'Sorry, Stella, I didn't mean to accuse you of being fraudulent – I won't mention it again.'

'I should have said my name to them, to him – Henry. I should have stood up and been proud of who I am.'

'Sometimes our instincts know us better than we do.'

'I was going to say it tonight but the time wasn't right. I can't keep lurking in the shadows like this. I spend my life defending people, animals, causes, but when it comes to me, I just abandon myself – it's a theme, the abandonment thing.'

'Whoa! Back up,' says Peter excitedly. 'Back up. Something *is* going on here, isn't it? What was it you needed to tell him?'

'I was going to tell them who I was.' I take a gulp of brandy. 'I was just about to tell him, but we'd all drunk too much and they were fighting…'

'What, Stella, what do you have to tell Henry?'

I breathe in, look into the night and back at Peter. 'I wanted to tell Henry that he's my father.'

Peter takes a long swallow of brandy. 'Henry Hardwick?' He looks at me as if he's waiting for me to pull a mask from my face to reveal a monster beneath. 'He's your dad?' He laughs hesitantly. 'You for real?'

'I never met my biological dad. All I knew about him was that his name's Henry Hardwick and he was a lawyer living and working in London. And that he kind of looked like… *that* man. I saw him in London last week and I had nothing better to do, so I followed him out here.' I hold up my glass. 'To happy families!' I finish the brandy in one.

'So he has no idea who you are?'

'I don't think so.'

'Does he know he *has* a daughter… like… at *all*?'

'Yes, he saw me, once, as a baby, and then another time I went to his office but he had me sent away. He had a restraining order on my mum so I was careful not to get her in trouble.'

He cocks his head. 'The bastard.'

'No, that's me, the bastard.'

Peter half laughs as he scans the horizon, piecing all this new information together.

'I'm here to get answers.'

Peter looks at me warily. 'Uh-huh. So what do you want from him *exactly*?'

'I want him to put his name on my birth certificate. It's just a little thing, but symbolic. My mother's parents turned against her when it happened so it would mean a lot to her. I thought I'd come here and make him do that one thing, and I needed a holiday. But when I first met him, by the pool that morning, in front of you and everyone, it didn't feel right to do it then so when Roy came up with me being someone called Banks's daughter he gave me a cover.'

'So, that means,' Peter laughs, 'he didn't know, when he toasted the bridesmaid at his wedding, that she was his daughter?' He rubs his chin. 'Well be grateful you don't look like him. Your mother sure must be beautiful.'

'Why thank you, Mr Lyle.'

He touches my face. 'You really are very cute. And kind of… surprising.'

I bring my lips a few inches away from his neck.

'That feels so good…' he whispers. I move around, kiss him on both cheeks because his face looks so symmetrical against the night sky and because the relief of telling him my secret is immense.

'I believe there are no accidents in this world.' He tosses back the last drop of brandy and brings our eyes level with each other. 'You are a very brave, *very* special person.'

Taking my hand, he leads me to his bedroom. The sheets on either side of the bed are turned down to make an arrow-head shape.

'Come.' He turns me around and unzips the back of my dress while planting little kisses along the back of my neck. The dress drops to my feet. He strokes my arms right down to the insides of my wrists. He leans against my back, his arms closing me in. I twist around, breaking his grip.

'While we're being honest and open with each other,' I say, 'you've got a nerve, going to reception to find out where I was staying in and then changing rooms to be next door to me.'

One side of his mouth curls. 'You heard the cicadas.'

His kiss sweeps inside my dizzy head. He tastes of brandy, saltwater and tropical fruits.

We continue untangling ourselves from our clothes, all the time using our fingers, tongues, feet – anything with a nerve ending – to feel each other's body. His fingertips set off charges. He drops on top of me, kissing my breasts, my thighs, my ankles. He becomes more frenzied in his kisses.

We breathe hard, excited by what's new and what's familiar in each other. But when I draw back to see the whole of him, his eyes look blank, and he touches me like he's feeling for a light switch in the dark. Something's missing. It's intimacy. It's heat. It's love.

It's Joseph.

56

'I've wanted to do this since I first met you,' Peter murmurs, holding me tightly before pummelling, rotating, juddering like a machine of jets and foams and wipers – I feel as though I've activated a human car wash. He licks, splashes up and down my body, mechanically, joylessly, as if someone's standing over him with a stopwatch.

He smiles into my face, sits on my hips and looks down his chest to his hard bronzed stomach. He sweeps his hand over his pecs as though he's presenting me with a sweet trolley. Lots of upper body strength. Peter's clearly very proud of his torso – and makes all the right appreciative sounds like people do in sex scenes on TV or French 1970s pop songs. I want to giggle. I want to call the whole thing off, but he has my legs trapped under his, determined to give me pleasure and I'm trying – really *trying*: this is my medicine. Everyone says you haven't got over a relationship until you do it with someone else.

'I like you so much, you know that, don't you?' He then stretches out, holds his body weight on his elbows. 'In yoga they call this the "plank" position.'

I circle my fingers over the mounds of his chest as if I'm about to shine him up.

'I wax.'

'Really?'

'Uh-huh. Makes me more ergonomic.' He prises my legs open and moves his fingers between them as if he has tentacles looking for something to sucker onto. 'You want some? You want some? Tell me how bad you want it.'

If I were honest, I'd have said, 'No, not really. I'd rather go back to my room and get past the first eleven pages of my book.'

'Come on, baby, you feeling this?'

'Yes, yes, I said yes. Do you have a…?'

'Huh?' he asks.

'A…?'

'Oh yeah, sure.'

Peter leans over the bed grappling for his trousers and takes out a packet of condoms.

'Let me…' My mother always told me to put it on myself so men can't pull a fast one.

'No, baby, just lie back and wait to be laid like you've never been laid before…' he says, applying the condom over himself. I lie back but I've lost the narrative. Peter has also lost something. I hear rubber snapping and the sound of another packet being opened.

57

Before Joseph, I hadn't had many boyfriends, just crushes that gave me the right amount of teenage drama without interfering with my school life. Keeping my mother out of trouble was my priority. I was also afraid of ending up like Mum. Every time I went out with a friend who happened to be a boy, she'd be following me out the door pressing prophylactics into my hands and making me promise not to go 'all the way'. From the first time Joseph and I kissed, I had one of those 'aha!' moments, when human existence on the planet all made sense and the reason for living was in my arms. Even after we'd been living together a while, I used to wake up in the morning and think: whatever the world throws at me today, however busy or crazy work is, or friends are, or the traffic or money worries, I know tonight we'll make love and that's the only thing that matters. Every day ended with us lying in bed together, connected, saying goodbye to the outside world and sealing ourselves into our own private universe.

Peter resumes his dolphin-like undulations while I wonder if there'll be a good film on cable.

He's propped himself up on his forearms over me, I have my legs around his back.

'Oh, baby, oh yeah!' he says, as I slide my hands over the two colonnades along his abs. 'I just keep thinking you're *Henry*'s daughter!'

'Try not to think of Henry Hardwick right now.'

'Yeah, keep doing that. But it's not him that puts me off so much, it's *her*. Oh yeah, that's nice, Stella. You have beautiful nipples.'

'Thank you. Do you think they're doing this right now?'

'Who?'

'Henry and Yuleka?'

The latex slides off in my fingers.

'This isn't going to work,' he says.

I'm relieved. Though I'm not sure where to put my hands now.

Peter peels himself from me.

'It's not as easy for men as it is for women: chicks can just lie back – with men, it's psychological.'

Chicks?

'We've both had a lot to drink. Let's call it a night, eh?'

'Let's call it a night. That a British expression?'

'It's a universal expression.'

'Whatever,' he says, kissing my ear, wiping his mouth and turning out the light.

58

As soon as Peter's breathing deepens, I slither over to his iMac and log on to my email account. There's a message from Joseph.

```
Sparks — don't believe the press. What
they say about me and Sylvia isn't true.
I was just about to explain when you ran
out on me. Are you in Barbados? WTF?
Kamilla says you don't want me to contact
you but I have to explain what's going
on. Can I see you?
   PS I love my compass BTW but it's
stuck until we're together again.
   PPS Elvis says, 'Grrrr.' He's with
your mom for the moment.
```

I write back fast, desperate, half crying with relief.

```
At the Paradise Beach Club. Barbados.
Find me. I realised that I should always
have trusted you, I was wrong and scared
and damaged but this time, let's make
this work and—
```

'Can't sleep?' Peter is standing in the doorway. I look up at him, my fingers still moving on the keyboard, tears rolling down my cheeks.

'Full moon,' I say.

'Oow-wwooooooo!' he howls. I don't even pretend to laugh. We both jump as a firework goes off.

'They're excited about the wedding,' he says, leaning against the door-frame.

'Henry and Yuleka organised fireworks?'

'No, the big showbiz wedding, next weekend. That blonde actress – was up for an Oscar – she's marrying…' he clicks his fingers in the air, 'I've forgotten his name. The Brit. Joseph… something.'

'No!' I thump the keyboard. 'No! He's not marrying her!'

'Take it easy. Maybe not, but… it's what I heard. Apparently there were scouts checking out all the big, fancy plantation villas to hire. It's been the talk of the island. What do you care? Come back to bed.'

'Sylvia Amery and Joseph West, they're *not* getting married!'

'Okay, okay, but I just got a text from a colleague of mine who flew in with an ABC news crew yesterday to cover it, but… if you know more.'

'I *know* it's not true.' I glare at him, defying him to stick to his story.

'Asari's aunt was commissioned to make the gluten-free cake with sugar-free marzipan.'

'Are you sure she said *Joseph West*'s wedding?'

'What's the big deal? You in a hurry to be a bridesmaid again?'

I scroll down what I've written to Joseph. Highlight it. Press: *Delete*.

59

And now here we are, a few hours later. The sun's up and our butlers are about to bring us coffee, polite conversation, and news of what the hotel has in store for us today. Neither of us stir.

Peter breathes deeply, but I can almost hear his eyes twitching under his lids. Beneath the disguise of sleep, we are both turning over the events of last night, reconstructing each move before having to face the day after the night before.

What happened?

Nothing, is what happened.

It would have been so much easier had we woken with the smug elation of having had sex but instead we are lying in the aborted remains of what was left half finished, and now our butlers, united in their complicity, are probably talking about how we like our coffee. Peter and I have jumped ahead of the natural course of dating, leap-frogged over all the fun bits – the coy initiation, serotonin overload, suspense, excitement – and belly-flopped straight into murky waters.

I hear my breakfast rattling on the tray. Ferdi knocks at my door. There's no reply. He knocks again. Peter turns to me with a mischievous sparkle in his eyes. I step out of bed holding a sheet over my body and peer out from the door.

'Ferdi... Ferdi...' I speak softly, so none of the other guests need be appalled by the orgiastic carryings-on in other rooms. 'I'm in here.'

I don't think for one minute that he ever expected me to answer my door.

Peter steps up behind me. 'We'd like breakfast out on the beach, thank you.'

'By all means, sir. One moment.'

Ferdi glides around Peter's room lifting up his terrace

furniture and taking it down to the beach. When Asari comes over, they set up the meal right by the shore. When Ferdi is about to leave the room, I follow him out into the corridor.

'Ferdi, I've heard rumours that there might be a wedding – Joseph West and…' I swallow, loath to say her name.

'Sylvia Amery. Yes, it's true. They've taken the Belle Reve Mansion, it's very near my village. Isn't it exciting?'

'Thanks. I just… wanted it… confirmed.'

'Are you all right?'

'I guess so.' I return to Peter's room while he runs through his Afro-Brazilian martial art exercises. I'm numb, shocked and can't even begin to work out why Joe would've written me that email when he was simultaneously organising his wedding.

Peter comes over to me, looks worried.

'I'm just not hungry. I'm sorry.' I slide my chair back. 'I need to sort a few things out.'

'You don't want to spend the day together? My plan for the afternoon will include crayfish, getting drunk and lots of rubber?'

What I had in my mind is to spend the day alone, wallowing in my grief. But I'm getting over Joe, so I have to do things differently: if he can marry someone else, surely I can eat crayfish, get drunk and appreciate the odd adrenaline spike.

'Sure.'

Peter puts his heavy, square hand on my shoulder and kisses my lips. It's a slightly exaggerated kiss to reassure me, and it works. This morning could have gone either way, but we are going to make the best of it. Moving on.

60

My room has been made up: clean white sheets taut over the bed, a refreshed vase of flowers and my few possessions neatly lined on the dresser.

I bring the phone to my lap and dial Kamilla's number.

'Tell me it isn't true about Joseph,' I say on hearing her sleepy 'Hello'.

'I don't know what to say, babes.'

I can't speak, just collapse under the weight of a killer heartache.

'Chas and I got a wedding invitation a few days ago, Joseph and Sylvia invite you to… blah, blah… It's in Barbados. And *you're* in Barbados! I just don't get why he'd do that! But there's a note from Joe – his handwriting – that says, "Please come. Everything will become clear. Can't wait to see you both. Kiss Kiss". That's sick, isn't it? I'm so sorry, honey.'

'So are you coming out?'

'No way! I wouldn't do that to you – celebrating his wedding to *her*?'

Kamilla's there on the other end of the line when tears stop me from speaking. For a moment, I wonder if I won't manage to pull it back, whether the pain will leave me on the other side of sanity, but after a few gulps of water and saturated tissues, I recover myself.

'I left a lot of messages with a 'Ferdi'? He sounds so cool.'

'He is. He's my personal butler.'

'Personal butler!'

'Yeah, it's horrible here.'

Kamilla laughs. 'I'll trade with you – I've been working in a house with no roof, it's snowing, the owners want to move in next week, I've started IVF and blown up like a balloon, I'm either crying or shrieking, Chas thinks he's going to be fired and every time I call you you're by the pool! But have you seen your dad yet?'

'I was his bridesmaid.'

We talk for about two hours until Kamilla has to attend to a load-bearing wall emergency.

'Stella, don't lose this chance to tell the fucker what you think of him.'

'Joseph or my dad?'

'Both.'

61

Peter's planned a personalised tour of the island with an afternoon's scuba-diving thrown in.

'Aren't you supposed to do lessons before you scuba-dive?'

'Nah. That's just for tourists,' he replies.

From the ridiculously oversized Land Rover Peter's hired, he points out houses, waterfalls, secluded coves and bars, all landmarks from his childhood holidays, until he slows down at an enormous white house that's built over an entire headland.

'That was my parents' home.'

Peter does a sharp three-point, stopping the car under a bush facing away from the foreboding gates protecting the mansion. He gives me the nod to exit the jeep, whispers, 'Stay down' before leading me through a gap in the fence hidden by a laurel tree.

'All clear,' he says, moving fast and low towards a front porch made from carved balustrades holding up weighty curtains of bougainvillea.

'Did you know that like the poinsettia, the coloured part of bougainvillea is not the flower, it's the bract? The actual flower is inside, it's tiny and white.'

'Watch your footing here. There could be traps.'

We climb around big cane sofas, armchairs and tree trunks forming arabesque patterns winding up the side of the house. Peter points out his bedroom, his parents' suite, the dining room, library. His index finger moves over to the empty swimming pool to the 'lookout' he built as a child.

'They just decided one day they preferred St Barts and let developers buy it. Didn't even ask me. When your folks do stuff like that you realise you mean nothing to them.' He snaps off a piece of dry-rotten windowsill. 'They can't look after anything.' I

put my hand on his shoulder. 'I'm saying this, Stella, because…
you think growing up without a father was the worst thing that
could happen, but sometimes, growing up with one can be just as
difficult. Remember that.'

62

We arrive at the Starfish School of Diving run by Peter's friends, Nick and Tandy. Turns out, Peter's kind of a cult figure here in Barbados – people all seem to know him, want to touch him, ruffle his hair or slap him on the back – but few seem to have any idea what he does or where he does it. I mentioned to him that whenever anyone says, 'How's living in New York?' or 'How's that movie you were producing?' he doesn't correct them. Why doesn't he tell them about his work in the war zones?

'Long ago I realised that if you choose to spend time abroad, nobody *really* wants to know anything about your life. It's like hearing an account of someone's dream or recent illness; mind-numbingly tedious. Who cares? I keep my horrors to myself. And maybe one day I'll settle somewhere long enough to write a book about it all, but even then, no one wants to hear about a war going on somewhere else, they're just glad it's not happening to them. What they don't realise is that it's always going on around us, just on different levels.' He makes a click with his tongue. 'You got enough sun cream on?'

We load up the speed-boat with cold beers, family-sized packs of tortilla chips and speed out to sea.

Peter's friend, Nick, who as well as jointly running the school works for a marine research company, and I strike up a friendship based on our love of animals and ecology, so much so, he refuses point blank to let me scuba-dive without any experience, which is a relief.

'Pete! She can't use an aqualung without lessons – you're crazy, dude!'

'She swims good.'

'No, man. You guys go down and I'll give her an introductory lesson. Stella, I have a facemask with an extended snorkel. We'll go through those reefs, you'll see plenty.'

'Yeah, well, don't show her too much, Nick,' says Peter. 'I'm kind of attached to this one.'

'That's why it might be good to keep her alive.'

The boat stops once the mainland looks like a toy in the distance. Peter leads me to the edge and rolls backwards into the water. Tandy follows. I jump in after him and tread water. It feels good to kick the sea, stamp out the residue frustration of last night. Nick tumbles in after me, gives me the thumbs up.

The two of us, with our long snorkels and masks, move through the underwater universe. It pays little attention to us, that world of colour and variety.

Once my head is above water again, I look back at the quiet coastline. There's nothing around apart from another diving school where a lone student takes off his mask, laughs a little and nods to his instructor. He's young, dark and familiar – when he catches me looking at him, his expression changes. His smile drops and his eyes dart away like he's been caught out.

'You know him?' asks Nick.

'I don't think so. Maybe he's at the same hotel as me.'

He was watching Henry and Yuleka's wedding and I've also seen him somewhere else.

Our next stop is a shack bar which Peter claims makes the world's best grouper sandwich. The swimming experience followed by the beer and fish has lifted our moods.

'I'm still rocking with the boat, is that normal?'

'Sea legs. I've got a remedy for that.' Peter grins. 'I'll concede to doing something nauseatingly touristy – something I wouldn't do for anybody else.'

The rum factory is a relief from the glitz of our hotel if you ignore the three coaches waiting outside. There are huge signs from the 1950s and everything stinks of sweet alcohol. The tasting glasses are still warm and sticky from the previous tours but Peter and I go at it as drunkenness takes away that viscous layer of awkwardness between us, and neither of us wants to spend a sober evening together.

At dusk we make our way back to the jeep, giggly and light-hearted, each carrying a bottle of Mount Gay rum. I walk slightly ahead of Peter when he stops to help a couple load their car and tells them about a great restaurant he knows.

'Stella, I need to go back... use the toilets. I'm not feeling...' He winces, hopping from foot to foot.

'Oh, sure, take your time.' I try to look sympathetic and avoid wondering if he had the squits when he was in his wetsuit.

Fighting the effects of the alcohol and dodging the green monkeys swinging through the branches, I see a jeep gliding all over the road.

There are about five of them. One passes a map to another in the back seat. They're all singing along to 'Ain't No Mountain High Enough', which is being played at full volume. One of them looks out of the window.

It's Joseph. The way he turns his head, his dark hair brushing the side of the window. It stops my breath. I want to call out to him but the car drives away.

'You okay?' Peter brings me back to reality by tugging at my arm. 'Stella? What is it?'

'Nothing... I... I just thought I knew someone in that car.'

'Don't tell me, more of your family showing up on holiday with us.'

Peter puts his arms around me and kisses my ear. I don't want him near me. I want Joseph. The fleeting vision of him suckered onto my retinas is dragging me all the way down the road.

A hit and run and there's nothing left of me.

'Maybe you need to use the toilets?' I break from Peter's grip, look away from him. 'I sure can't make you out, girl, but I'm not giving up,' he says.

63

I spend the night with Peter again. After our ritual of nightcaps and chat, we undress and lie in the dark together.

'You okay just to snuggle?' he asks.

I wish I were, but having this other man next to me makes me miss Joseph more.

'I'm not the kind of guy who can meet a wonderful girl like you, make a home in one place and stop moving. I'd feel like a target, y'know?'

'But that's not at all what I want either.'

'Girls say that, but… Remember what Tandy said about sharks, if they stop swimming they sink and die – that's me, baby.'

'Thanks for sharing that with me, but there's nothing to explain.'

He moves his legs across mine. 'Maybe one day someone will put a gun in your mouth, you'll hear a click and you'll know how it changes everything.' Peter lifts the sheets up over me and starts tucking me in. He kisses my eyelids. 'I've wanted to do that all night.'

'That's sweet.'

'I'm not *sweet*, Stella. I'm anything but sweet. But I wouldn't have stopped last night if I didn't feel something for you… I just can't fake it with you. I can only fuck people I hate.'

I focus on the shadows and try to slide away from him without him noticing but he traps me in his arms.

'Please stay,' he says, reading my mind.

Before I fall into a deep sleep, the last vision I have is of the man in the Land Rover who looked like Joseph. That smile, the turning of the head, the way he was able to capture Joseph's

'Josephness'. Every night we lived together, the last thing we said before we went to sleep was 'goodnight' and still, I can't break the habit. Wherever you are Joe, *Goodnight*.

PART FIVE

LOVERS

64

Sorry I haven't written for a while, stuff's been going down. Mum and I had a big row last week so I went to stay with Kamilla but then I had a feeling something was wrong. Luckily I found Mum in time. She'd taken pills again so I called the ambulance and they saved her but they think she might lose the use of her kidneys. She's still in ICU. I visit her every day but if she gets worse I might have to go into care again, but meanwhile I'm here at the flat and no one's got involved. Don't think I'm partying and having all my friends over – I'm actually revising for my GCSEs which start next week.

Big news. The other day there was a knock at the door – I wouldn't have answered because quite a few of the flats here have been burgled recently but it was a little old lady – I know, I know you shouldn't trust people but... anyway, the old lady had a cake and a bag of presents in her hands. She was looking for me! She was Granny Tyler! Mum's mum. She said 'Happy Birthday' because it was my sixteenth birthday! Did you think of me? Over tea and cake, we curled up on the sofa and she told me all about her life and how sad she was that her husband wouldn't let her see her daughter, Mum.

When Nana Tyler's husband died, the first thing she wanted to do was get back together with Mum and me. For all these years she'd wanted to see me, her granddaughter, but she'd been too afraid of her husband's rages. Now he's gone, she's sold her house and wants to get a flat in London and study horticulture.

We all went to see Mum who was awake and sitting up with Robert Atkins, her boss, who paid for her to have a private room. His wife died recently and Abigail and I think he wants Mum to marry him although he doesn't know how messy she is and how much her debts are. Anyway, Robert has promoted her to Assistant Editor (a little pay rise!) and she's even getting Thursday afternoons off for her group therapy sessions and can pick me up from school which will be mortifying for me as I'm in Year 11.

Robert says I'll be a great lawyer after reading the letters I wrote on Mum's behalf since she's been away! I've chosen the subjects, everything I'll need to go to uni to study law which I want to do but also it makes Mum happy. What subjects are your sons going to choose? Where are they thinking of going to university?

Lots of love, Stella xxx

65

'Today is the day you talk to Henry,' orders Peter as we follow a hummingbird into the breakfast room. He points to a table next to a blue jacaranda tree set with the napkins folded to look like doves.

'They're here.'

Before I can ask who, Yuleka strides over.

'Well! Look at the two lovebirds. I just said to Hard Dick there'd be no fun people around at breakfast time – and look who I've found! Oi, Henry, say good morning to Stella and Peter.' My father acknowledges us with a shake of his teaspoon. 'Darlings, you must sit with us.' She calls over to Ferdi, 'Boy! Set these two a place at our table.' Ferdi and I exchange a look. 'He's a bit of all right, your one… hmm? Deeelicious!' she says, pointing to Ferdi as if he were a ripe melon. 'Look at ours: he's like a big, fat hippopotamus and just as bloody slow.' She wipes hair from her mouth. 'And I think he's taking drinks from our mini-bar. I'm going to put poison in one of them and if he pukes everywhere we'll know I'm right.' She sits Peter down. 'We were wondering where you two were yesterday. We all had breakfast at three o'clock in the afternoon! Can you *believe* it? Then we did the glass-bottomed boat thing with Bunny and that man – what's his name? Then we went down into a grotto, saw a deserted island and had an English cream tea – all in time for Happy Hour!' She kisses Henry loudly on the top of his bald patch like an old dowager would her chihuahua. I break into my roll. 'Okay, the breakfast bar! You guys, don't go anywhere – I'll be back!'

'And that's a threat!' says Henry, which makes Yuleka screech: 'You hear what he said? "That's a threat!" Big Shot, you are *so* funny!' The two of them knock into the cold-meat platter.

'*Sure* he's your dad?' asks Peter when they're out of earshot.
'We'll find out today.'
Peter raises his coffee cup to me. We chink the rims together.

66

'What is it about buffets that make people fill their plates four times as much as they usually would?' asks Henry, as a guest holding up a colossal plate while munching on a croissant passes our table.

'No limits, I guess,' says Peter. 'Starts off like you've hit the bounty – every permutation of breakfast imaginable, but after the first few bites it just becomes an endurance test.'

'I read somewhere it's mostly animals that live in proximity to humans that overeat,' I add.

'You'd think some of these people have never seen food before.'

'They probably haven't, darling.' Yuleka groans. 'The people at this hotel are so *common*.' She scrapes the fish from her plate into a saucer. 'Henry, this is smoked *trout* not *salmon*. Typical.'

'Poor baby,' says Henry, patting her wrist.

'What do you do in London, Stella? You work or you a party girl like me?'

'I'm a lawyer.'

'These career women, eh, Peter?' Masticating on pieces of bread roll, Henry levers a dollop of scrambled eggs onto his fork, dumps it into his mouth. 'What area?'

Peter watches me, eyebrows raised.

'Family law.' It's not true but lays down a trap. I stick the knife into the butter and slice it down the middle.

'Oh,' he says. 'And do–'

Yuleka pushes her head in front of Henry's. 'You should help Henry then, he's in a legal battle with his two boys because they say he has to give them *and* that blood-sucking ex-wife *everything*. He worked so hard all his life for them, you know, and now he wants to enjoy himself, they don't like it. The selfishness!'

'I'm sure Stella and Peter don't want to hear about my problems.'

'They do! Don't you, darlings? She's interested. She's just as disgusted as I am, aren't you, Stella? Poor Henry. They call me – the woman he loves – they call me a "gold-digger". Yes, they actually said that. Can you imagine how hurtful that is to Henry? People find true love and all you get is jealousy and suspicion. What losers.'

'Don't get yourself upset, dear,' says Henry, brushing away a crumb from her cheek. 'They don't know her, that's all. Anyway, I thought we weren't going to talk about them on our honeymoon.'

'I know, I know. I'm positive energy, a *chi.* They are negative, *chang* – chi-chang, yi-yang – whatever, they are bad,' she says. 'So can we go back to the George V on our way back?'

'I do a lot of paternity cases,' I say to no one in particular.

Yuleka takes out her make-up compact and puckers up her lips. Then she starts scrunching up her hair so that it stands out like antennae seeking more scintillating company.

'What's that?' she mutters absent-mindedly.

'It's where the children of men who've been abandoned trace their fathers and sue them for back payment, maintenance, damages…' I let this hang in the air. I look at Henry who doesn't even appear to be listening while his new wife brushes away slivers of croissant from the top shelves of her breasts.

'How do you find these fathers?' asks Peter, leading me.

'Oh, private detectives, banks, DNA profiles, tracers. We always get them in the end.'

'Good for you!' cheers Peter.

'Bravo,' Yuleka adds.

Peter looks to Henry who taps at a breadcrumb on the table

while looking out to sea. 'Terrible thing that, to abandon a child. Don't you think, Henry?'

'Monstrous,' Henry agrees, mopping up the last of his scrambled egg onto a triangle of toast.

Peter looks at me – this is the moment.

I put down my bread knife and sit up straight. 'Actually, I was interested in this type of law because my...'

A figure jumps out of a bed of giant pink begonias, right behind Henry's head. Henry and Peter wait for me to finish. 'I never... met my...'

Someone waves at me while holding a plant in front of their face. The shape moves and a coconut comes crashing down. The person peers over the plant again. It's a woman – long red hair, wearing a hat and large square sunglasses. When I look up, she ducks back behind the plant.

'Stella, you were saying?' asks Peter.

'Yes. I was interested in family law because I...'

'Because you...?' Peter nudges me.

When I look again, I see a hand shoot out of the topiary and wiggle its fingers, motioning me forward.

'Excuse me a minute,' I say.

Peter tries to catch my wrist but I tear off towards the bushes, hearing Yuleka say, 'Probably cystitis, hmm, Peter? You naughty boy!'

Crouched behind a rhododendron trunk holding a large waxy leaf to her face is my mother.

'I'm in disguise.'

'What are you doing here?'

'I'm going to be fifty next year,' she says, flicking at an ant.

'It's time that I… don't I look stunning as a redhead? Ow!' She leap-frogs in the air. 'An insect bit me on the–'

'Who's looking after Elvis?'

'Dot. Dot Preston, your old dog walker. She's had a heart stent put in.'

'I'm glad she's getting better. So, Mum, I know you're going to be fifty. You came all the way to Barbados to tell me that?'

'No. I came to see *you* – but I also came to see *him*.'

We both look at Henry who is now crouched between two bowls of fruit, his mouth wide open for Yuleka to throw grapes into. 'You know, Stella, I spent half my life believing we were meant to be together, I don't want to spend another fifty years always wondering.'

'You've met him?' She presses her fingers on my arm to keep me still, concentrating on Henry.

'I was his bridesmaid.'

'His what?'

'I'll tell you about it later, but he doesn't know about me. I was just about to tell him when I saw you decimating the shrubbery.'

'Is that *her*? The new one?'

'Yes. You know?'

'Caroline – his ex – she told me. We've been speaking.' Her wig slips forward as she looks at the ground. 'His sons are suing.'

'I can't believe you're here.'

'You gave me a lot of money. I was worried. Then Joe told me you'd gone to Barbados. I did a little research. Apparently he left his wife for her… really? *Her*?'

'Stella?' Peter is looking over in my direction, waving his napkin at me.

'Who's the dish?' Mum points at Peter.

'Just a friend.'

'I see,' she says, not breaking her stare from Henry and Yuleka.

'He's not happy, I can tell.'

There's a rustle in the bushes and, 'Miss Stella?'

Mum and I both jump to see Ferdi standing behind us. 'Is everything all right?'

'Ferdi, this is my mum, Florence. Florence, Ferdi, my friend.'

'Enchanted to meet you.' They shake hands. 'You didn't tell me that your mother was staying with us. Here, let me add another place to the table…'

'No!' we both squeak. 'She's here in *secret*. That's why we're whispering,' I say. Ferdi closes his eyes, showing me he has a full grasp of the situation.

I gesture to my barely touched breakfast. 'Ferdi, could you…?'

'Leave your beautiful mother to me – and your secret. Come this way, Stella's mum, though you look more like *sisters*.'

'Thank you,' she says, holding out her hand. 'Stella, I don't want to see you again until you tell Henry who you are, and if you could get me some of those little shampoo and shower gels from your hotel, it would–'

'Go!' I say, as Ferdi half carries her out of the flower bed.

67

'Ah! Here she is!' says Henry when I return.

'Sorry about that – just had to see if that begonia was real or plastic.'

'Probably plastic knowing *this* place.' Yuleka's seated so close to Henry that she's crushing his hips. 'This resort is so crappy. Have you seen the towels, they are so small they don't even go all the way around Henry, yesterday in the shower...'

While she lists the hotel's deficiencies, Peter sees me scowling at the bush where Mum's still talking animatedly to Ferdi. He mimes 'What?' I don't answer.

'I took the liberty of filling your dish while you were checking the authenticity of the plants.'

'Thank you.' I try to look at Peter but am once again distracted by Mum's red hair and Ferdi's laughter.

The waiter brings over a coconut-and-mango salad.

'Stella, you were telling us about the scum who abandon their children. Please go on,' insists Peter.

'Well! That was ab-so-*lut*-ely scrummy!' says Henry loudly as he puts down his knife and fork. He lurches out of his chair, scraping it across the floor.

'Henry, where are you going?' asks Yuleka.

'Enjoy your–'

Yuleka leans over the table to us: 'Probably another toilet emergency. Henry can't digest fruit very well. Flower girl and Hot Peter – *later*. And that's a threat.' She backs away from the table. 'He shouldn't have had that third Toulouse sausage – if you know what I mean! Oh, and...' Henry's almost out of the room as she twirls around and calls back '...there's a picnic lunch on the other side of the island where friends of the Templeton-Crests have a private beach. We're getting there by boat. It's gonna be a wild parrrrrty! You gotta be there. No running away this time, eh!' From the foyer we hear her calling, 'Henry! Wait!'

Peter waves for more coffee and the rest of the cooked breakfast. A broad grin moves across his cheeks.

'That's your father. Running away.' Peter smiles.

'Don't be silly, the fruit compote disagreed with him.'

'What did it say?'

I smile back at him, despite myself.

'No, really. You got him, Stella.'

'But I didn't have the chance to say anything, I would've but–'

'But, look, this is interesting…' Peter points to where Henry was sitting. He'd dropped a camellia flower when he left. All its petals have been removed, bruised and crushed, the little green leaves have been curled back and forth repeatedly and each stamen separated, stripped and rolled into a dark ball. These are the remains of a cruel and deliberate mutilation – could it signal some kind of conscience?

68

Ferdi appears behind me, feet together and hands clasped behind his back. But his lips can't suppress an excited grin.

'Okay, where is she?'

'She's staying at the RumBah Inn. I took her back there myself. She's a very funny lady, your mother, and so kind.'

'She's also completely mad.'

'Mad, but in a good way,' he muses. 'I made her one of my mother's special drinks. She had three!'

'Did she say what she was doing here?'

'Yes, yes, marvellous answers. Let's see… She wants to "re-evaluate her life goals" and go zip-lining.'

'Couldn't she do that at home?'

'Zip-lining?'

'No! The *re-evaluating*!'

'Why don't you ask her tonight at dinner? The RumBah do the best grilled crayfish. She said about eight?'

'Great,' I groan.

'Is there anything else I can do?'

'Keeping my mum out of trouble is a full-time job, believe me.'

'I will devote myself wholeheartedly to the task.'

'Try to keep her away from sugary drinks. And alcohol. And karaoke.' Ferdi's already bouncing on his toes ready to get back to his charge. 'One second, Peter and I are going on this boat today. Apparently there's a party?'

'Johnny Mansard's party. He's one of the richest people in Barbados – owns a chain of shops all around the world. You shouldn't miss a chance to go to his private island.'

'Ferdi, you're smiling an awful lot this morning.'

'I must admit, finding you and your mother crouching in the

bushes has tickled me a little. And I've had a glimmer of hope for my career in the movies.'

'Why's that?'

'Remember you were asking about a celebrity wedding on the island? I said that it would be Joseph West and Sylvia Amery's wedding? Well, very near my village is a beautiful old colonial home that was hired two days ago at a moment's notice. All the big hotels have been receiving bookings from very prominent names. It's very exciting. It's a hope, eh? You know who Joseph West is, don't you?'

'I do.'

'I'm not a fan of hers but he's a fine actor. If he's here, maybe… it's silly, but you have to dream.'

69

Before leaving for the yacht party, I check my emails. Claire wrote to say she's barely left the office since being made partner and that Happy was the only person she could talk to. Tash informs me that she was forced to use all of my deposit to buy a new vacuum cleaner, and then, in all the spam, phishing, animal rights petitions forms, something from Joseph.

> I guess you're not picking up emails or you'd rather believe social media stories about Sylvia and me. I'm beyond apologising for all the press that's rained down on the people I love. The film grossed out so I've agreed to one last publicity stunt to 'launch the Hollywood thing' and get established in the US. So I'm just writing to you to warn you that the news might be particularly bad over the next week or so. Please don't believe anything you read — it's all part of Rebecca's show. Hopefully you are somewhere where they won't reach you — I can't. In two days I'm taking a month's break until I start filming again. After that, yes, I am going to move to LA for my career, for the privacy and there's nothing for me in London without you.
>
> Elvis is at your mother's. Can you call her? She doesn't seem to be answering.

```
    I reset her central heating thermostat
 — it was 42 degrees!
   What happened?
   Your West Star
```

'Ready for lunch?' Peter sings.

'You look happy. Good news?'

'Yeah, actually. *Inside Hollywood* has asked if I'll cover the Joseph West and Sylvia Amery wedding. It's not my thing but...'

70

The sky is petulant, refusing to let the sun push past. There's a taste of tin in the air, it sticks to my teeth. Peter warns me, as we sit in the back of an old Bentley convertible, that cloudy days are the most dangerous for burns. He says that people don't protect themselves enough from threats they can't directly see. He dabs sunscreen on my nose. His movements are careful, gentle. In a few days Peter and I will say goodbye but I'm still waiting for us to meet.

We pull up at the Templeton-Crests' hotel, which has a glass lift going down to the sea. It's where Yuleka said she'd prefer to be.

Bunny's chauffeur jumps out. As the sound of his footsteps disappear, Peter and I absorb the silence. The hotel isn't that different from the Paradise Beach Club but the pool's bigger and bluer and some of the rooms are on the sea linked by glass pathways.

'I'll try and get you a moment with Henry alone, so you can say your stuff. I thought you were going to this morning but then you darted off... were you okay?'

'Something came up.'

'Remember, Stella, you've met your dad now, you don't have to confront him if you don't feel comfortable about it. I mean, it's for *you*, not him.'

I watch a young couple in tennis whites walking hand in hand to the courts. I wonder if I'll ever be able to see two people in love and not think of what I lost.

'You *really* okay?' asks Peter, taking the ends of my fingers and pressing them gently.

'Not saying anything would be worse than saying something, so, I'm ready.'

'Just remember, you cannot control consequences.'

'Wise words,' I say, squeezing his hand back. 'After all you've seen in wars and conflicts, you must think I'm so pathetic.'

'The big stuff's easy. It's these private battles that really test us – *les petites misères de la vie quotidien*. But I know you'll be great.'

Peter and I sit quietly again. Something's going to happen today.

We hear Bunny before we see her. She emerges, propped up by the chauffeur, Martini cocktail in hand. Seeing us, she goose-steps towards the car. The chauffeur runs alongside her, panicked. As she gets closer I see that her mascara wand must have missed her eyes – her cheeks look as if she's slept on a Chinese newspaper. She has only managed to do up the alternate buttons on her shirt so there's a large diamond-shaped opening through which we can see her skin dragging into her bra.

When Peter opens the car door, she shouts over, 'Do you know, my husband hasn't fucked me for three years?'

'His loss.' Peter waves her into the car. She trips over her skirt, lunges forward spilling her drink. Seeing me, she slurs, 'Urgh. *Her.*'

I jump out and take the empty seat next to the driver while Peter helps bring her in and the two men twist her limbs round so that she is folded at Peter's side. She lifts the drink to her lips and spills some down her front. She snorts, rolls her head onto Peter's shoulder and waves for the driver to continue. Every once in a while, she glares at me, sneers and mutters, 'Pfft.'

'Roy not coming?' asks Peter a few minutes into the drive.

'Pfft,' she replies.

'Lord T-C cannot go on the boat: it is not wheelchair accessible,' says the chauffeur. 'He's playing in the bridge tournament.'

'Pfft,' adds Bunny, raising her hand up over Peter's head where it hangs suspended like a chicken's claw until she brings it down over his hair. 'He hasn't fucked me in years.'

Peter ignores her petting him but his indifference only exacerbates her. She starts making circling motions with her finger around the outside of Peter's ear. He swats her off. She looks out of the window again.

'He doesn't find me beautiful anymore. I used to be, I used to be... but not anymore,' she slurs before a tear runs down her cheek.

71

We reach the harbour and spend a few minutes helping Bunny out of the car. Once standing, she comes to life, rotating her arms and telling us to 'Get off'.

'Do you think she'll be all right?'

'Who cares?' Peter puts an arm around me and points to where we will be spending the rest of the day. 'That's our ship! Fantastic, isn't she?'

The three-deck yacht bobs as if impatient to get on with its journey. The boat is one of the largest in the harbour, gleaming white and navy blue with polished chrome, she's called *Credit Crunch*.

'You *sure* Bunny's all right?'

'Nope,' he replies, and then flings his arms in the air and calls out, 'Hey, Johnny!'

'Ahoy there!' answers a man on deck, waving to us.

Our host has brilliantly blond hair and wears a brilliantly blond suit, a deep tan and has four long white hairs sprouting from his chest. He canters down the shining gangplank to meet us.

'Heyah!' he neighs, giving me a hand over the coiled ropes. 'Watch your ankles on these!' He smiles, displaying thousands of pounds' worth of dentistry.

Peter doesn't take his hand but leaps up to the boat in one easy sprint. The two men clasp each other and I am once again struck with how easy Peter is with everyone. Johnny puts an arm around the two of us and walks with us along the deck.

'So, tell me all about the…' He stops and murmurs, 'What the…?'

A crowd has gathered, all looking down into the marina. We move quickly towards the commotion and focus on the sandy mud between the boats. A huddle of Caribbean men are dragging something large and heavy. It looks like a dead body. Tourists click away at their phones. Someone whispers that it's a child, another insists it's a baby whale. We hold our breaths. We lean right over the railings, craning our necks as far out as we can yet holding tight in case we need to pull ourselves back.

'I think it's alive,' says Peter, who is videoing the scene.

I frown disapprovingly at him. 'Peter, this could be–'

'A story,' he says, moving my head out of the way.

All at once the crowds by the waterfront jump back. Hands cover faces and children are told not to look. The men start pulling at once. There's a cry and I see a long leg jutting out of the water to kick one of the men – it gets him where it hurts most and he doubles over in pain, the other boatmen roar with laughter.

Whatever they're dragging in from the water, it's very much alive. An arm shoots out this time, grabs a man's shirt and shakes it. Then I see what the great weight is. It's not a murder victim, a giant fish, the remains of a pirate or a treasure chest: it's Bunny Templeton-Crest. She's going through the motions of breaststroke in the mud. The men try to catch hold of her.

'Bring her up here, boys!' orders Johnny. 'She's one of mine.'

It takes five of the crew to lift Bunny up and lead her back towards the dockside where she is hauled up by Peter and Johnny. The men drop her first on the deck where she wipes at the mud in hard punishing motions. Everyone watches to see if she can stand unaided.

Johnny kisses her cheek. 'Little early for a swim, my dear. We were going to wait till we got to the island first.'

'Ya!' She spits mud from her mouth.

'Come on, up here, there you go! Wonderful to see you again!' He takes her hand and shoos away the men who were holding her.

'So where's Roy, m'lady?' asks Johnny.

'He's…' She screws up her face and waves her hand around, vaguely.

Johnny smiles sympathetically. 'What a shame. Next time, eh?' He grabs hold of her again before she falls back. Then she turns, embarrassed by her lack of agility and tries to march ahead of us. She trips over her skirt and goes to grab hold of Peter to break her fall, and then she looks up at him again, sneering. She holds on to his lapels and tosses him back and forth unsteadily, shaking him.

'Don't. Laugh. At. Me,' she says angrily. Peter bats her hands away from him while Johnny takes her by the shoulder, leading her away.

'Bunny, I'll get someone to help you change into something dry.' He signals to a young Bajan woman. 'Gracie, could you take Lady Templeton-Crest to Ottoline's room, help her freshen up.'

The three of us watch as Bunny stumbles away, propped up by the maid.

72

'My parties are known to *end* with women jumping into the water, not begin!' Johnny laughs. 'It's sad because she was once a real beauty.' Johnny looks at Peter. 'So! Ya'll right? It's been a minute.'

'Too long, old friend, yeah, life's pretty good.'

'And who's this lovely young lady?'

'Johnny, please meet my friend Stella.'

Johnny gives me a beaming smile. He is about to say something when the definition of ravishing appears behind him.

'Who *was* that woman?' she asks. Johnny puts his arm around her waist. 'Lady T-C. One of the old Antigua gang, her husband drives a wheelchair.'

'Looks like she could do with one too.'

'Gracie's helping her change. Stella, Peter, let me introduce you to Kimberly. Kimberly, do you remember I told you about Peter? His parents used to own the old colonial sugar farm on the headland.' She nods vaguely. 'Anyway, you guys, Kimberly, she's half Brazilian and half Dutch.'

'Danish,' she corrects.

'My little Viking,' he says, winding his arm around her mother-of-pearl-tinted waist. Her smile's so perfectly symmetrical it makes me want to giggle.

Johnny looks up at the sky. 'Damn awful day. They say a storm is in the air. Look how the water's all stirred up. Let's hope the sun'll break through, eh, but first, my dears, drinks.'

The rest of the party are on top deck. Most look like Johnny and Kimberly apart from a group of older Russian men playing poker with a cloud of nubile girls wearing impossibly high heels and little else. I stop scanning the guests when I come to Henry Hardwick wearing a sailor's hat. He is talking to a small, animated man in a Breton T-shirt and an enormous camera around his neck. Henry nods distractedly while exchanging an empty champagne glass for a new one from the waiter's tray. Their conversation seems to be winding down, both men swivel round to examine the rest of the crowd, and then he sees me. He looks straight at me and turns away. There's no sign of recognition, smile, squint of displeasure even, nothing. In that split second, he might have pulled out a laser gun and zapped me under the sternum. But I remain standing, watching my father.

Bunny reappears as though she'd just stepped out of a time machine to a restored version of herself from twenty years ago – she wears a vibrantly coloured dress with all her hair piled on top of her head pinned in with fresh flowers. She swans past us nodding at someone in the distance.

Peter claims not to know anyone, although hardly a second goes by without someone breaking into our conversations and hugging him. Then I hear a shriek.

'Pete! Pete!' We turn as a girl races towards Peter and throws her arms around his neck. Was she a girl he could fake it with?

I sip my champagne, look out to sea and hope not to appear too curious when I'm introduced to Ottoline.

73

'You're from London. Oh my God! So am *I*!' Ottoline holds out her arms as if this is the most incredible coincidence. 'Don't tell me… not Chelsea too?'

'Sorry, not Chelsea.'

'But I'm sure we know some of the same people. What's your name?'

Peter cuts in giving my false name.

She asks for it again, bewildered that she's never heard of me. 'Stella *Banks*… Stella…' Peter and I exchange a knowing smile. 'Do you know Oscar Cox-Pollack? Sophie Hampton? Drew Stapleton-Fox? Caz… not Caz? Rebecca Hobson? Okay, but you must know Tash, Tash McKendrick…?'

'She used to be my flatmate.'

'Oh right! So you must know Joseph West?'

'I've met him, yeah…'

'Have you heard he's here? Here! On the island! He's marrying Sylvia Amery this weekend. I'm desperately trying to get in touch with Rebecca but it's all so incredibly hush-hush and we've been out to sea, but it's going to be *fucktastic*!" Ottoline squeezes Peter's arm in excitement. 'Let's all go together!' She turns to me. 'I thought you'd know Tash – she knows everyone! I was at school with her.'

'Well, never rent a room from her.'

'Wouldn't dream of it.' Ottoline laughs and announces that we should go and make mojitos. 'Really fucking strong ones!'

In the 'Captain's Cabin' we clink our glasses together. 'Let's drink to… things getting fucking better!' Ottoline says, taking large gulps from her glass and swearing loudly every time her pimento separates from the olive. She tries to impale it with a toothpick but the miniature skewer slips from her hand a third time and the olive escapes. I notice her fingers are trembling and there are tears in her eyes.

'Hey, you okay?'

'I'm fine… I *will* be fine… things are getting bet…' She shakes her head, unable to speak.

'Come on, Ottie, get over it,' says Peter impatiently.

Ottoline leans over the counter, looks longingly out to sea.

'Peter… Peter,' she repeats. 'Peter, I haven't seen you since… since the fucking Grand Prix!' He nods, lifts his drink to hers, clinks them delicately together so they ring out. The two of them look into each other's eyes and for a moment I wonder if they've completely forgotten that I'm here.

Then Ottoline grabs an unopened bottle of tequila.

'Shots!' she exclaims, dragging her glossy hair repeatedly back from her face. 'It's just… fuck… Peter, you know…' She half laughs but lets out a cry instead. She lowers her voice so that I have to bring my ear to her mouth. 'Didn't Peter say anything to you? Just check the door, Pete, see no one's listening.' She downs her drink in one. 'God! It's so brilliant to have someone to talk to!' she exclaims. 'I'm so glad Peter brought you, I've been going out of my fucking mind for some decent girly talk! Oh God!' She stamps her foot in an effort to regain emotional control. Then she lowers her voice again. 'It's just… I've been with Johnny for ages, you know, we've had a party every night for the last four years. Anyway, it was one of those "When I'm in London I'll always call you" sort of thing, but *more* than that, wasn't it, Peter, more? I decorated his place in Mallorca, I'm the one who goes to his kids' parents' evenings when his ex-wife's having implants put in her buttocks, and as the years went by I really thought…' she taps her bare wedding finger, 'you do, don't you?'

I gulp back a thimbleful of gin and tonic wondering why I didn't push for Joseph and me to marry.

'So last week he says, "Drop everything, I *really* want you to come out to Barbados, I've someone important to introduce you to". Of course, I thought, this is it. This is really fucking it! And you know who this person I've got to meet is? Kimberly, his new girlfriend! And that's it. Just fucking wham! Bam! No warning, fucking nothing. And I'm left here passing around the nibbles!'

'You knew this would happen...'

'But we were so good together and I... I'm going to be thirty in three years! And here I am, staying on this bloody boat, organising her shopping trips and yesterday...' she chokes on the tears, '...yesterday I helped him put mirrors up over their bed so he could watch them *fucking* fucking! Can you believe it?' Peter gives her a kiss on the head.

Kimberly taps her nails on the glass door.

'Ah, so this is where the *real* party is.' She looks at each of us sensing that we were most probably talking about her. 'Peter, we need you to translate for Mr Kawasoto... sorry, girls, if you can spare him.'

Peter looks to me to check that I can cope without him being there. I wave him off; Ottoline is like a little piece of home. Even if a little too close to home. The humiliation of being jilted for a beautiful blonde is all too familiar.

Ottoline wiggles her fingers to say goodbye, trying to avoid eye contact with Kimberly.

Ottoline puts two ice cubes in her mouth and pours the Martini between them.

'Peter speaks Japanese?'

'Course not,' she answers, shaking her head and dribbling, 'he's just very charming. Where did you meet him?'

'He has the room next to mine at the hotel...'

'A holiday on your own. I'd never be brave enough.' She makes us another drink.

'I came out here to recover from a break-up so I do know how you feel.'

'Oh, we haven't broken up! God *no*!' She laughs at the thought of it. 'This is just Johnny on some Victoria's Secret model jag. He'll get over it and I'll be right here.' She shuts her eyes and sways. 'The boat's started moving. I should see if everyone's all right for drinks. You have such beautiful eyes. Peter really likes you, y'know.'

'Do you know Peter well?'

'Peter? Oh yeah, I *know* Peter.'

'Is there anything I should know about him?'

'Oh he's fab. Fun. Fucked up. Just don't expect him to call you when you get home!' Then she clasps her hand over her mouth. 'Sorry. That was an awful thing to say. Fuck. Don't listen to me... I'm just bitter and twisted. He looks besotted with you and he's got to settle down at *some* point.'

'It's okay, he's told me all about not being able to make any commitments. What with his job and everything...'

'His *job*?'

'Being a war journalist.'

'A *what*?'

'A war reporter, you know, Iraq, Syria, the Ivory Coast and...'

'Who told you that?'

'He did. He's married to his work–'

'Peter – *work*?' Ottoline is laughing so hard she spills some of her drink down her front. 'Oh my God! Sorry, sorry, but that's so funny!' She snorts before saying, 'I was worried that I was clinically depressed because I haven't laughed since last Christmas – you've cured me! Thank you!'

'Why's that funny?'

'Peter's never had a job in his life! He lives off his parents who are totally fed up with him. That's why they stay on another island when he's here. He's a complete dropout! A war journalist? Is that what he told you? Oh dear.' She wipes the tears from her eyes. 'Men! Now I've heard it all!'

'But he told me about how he's travelled all over the world writing about…' As I speak she wrinkles her nose, grins. She's more surprised that I would believe his stories than that he would lie.

'Stella, he's in Barbados now – where's the war?'

'You mean…?'

'Sorry, I shouldn't have said anything… but you took me by surprise when you said that about him being a…' she can't speak for laughing, 'journalist. That's so hilarious! Hey, he's just a *boy*.' She taps the side of her head. 'Take the sex and run!'

Peter circulates, so handsome standing on deck, so plausible. He sees me looking at him and raises his glass before returning to a conversation. His head moves up and down, his champagne glass is slightly at an angle as if he is so absorbed in the speaker's story that he has forgotten his drink, but I doubt he's even listening. Peter calls me over and introduces me to a small group of American investors who are hoping to buy beachfront properties out here – Peter, of course, knows just the place and a deal is in the offing. As soon as there's a lull I slip away, but Peter follows me.

'You okay?'

'I've had a little too much to drink.'

'Ottie's a lethal bartender. She talk about me?'

I shrug.

He knows.

'You know, she's not so innocent… you can't always believe her. She's trouble. I'll tell you about her later… just let me say one thing. She doesn't take rejection well… not from Johnny, not from *me*… y'know what I mean? What she say?'

'Would you get me another drink? Something soft.' I try to give a perky, flirtatious lilt to my request but it comes out spiteful. He puts his hand over mine, it's clammy.

'Whatever you want.'

I watch the foam trail gather until I sense there's someone behind me. I brace myself for Peter again, but it's Henry, thankfully without his sailor's hat.

'I see you found us,' he murmurs. 'Quite a mixed mob, aren't they?' He pauses to watch a woman kick her leg over the head of a man in a Tarzan outfit.

'Yuleka said you weren't feeling well at breakfast, better now?'

'Sorry about dashing out like that. Too much celebrating.'

'Well, it's only once in a life– well, maybe not.'

'True, you can only marry *twice* once!' He looks wistfully at the sea. 'We're eating on this chap's island, I gather.' We both look out to a cove where the boat is heading. 'Quite a racket Bunny was making earlier, what?' He grins, showing me dark-brown stains between his teeth. The way he speaks so dismissively of Bunny reminds me of all the men who laughed at my mother when she embarrassed herself in public.

'She just had a little too much to drink, that's all. Can't be easy, caring for someone with a disability.'

'Ah. Someone said it was a suicide attempt,' he says.

Peter returns to my side with a drink. An open passenger boat packed with tourists passes. The crowd looks up at us, a few take photos. Henry waves at some of the children.

'Henry! Don't look at them, they're nobodies!' Yuleka snaps. She's wearing Henry's sailor's hat and a bikini that looks like it's been made out of roadkill.

'Stella, my dear! Peter, darling. Henry says I look like Ursula Undress…'

'Andress,' he murmurs. 'She was a Bond girl.'

'And I'm a bondage girl! Watch me!' She skips off to the other side of the boat, clambers up the mast, arches her back and thrusts her breasts forward. 'I'm the queen of the worrrrrld!'

'Good God. Get down!' demands Henry.

'I'm the queen of the world!'

'Christ! She's going to fall in!' says Henry, rushing over to her.

Peter whispers in my ear, 'Like she could sink with those jugs? I don't think so.'

We watch as two men help her down. The Russians pop the cork of another Bollinger.

Peter touches my back. 'Hey, we still a team?'

'Course.' I don't know who he is, this Peter Lyle, but right now, he's all I've got.

'When are you going to tell him?'

A swell of water lifts us up in the air for a second before we drop down only to be heaved up again; the crowd cheers.

'Soon,' I say, steadying myself against the side rail.

'We're here. Look.' He points in the direction of the island.

I swear I had this view as my screensaver once. The chunk of land the colour of farmhouse butter surrounded by turquoise waters. The sides are sheer, dropping down to a deserted cove protected by monster palm trees and Technicolor flowers stretching out from oversized leaves. The boat slows down for us to make our way onto the tenders to take us out there for lunch.

I scan the cove, a wall of big square rocks and then the cave which looks like a black hole until we get closer and I see a line of men in white uniforms waving to us from the shoreline. A red-faced man in a black suit peers at the boat, gesticulating to the waiters.

'You're gonna love this, Stella. Inside the cave is a lagoon, that's where we're having lunch,' says Peter.

75

'Hey, you two, jump in!' shouts Ottoline from a dinghy bouncing on the water. She's sitting with an Indian man I've seen on TV cookery programmes. We edge down the rope ladder and step in.

The chef makes room for me and offers me his hat. 'You have such beautiful skin. You must be careful not to let the sun get to you.'

Peter begins to tell them the story of our first night on the beach and how my tan washed off. In one of the other dinghies a group are talking excitedly about the West-Amery wedding, but I can't catch what they're saying. We're joined by two of Kimberly's friends, their legs are so long they have to dangle them over the edge of the boat. On the count of three, our engine starts.

After a few minutes we paddle to the sand and wait on the shore for the others as the sky thickens into a bilious yellow.

The sand is so hot that Ottoline and I have to skip to get to the cave. Inside are vast ceilings and luminescent pools of water. The walls are covered in burning candles. A quartet in black tie play Vivaldi's *Four Seasons.* Further in, there's a quiet waterfall lined with shards of light coming from lanterns overhead. In the middle is a deep pool, reflecting candlelight. The air is close, warm. One person calls out and listens. After that, no one can resist the urge to call out and hear their echoes. One woman sings an aria from *Turandot.*

'What a place!' says Henry, dwarfed by overhanging rocks. He leans his hand against a gigantic boulder to catch his breath while Yuleka begins the lengthy exercise of unstrapping her heels.

A man wearing a pink one-piece bathing suit stands next to us taking photographs of the crystal blades drooping down from the cave's vault-like ceiling. Peering over his horn-rimmed glasses, he springs into a lecture in sedimentary petrology. 'People don't appreciate that Barbados has one of the most impressive underground worlds. They come here on holiday and leave without any idea that the island's geological composition is eighty-five per cent sedimentary rock.' I follow his finger pointing over the rocks. 'Coral reef limestone. See? You see, there? Unlike many other Caribbean islands, there is no volcanic rock in Barbados, making it ideal for cave formation. Places just like these flourish beneath the surface where water can create cavities in sedimentary rock and exposed coral reef. Not only are they geologically fascinating but many were used as refuges for runaway slaves escaping the sugar plantations. This is a particularly splendid example, I'm very grateful to Mr Mansard for permitting me to see it.'

'So it's all natural?' asks Henry.

'That's what I've been saying,' he answers irritably. 'Watch out for the bats.' He walks off, his feet slapping over the wet sand.

'Dickhead,' says Yuleka after him. 'You know what, guys, it reminds me of that Italian architect who makes the buildings that look like ice-cream cones. What's his name?'

'Gaudí,' says Henry weakly. We stand together as the pools of lime-green water flicker in the light. 'And he's Spanish.'

'Catalan,' I say. 'He lived mostly on lettuce leaves, olive oil and nuts.'

'Gross.' Yuleka shrugs.

Peter's hands brush down my back. 'Wanna swim, look for hidden treasure?'

'You might find a few skeletons of runaway slaves,' says Henry.

'Do you have any hidden skeletons we could find, Henry?' asks Peter.

'No, no, no flies on me.' Henry laughs.

'We'll see about that,' Peter retorts.

Peter and I strip down to our swimsuits and rush into the warm water. He catches my toe and whispers urgently, 'Kiss me.'

'I warned you about him!' says Ottoline, who suddenly appears at my shoulder. She leans into us holding her wraparound skirt into her legs.

'Ottie, gimme a break, or...' Peter threatens to splash her.

'I hope Stella's got a life-saving pack fully equipped with oxygen mask. I warned you, girlfriend! He's one of those beasts who swallows girls up.'

'Only if they taste good enough...' he says, without his usual cheeky smile.

Ottoline looks away, bored by this line of flirtation. 'Cool place, huh?' She raises her sunglasses above reddened eyes and drags a hand through the water.

'Johnny plans to build a hotel here one day but right now it's too dangerous to be open to the public. Once the tide's in, there's no way out except by boat. Not sure I feel all that safe. Johnny's captain said we shouldn't be out here.'

'Peter!' shouts Bunny. 'Help me open this Pol Roger!'

Peter squeezes my hand. 'Be right back.'

As he wades over to Bunny and the rather drunken gathering of older men surrounding her, Ottoline says, 'They go back a long way, Peter and Bunny.' We watch as Bunny lassoes her arms across Peter's shoulders and I realise how naïve I've been.

76

After bobbing around in the natural hot spring, I dry off and make my way to the feast laid out on a long flat-topped rock. There are piles of oysters, lobster claws and mussels lit up by opulent candelabras all around us. Johnny sits at the head of the table, dismantling a crab, with his new love on his right and her predecessor, Ottoline, to the left.

Peter's settled on the other side of the rock next to Bunny while I've been placed between a property developer and a plastic surgeon. As we dig into platters of seafood, the air changes from fresh sea breeze to breathy stillness. Looking down to the entrance of the cave, I see the sky outside has turned slate grey.

I watch Henry through the crowd: the way he listens to people, anticipating their punchlines, how his foot will surreptitiously scratch at a mosquito bite on the calf of his other leg while he pretends to be really interested in what's being said, how when he inhales from his cigar he crosses his eyes like a comic-book character.

Was it just *a* father I wanted, or was it him, *that* father, *that* man, Henry Hardwick?

I must have sighed out loud because Yuleka taps me on the arm and says, 'You're in love. I can tell.' She leans across a man wearing nothing but a thong to bring me eye level with her. 'I've been watching you and I'll tell you something, I studied psychology, it's one of my degrees, so I can say for sure,' she tightens her clutch on my wrist, 'he loves you too.'

'I'm not so sure,' I answer, wishing she'd drop the subject.

'I've got an idea. When the sun comes out again, let's use my ylang-ylang essential oils on him, shoulders, back and then, whoopsie, go lower and slower and we'll do the massage of four hands down there. I learnt it in Thailand. After that, you'll see how much he cares. I did it with Henry… now look at us.'

'Yes, look at you.'

'You know he was married before?' she asks, peering into her crustacean. 'To the *Cockroach*!' she says, cracking down on a claw. 'These days are the first happy days he has ever lived in his life. Imagine!' I look over at Henry, who's opening his mouth wide for a forkload of potato salad. 'That Caroline, she's obsessed with me.' Yuleka sucks in the juice from the lobster's claws, one by one.

'What are his children like?'

'*Those* two? *Children*?' She swings her index finger from side to side in front of my face and tuts. 'Not *children*, they are *mutants*.' She stabs at her salad before adding, 'They are just like her. Grabbing, selfish… they don't love their father… they just want a human ATM machine. They do nothing but sit around moaning that he wasn't a good father to them. That poor man, he suffered every day until he met me,' she says, pointing a tentacle at Henry. 'Hey!' She rattles at my wrist. 'You and Peter should do it, get married in Barbados. Don't do it on the beach like we did, though, too many people hanging around and too much sand. Oh, and get them to release fifty white doves. Henry didn't wanna do it because he said it was too expensive, I bet that Johnny wouldn't have held back like that but Henry's so cheap sometimes.'

'Did you hear about some old man marrying a lap dancer on the beach?' asks a man wearing pink sunglasses. 'Everyone was saying it was quite hil-*ar*-ious! Really tack–'

'Hey! That was us!' Yuleka cries out. 'It was our Wedding of a Thousand Dreams! I was in a red bikini top and G-string, red suspenders and a see-through dress – *everyone* said, "Yuleka, you are *the* sexiest bride ever!" But *he* wore shorts and white socks!' A few people laugh. 'Long socks too!' She leans back in her chair, adjusts her breasts and holds up a champagne flute. 'Ha! And *he* had…' she stops to laugh at the memory, 'his stomach, my darlings, stomach out here!' she puts her hands over her belly and blows out her cheeks.

'I think they've heard enough about our big day.'

But Yuleka's on a roll. 'This French bird next to me, she goes, "Yuley, I dunno 'ow you gonna find his *zi-zi* on yourrrr wedding night!" His zi-zi!'

On my other side there's a group gossiping about celebrities and it doesn't take long for one of them to pipe up, 'I heard that Joseph West – you know, the *Replacement* one, British, in everything – is getting married on the island to Sylvia Amery.'

'No way! She's gay.'

'You know, I heard that too! But–'

The man in the black suit claps his hands authoritatively and announces that we must leave immediately – there's a storm coming.

When I ask if anyone's seen Peter, I'm pointed to Johnny's boat. People are piling into the tenders to continue the party away from the churning sea. It's already dark enough to see the disco lights blinking from below deck.

Once I climb back on the boat, I find the narrow corridors that lead to the sleeping cabins and follow what sounds like Peter's voice. I wait outside the door until I can make out the rhythm of his speech. I knock. No answer.

'Peter?' Again, no answer. Then I hear a glass rolling on a table and falling. There's giggling.

'Hello?' I listen for footsteps on the other side of the door.

There's the clunk of the lock being turned. The door opens and Peter stands in a dressing gown, his hair wet and ruffled. Behind him there's a divan strewn with pillows and a fur rug. Peter puts his arm out to stop me moving forward. The body disentangles itself from the cushions and throws. It's Bunny, naked. She slides out from the bed and walks towards me, a smirk on her face. It's like being confronted by a six-foot lamb chop left too long under the grill. Her expression is distinctly post-coital – her hair is still plastered against her neck with sweat. She snarls with lips that are enflamed and wine-stained.

'Run along now,' Bunny slurs, leering at me as if I were some insolent maidservant hanging around for a tip. 'And say hi to Daddy Henry for me, won't you?'

'Hey, don't–'

'Leave her!' Bunny says sternly. 'I said, Peter, stay here!'

I stride down the length of the boat, up the stairs and jump onto a dinghy bringing people in from Johnny's island. Seeing that Henry isn't on board, I ask them to take me back to the cave. I have to finish what I came here to do.

Back on the beach, there's a scramble to fill every boat of every kind. The sky is black overhead, inside the cave, it's even darker. The banquet has been dismantled and the candles are burning out. There's only Henry, Yuleka, and a smattering of people left.

'Stella, can you help me get Henry up?'

Henry is smoking a cigar on a large rock, which has been carved out to make a stone armchair. 'This man eats and drinks too much,' Yuleka says between puffs as we try to lift Henry to a standing position.

'Sir, you need to leave right now,' urges one of the crew.

'Can't you see we're trying? Hey! Come over and help!'

Yuleka slumps down at Henry's feet while he pours himself another drink from a half-empty magnum of champagne.

'Look, she's nagging already.' He chuckles to a straggler.

The other man pats him on the back, says, 'See you on the other side, mate,' and makes his way out of the cave.

Yuleka hisses, 'Henry, I'm going. You stay here and drown, okay?'

She stamps over to the cave's mouth and waits. Henry attempts to stand a few times but falls back down again. 'Henry, come on! Please! You're embarrassing me.'

'*You* embarrassed *me* today.'

'Ugh! What are you talking about?'

'You. You made fun of me and my socks.'

'Henry, I'm not hearing this now, get me? There's a speedboat going straight back to the hotel, I'm taking it. Maggie said there's a carpet sale in the foyer. *Now*. It's going to rain. And Roy will be looking everywhere for Bunny, what do I tell him?'

'Let's just wait for Johnny's boat.'

'What are you talking about? Henry, look! It's leaving!' True.

The sea is now covering the sand that we strolled over earlier. Johnny's boat appears much further away than it had been before. 'Henry, I'm going. Okay? You stay and die.'

'I haven't finished my cigar. Stella, you're not scarpering off just yet are you?'

This could be my only chance to tell Henry who I am, so I answer, 'I'll join you, one more for the road.'

'Good girl.' He pours me a glass of champagne.

Yuleka glares at me. 'Did you hear what I said?'

'*Chill out*, as they say.' Henry then pulls a face at her before singing 'When a Man Loves a Woman'.

'It'd be a shame to get those Blahniks wet. You go on, we'll catch you up,' I suggest, trying to sound relaxed.

Yuleka turns to me, at first in defiance, then relief. 'Sure, Stella? I would like to buy a carpet and I'm getting cold. Henry, enjoy the storm.'

'Clouds! Big deal! See, Stella's here. Us Brits don't panic at the first drop of water. Maybe we do eat too much potted shrimp, but at least we know how to fight.' He hums 'Drunken Sailor' to himself, too drunk to see the grey plumes of clouds gathering over the horizon. Henry listens to his echo throughout the grotto. Yuleka stomps off, her heels sinking into the sand. We watch her climb into the tender as the driver turns the engine.

'She buggered off then?' Henry asks, looking around the cave.

The boat skids over the sea, which is coming alive with a specific maliciousness. Soon we'll have to make our way over the rocks to wait for someone to come for us. I turn to Henry who's checking to see if his cigar is still lit.

'It's just us now,' I say.

79

Henry settles back into his rock as if it was an armchair in some Mayfair gentlemen's club. He grunts and takes another gulp of champagne. One of the candles slumps to the ground soon followed by the rest.

'Think I showed her, didn't I?'

I pick up my bag and settle it on my shoulder.

'Henry, we should get going. The water's nearly ankle high already.'

'I'm…'

He clamps both hands down beside his buttocks and tries to push himself off. I watch him lumbering over the rocks to collect his belongings. He returns to his seat and slowly brings a sock up to his foot. After a few failed attempts, he searches for his shoes. One is sinking in a small rock pool and the other bobbing out to sea. Spray covers his glasses.

'You sure they've *all* gone?' He squints at the heavy sky. '*All* of them? Even Peter?' He takes his glasses off, cleans them with the ends of his shirt. 'I didn't appreciate what she said. About me. I've put on a bit, but… still…' He juts out his paunch to the wind and grimaces. 'It's bloody dark in here. Hot too.'

Every wave in about seven crashes hard against the cave's mouth.

'Quite a lunch, quite a lunch,' he mumbles. 'He can't be short of a bob or two, what? That Johnny. Must have cost a fortune, all that drink, that *boat*. I thought it was too big, didn't you?' He wipes his brow from where the sea is flicking water at him. 'That's what's got her. Seeing all these super rich. Shouldn't have brought her here because now she's caught on to the fact I'm nothing as flash and fun as these types. Probably off with one of them right now.'

I climb off the rock I've been sitting on and walk over to Henry who seems engrossed watching droplets of water pitting the pools by his feet.

'Take my hand. We need to leave the cave very soon, step over the rocks and get to the cove. The tide's coming in fast.'

'Seems a waste of water, eh? Falling into the sea,' he says, his syllables merging into one. 'Don't look so worried, any minute now—'

'I'm Stella Tyler. Your daughter.'

'Hmm? What are you on about?'

I say it again. 'I'm your daughter.'

He wipes his forehead. 'I've only got two boys. They're a handful enough. No others.' He tries to lift himself up. 'Come here. I won't bite. Just need your shoulder to lean on. Get out of this place.'

'Henry?'

'Hmm…'

'What did you do with the letters I wrote to you?'

'What are you on about?'

'What did you do with them? The letters, the Christmas cards, the pictures, notes, poems, school reports? They were sent to your office. They were for you.' He looks behind him to see if I'm talking to someone else. 'Your daughter? Have you ever thought about your daughter?'

Henry slaps the water around his granite chair. It's almost up to his knees now when he sits. Outside, the waves are almost deafening, but inside, the cave is quiet but for the rasping foam.

'My… my… where are my—' he slaps down the water, '—glasses. I can't see a wretched thing! Damn bloody storm. Damn bloody women!'

'Henry, I'm Stella. Your daughter.'

'I don't know what you're bloody on about.' He peers at the

cave's mouth, where the boat had been waiting. There is nothing now but rain, not even space between the hurtling drops.

I stand before him. 'Florence Tyler.'

'Huh? She at the lunch today?'

'No, Henry, she wasn't. Florence Tyler. She was a secretary at your chambers. You had an affair with her while you were engaged.'

'Damned hot in here.' His eyes tighten as if under a blinding light. He pads over again to the cave's entrance in a waddle that makes me think of a duck-billed platypus.

'Look, do you think they're coming or not?'

The dark sea surges towards him. His breathing is shallow and his cigar is soaked.

'You met me as a baby.'

'Stella,' he says. He closes his eyes and opens them again. 'Stella, my daughter. Florence's daughter.'

'Yes!'

'No bloody idea what you're talking about.'

80

Light billows out of the tunnel behind us. I brace myself for an angel or cannibals or pirates. The glow widens, lengthens, and is followed by a moving shadow. Henry and I stare as a ghostly figure with long hair creeps forward until a voice comes from behind the torch.

'You *don't* remember *me*, Henry?'

'What's going on?'

'It's me,' says a woman's voice.

'You?'

'Mum?'

The black stone behind the shadow turns white, and Mum appears. She's no longer wearing the wig. Her hair is swept back and her eyes are bright.

'Mrs Wombat?' asks Henry, squinting into the fog.

'Mr Wombat!' she cries and laughs at the same time, skips over the rocks to give me a hug. 'Oh, Stella! Henry, this is *our* daughter.'

'Mum? Mum! What are you doing here? Have you been here all this time?'

'Ferdi said you'd be on the boat so I came to find you. When there was all that hoo-hah with the woman falling in, I slipped in like a stowaway and came out here. You can go even deeper into the cave, I made a little room for myself, so cosy. Oh, and I have a life ring – we really need to get across soon.'

My mother once hid in the Belgravia home of a minor royal for about three weeks before one of the occupants called the police, so I'm confident she can survive in small spaces undetected.

She takes a better look at the man she mourned half her life for. 'Henry, where's all your hair?'

He slaps the top of his head. 'Gone.'

'Though I bet there's still plenty on your back!'

'It *is* you! I thought–' His words are half-stolen by a blast of wind which drags the skin away from his face. The rain has stepped into a faster, harder gear. Henry staggers, half-blind without his glasses.

'I saw you once, on *Blankety Blank*. So brainy.'

'Did you? In '94? I so nearly won that game. Have you had your teeth capped?'

Henry puts his hand up to his mouth.

'Goodness! You've put on a bit a weight!' says Mum, looking at his protruding belly.

'But you! You hardly look any different, Mrs W!'

'Do you remember?'

'I do, Florence, I do,' he answers, his voice breaking with emotion.

It's time to give this reunion a little context.

'Henry, I remember sitting in your office, waiting to see you. I was eleven years old, and you sent me away. Your secretary said you were busy. She put me in a taxi with an envelope full of cash.'

'I've no recollection of that,' he whispers, bewildered.

Mum's eyes brim with tears again. 'How could you?'

Henry shakes his head, mumbling, 'What's the point? What's the point in going over the past?' His floating shoe knocks against his leg. He picks it up and empties the water out of it, then throws it back in the water.

'Henry, just acknowledge her, it's all she wants. There's only the three of us here. Remember the "cuckoo clock"?' Henry chuckles into a pool of water. 'Remember the "worm that turned"?' He smiles wider, breaks into a laugh. Mum joins in.

'What cuckoo clock? What worm?' I ask, though not sure I want the answers.

'I'll tell you when you're older.' Mum wades in closer to Henry. 'Remember the way we loved?' Henry doesn't answer. 'You said you'd leave Caroline for me, that you wanted to be with me forever!'

'For goodness' sake! That was *years* ago! I can't remember what I said!'

'You broke my heart.'

Mum's cheeks are wet from tears, not just rain.

'She has those dimples, like you do. Quite a stunner! But what d'you expect with parents like us?' The two of them knock their foreheads together, giggling. 'Sorry about all that, back there,' he says to me. 'It was a shock… I always wanted to find your mother again, but I was too ashamed, how could she ever have forgiven me? How could it ever have been the same after what I did? And she had problems – admit it, darling, you did do some rather nutty things.'

Flares of lightning bounce around the horizon.

'Hmmm, Mrs Wombat. Psychiatric care, they said.' He shakes his head. 'Florence, my Florence, my precious Mrs Wombat!' Henry folds his arms around her.

'Mr W, you've even got hair growing out of your ears.'

'Oh, I know. And–' he shakes his chest, '–man boobs. Time has a dreadful sense of humour. Mrs Wombat, I'm an old bird now, but oh! I don't feel it, right now, right here with you!'

A wave hits them, they nearly topple over. We have no option but to keep retreating into the cave where we can stand without being engulfed by the rush of water. Mum said something about a life ring and unless we get it soon, we might be ending our days here.

'You didn't trust me, Henry.'

'I wanted to! But to stand up to my father… all the plans they had for me. And not just him: the house, the firm, the future, Caroline's family…'

'But you didn't *love* Caroline!' says Mum, looking so young and frail. Both of them are half crying, half laughing.

'Love? No! But she was a *nice* girl! I *wanted* to love her. I thought I could if I worked hard at it. Hard work brought me success in everything else, why not a marriage? And Florence… you were too young, too sweet, no background to speak of and then…' he dropped his head and swallowed, 'you got pregnant.'

I look away as I'm introduced to their story. 'It nearly killed me, Henry,' cries Mum as he squeezes her tighter.

'Sometimes you have to choose to go with your head or your heart. I'm a lawyer, Florence, I count on reasoning.'

The sea is now lapping at our thighs. We must get out of the cave.

'I had to do what was appropriate–'

'But not for *you*.'

'But not for me,' he says, looking into her eyes. 'Or us.'

'And now, Henry, this marriage, what's this about?'

He falls back against the rock behind him, out of the light. 'I've made a big bloody mess,' he says, exasperated. 'What a bloody mess!'

'Oh, Henry!' says Florence as he buries his face in her hair.

'I had a weak moment, got involved with this woman. I was feeling old and bored, got a little carried away and then it all got so real. I was *defending* her in a court case – do you know how bad that could look? She *had* me. She *scared* me! Then next thing I knew, she told Caroline about us. Then Caroline started suing me for divorce. I didn't know how to stop it all. I had nowhere else to turn… but to… that… creature. If I hear her say "Bravo!" one more time… It was all Caroline's fault. She should have–'

'Henry! You are not worthy of my love until you can accept responsibility for what you've done!'

'Oh, Mrs Wombat! Don't rattle me!'

'Henry!'

'Oh, darling one, if only I'd trusted us. Trusted love!'

'Could you carry on this conversation somewhere we might not drown?' I ask.

Mum lifts her face up to him, their lips touch.

'I'll get the life ring,' I say, though no one's listening.

I leap down the stone corridors between the mouth of the cave and the lagoon. Over the rocks, I see the lair where Mum has been hiding. She'd somehow helped herself to food, two crème brûlées and half a bottle of champagne. I find the life ring and drag it back to where Florence and Henry are kissing.

'Can we move this along, you two?' I am no longer able to keep the urgency out of my voice. 'Mum? *Dad*?'

Mum jumps as a wave leaps up to spank her thighs. 'Oh my God! We've got to get out of here!' She holds us both by our hands and leads us out of the cave.

81

The rocks we have to climb over are almost fully submerged with waves edging forward at a hard, fast rate. The rain stings my skin, making it difficult to see ahead. But through it all, I hear an engine and see a fuzzy light moving towards us.

'Look!'

A speed-boat bounces over the tops of the mounting waves.

Henry and Mum tread fast, arm in arm, towards our exit.

I carry the life ring over to them.

'Mum, the life ring, it's too small for three. You two go ahead, get on the boat and pick me up.'

'I'm not leaving you here!'

'Mum. Go. Quickly so they know we're here.'

'We're not leaving you,' says "Dad". 'You girls go, get to safety.' He gives Mum a long kiss. 'Listen, both of you, don't waste time. Go. Together. Take the life ring.'

'I'll be fine. Just go!' I say. They look at me. Mum shakes her head. 'Mum! Go! There's someone arriving now – I'll follow you.'

'But... I...' She tries to argue as I push her into the water. 'All right, darling, we'll get the boat over. We won't be long.' She takes a little rucksack off her back and pulls out a pink rubber bathing cap.

'What are you doing?'

But it's obvious as she pulls the cap on and carefully pushes all her hair inside.

'I only had my hair done a few days ago, you know what seawater does to it.' Cap on, a little stretch and she declares, 'All done.'

'We'll get someone to you straight away,' assures Henry. 'Here, Mrs Wombat. Hold it. We can both cross over now!' Henry grabs on to one side, my mother the other. 'Okay? Ready to swim over?'

Mum hugs me, when she lets go, Henry stands in front of me. He puts out his arms and I hold him. It's a lot of flesh, and he's trembling, but it's comforting to be held by this man, my dad.

'Stella. Henry. Look…' and Mum starts crying '…after all these years – *a family*.'

82

I wade out with them as far as I can and watch Henry and my mum paddle around the rocks to the cove. As the waves move with increasing power sometimes they are just spinning in the same place, but eventually, kicking hard and holding hands, they move towards the beach on the other side.

I cling to a rock on the outside of the cave that's rugged enough for me to grip on to. The speed-boat will return for us any minute, I think in time with convulsive shivering.

There's a light shining from the other side of the island but I can only open my stinging eyes enough to see Henry and Mum collapse on the sand. They're safe. When I look again, they're jumping up to wave their hands at me. I try to wave back, losing my strength.

Another thrust of saltwater hits the back of my throat followed by a punch to the head. For a few seconds, I sink below the surface. I remember the breathing exercises I did with Nick at the scuba-diving centre. I hear him saying how the greatest killer in water is panic.

As I rise up again over the rock I'm clinging to, I draw in a mouthful of wet air and see headlights making wide white arcs through the mist. It won't be long now until we're rescued. Even blinking is exhausting. At one point I lift myself up to see the lights moving along towards the cove. Whoever is out there will be with Mum and Henry any second.

The next time I look over, I can't see Mum, just Henry. When I wipe away a splash of water from my stinging eyes, all I can see now is one figure. A flash of lightning lights up the whole sky – for a moment it's like broad daylight – all at once, in the phosphorescent glare, I catch sight of Henry on the ground, a man, a flash of something red and a trail of black exhaust.

Clouds like a fleet of zeppelins hover over the coast. The last amount of reserve energy is all I have to keep me clinging to the rock, but each time I slip, it takes more out of me to get back on. Breathe evenly, keep calm, stay awake, but something is pulling me down and the night sky is closing in.

PART SIX

THE CALM AFTER (SORT OF)

83

An overhead fan gently flicks through the seconds. Cool sheets, playful waves brush against the sand. The room-service trolley bustles down the corridor. The hotel room. I begin to open my eyes. Shutters half-closed and Mum silhouetted against them.

'You're awake,' she says, breathless with relief. 'How are you?' I must have been unconscious for a few days because she already looks different. She is sun-kissed, her hair a shade paler and she is wearing a grass-green dress which goes with her eyes. She keeps her hand on my brow.

I close my eyes again as images of the last two days download themselves in erratic batches – Mum and Henry in each other's arms; the two of them swimming away; being under water; losing my sense of whether I was going up or down in the sea. Peter and Bunny. The sharp pain of seawater lacerating the back of my throat. Seeing someone with Henry – who was with Henry? Then blackness ripping through my lungs. Lights. Being carried. Then nothing.

'Okay. You?' I manage. Mum turns my palm down, strokes it. 'We're going to be fine. You're on lots of anti-inflammatories, painkillers, all nice things. You've got a possible broken rib and some very bad bruises, there's that cut on your foot and your lungs had water in them… but nothing a little rest won't sort out.' She sniffs as a tear balances on her eyelid. 'I should never have left you.'

I hold her fingers and again feel the sensation of dropping down into the water.

'Henry. Is he okay?'

She turns to the wall. 'He was found dead.' She rests the back of her hand against my forehead. 'They think he had a heart attack. Apparently he fell – fell back – and with the shock, his heart gave out.'

'Heart?'

'His silly, scared, confused little heart, yes. He was keeping watch over you while I'd gone to get help, and…' She can't speak for a moment. She opens one of my pill packets, swallows a couple down with her rum punch. 'Did you know rum punch is one of the oldest mixed-drink recipes, started in the seventeenth century?'

'And it was slaves in the Caribbean who discovered that molasses could be fermented into alcohol and distilled. Who was the other person on the beach?'

'Hmm? No, I never saw anyone else. I know there was that speed-boat but they must have driven on. We think they saw us and called the rescue service.'

'I saw a man. With Henry, someone.'

'No, petal, he was alone. Alone. Poor Henry. Just when he was beginning to realise how much time he'd wasted by trying to do the right thing rather than do *his* thing.' She weeps quietly, mumbling something about how we can get anything back but time.

'Do his family know?'

'They've been notified. Stella,' she leans her lips to my hand, 'he loved me, he loved me all along. He loved you too, in his way. I feel so blessed that we got to know that – that time in the cave, it was real, wasn't it? We had that moment even just for a few hours.' Mum's eyes are clearer and more alert than I'd ever seen them. 'We know what happened. *We* know. Secrets can't hurt us anymore. Rest now,' she says, tightening the sheet around me and turning out the light.

84

'Drink this,' says Ferdi, leaving another of his mother's specials by my bedside. My lungs burn as I swallow the drink. 'The results are back – you're lucky. But I knew that already.'

'Apart from this.' I slide back the sheet to show him the bruises on my legs. 'And when I breathe in, e*verything* hurts.'

'If I'd been there none of this would've happened. Miss Stella, I'm so sorry,' he says, wiping the condensation from the drink. 'Now. I looked up your flight online, all's in order. Meanwhile, your mother's captured the holiday spirit with impressive aplomb. I took the liberty of showing her around the island yesterday. And she swam – after everything!' He laughs as the memory comes back to him. 'She is the embodiment of true British spirit.' He chuckles to himself at some private joke. 'But most of the time, she was just here waiting for you to come around. She told me the whole story! I couldn't believe it! Henry! What a cad! What a fool to have given up on love because of what he feared from his family! And your mother could have had a career as a lawyer if he hadn't got her fired. Goodness!' He claps his hands together. 'Finished your drink? Oh, I forgot to ask, who's the mystery man who sent you flowers?'

'Huh?'

'A young gentleman came to ask about you – I didn't manage to see him, all very furtive, cornered one of the porters and then said to give you these.' I look up to the other side of the living room and see a huge vase full of flowers. Beautiful flowers, birds of paradise, red hibiscus – an impressive display. 'There's a note,' says Ferdi, following my gaze. 'Shall I open it?'

Was it possible that news of my accident had reached Joseph?

'Okay, it's written in ballpoint pen – can't help that. Definitely a man's handwriting. It says… "Was knowing the truth worth dying for? Maybe now you realise you were the lucky one. More than a friend".'

Ferdi passes me the card. Those three cryptic sentences are not written in Joseph's writing, nor his style.

'I've no idea who that's from.'

'The story was on the local news. You can imagine, the island's been abuzz with the tragic death of Mr Hardwick. Do you need anything?'

'No, Ferdi, just feed me morphine and let me hear the birds sing.'

'The hotel doctor wants to take another look at you. Oh, and Kamilla will call again tonight around–'

The door bursts open as Yuleka hurls herself through them.

'You!' A giant, prehistoric lizard gathering a mouthful of acid to spew comes to mind. 'You!' She rolls her head around the room to see if anyone else is around. 'You! How dare you tell lies about my late husband!'

Late husband, she's caught onto widowhood quickly.

'How dare you!' and with that, she picks up a pair of slipperettes and throws them in my direction.

'Yuleka, wha–'

'All because of *you,* he's not here with me!'

'What are you talking about?'

'What? Am? I? Talking? About?' She has the strangest expression; no longer the prancing young bride but someone – something – dark and dangerous. 'All along you planned to *seduce* him, ah yes, and then when he turned you down, you made up these stories about him, saying he's your *father*! You are crrrrazy! All because you are so jealous of me! But you, you, you aren't getting anything from us!'

'Yuleka, *you* left him in the cave. As I remember it, you wanted to catch the rug sale.'

'Another lie! Another *lie*! Oh my God, this girl! This cheap–'

'I gave Henry the only life ring.'

Ferdi stands up. 'Leave now.'

'You have committed four crimes against me.' She raises her long, sabre-like nails and points them in my face. 'Number one: you tried to steal my husband! Fail. Number two: you kill him! Number three: you tell lies. Oh yeah! Bravo! Bunny told me all about what you've been going around saying. And number four: I'm suing you for *slander*! Here's my lawyer... Where's...?' She whirls towards the door. 'Bradshaw!'

I try to put my feet to the floor.

'Bradshaw! He'll be here. Wait. Just you wait! He's the best lawyer you can get – he's known Henry for years and he'll make you pay. Bradshaw!'

'Yuleka, Henry *is* my father. He confirmed it before he died, to me and my mother.'

'Your *mother*? Yeah? There's a mother now? Who's she then?' She slaps her hands on her hips. 'You are sick! Sick!'

'Henry was my father. I came here, from London, to tell him that.'

She moves her face an inch from mine. 'You're not touching his money. If you even think about it you got another thing comin', girlfriend.'

'I don't want his money. I don't want anything from him but I want you to get out!'

A man in a black suit walks briskly through the door.

'Mrs Hardwick,' he says, taking Yuleka by the arm. 'Mrs Hardwick, please.'

'Here he is. Bradshaw, my lawyer. This one. Right. First off, I want you to sue *her* for slander. Those things she said.'

'Mrs Hardwick, may I suggest that we all–'

'Sue her!'

'Could we,' Bradshaw was sweating heavily into the collar of his dark suit, 'leave this lady alone?'

'Let me say something.'

'No, don't you speak to him! He's *my* lawyer not yours! You are a worm! A creepy, crawly worm!'

The lawyer takes a few strides over to me.

'Henry's last wishes were to acknowledge me as his daughter. He said–'

'Miss…?'

'Miss *Tyler*. My mother and Henry had an affair thirty years ago, before he was married. They had me. I don't want anything, just his name on my birth certificate.'

Bradshaw looks at me, and a smile crosses his face.

Yuleka stamps her foot. 'This man has come all the way from London to look after *me*! Not you! We will see you in prison!' I try to swat her fingers from my face. 'Bunny Templeton-Crest said you plan to blackmail everyone in the hotel! And we… we even asked you to be our bridesmaid at… our… beautiful Wedding of a Thousand Dreams!' She marches to the door, stops, then turns back to the lawyer. 'Now you leave me a widow in my prime!' She pushes away the lawyer and lunges back at me. 'You killed my Henry!'

'Henry *is* my father.'

Bradshaw raises an eyebrow at me, and nods, just enough to let me know he knew.

'Oh right! This again!' she splutters. 'Hello? Don't you think if he had children by other women I would have known? Henry told me everything about his past – we were soulmates – and… and you… You! You don't even have matching luggage! I am the next Mrs Hardwick with an estate in Nor– Nors– Northfiham…?'

'Norfolk, madam.'

'North-fuck. But you are a lying–'

'Come along now, really, come,' urges the solicitor, taking

Yuleka by the shoulders and moving her away. 'Mrs Hardwick is very tired now. Very emotional. Come along, Mrs Hardwick!' He sighs, exasperated, before turning on his heels out the door. But she doesn't follow. She leans forward, panting, gathering the strength to launch the next attack.

'You heard what my daughter said, get out now.'

85

Mum steps in from the doorway.

'And who are you?' Yuleka asks.

'I'm the woman Henry really loved.'

Yuleka drew a lungful of air. 'Oh now what?'

'I am the woman who gave birth to Henry's lovechild. He would have chosen me over Caroline but he was a weak, insecure man, but he *did* love me and he *did* love his daughter.'

'What d'you know about that dirty old man's ideas of love?'

'Enough. And I've learnt a lot more about you from your ex-husband, Gary Marnes – you know Gary? We all know who you are now.'

'Bradshaw! Sue her too.'

'You're not suing anybody. And don't you ever threaten my daughter again. Get out of Stella's room!'

'No worries bitch, there are some serious bad vibes in this room!' spits Yuleka. But before she makes it out the door, she locks eyes with me again. 'And you – bravo! This is the worst honeymoon I have ever had! Bradshaw, now!'

Her lawyer turns to follow her, muttering something that sounds like 'sorry'.

———————

We wait until the room is quiet again. A sparrow watches us from the window ledge.

'Did you see her face?' Mum gives Ferdi a high five. 'Stella! Did you?'

'When she heard the name Gary Marnes!' says Ferdi. 'Oh, Stella, you've got to read this exposé of her flagitious life! The minute Henry's death was in the papers, all the termites came scurrying out of the rotten woodwork! Miss Stella, where are you going? The doctor said–'

'Sorry, but I just need a little hobble around.'

'You're not supposed to, but...' muttered my mother, exchanging a look of concern before she leaps up and says, 'I'm late for the women's volleyball tournament.'

86

It is Happy Hour at the Paradise Beach Club's bar, though less jubilant with the recent death of a guest. The bar staff are in black and violet orchids are dotted around the tables. A few of the Templeton-Crest crowd are gathered at a far table, heads locked in a scrum though I can make out Peter's back. Judging by the build-up of bottles, they've been sitting there since lunch.

'Let me buy you a drink,' says Susie.

'Thank you.'

'No, thank *you*, because of you and all that's happened in the last few days, I'm suddenly a journalist in demand! And also, I was pretty pissed off you got with Peter but, hey, again, thanks to you I dodged a bullet there. Cheers!'

I sit on the terrace, sipping at a Coke, watching Venus rise up to take over from the sinking sun. Though fuzzy from the painkillers, I am preoccupied by the idea that I could have died and Joseph would never have known how much I loved him. Losing Henry has confirmed how fragile these opportunities to love are, and how synchronicity between two people is at an ever-shifting biting point. The parallels between myself and my dad are clear. We'd both lost those we loved because we'd been too scared to take the risk. We'd followed logic and protected ourselves, only to trudge alone through half-lived half-lives.

I hear the distinct squeak of Roy Templeton-Crest's wheels behind me.

'Miracle you survived ol' g-g-g-girl!'

'So they say.'

'You could've ended up like me, in one of these wretched things for the rest of your life. Or like ol' Henry. Not exactly what one p-p-p-plans on a honeymoon, eh? Apparently that woman of his is a piece of work. Old boyfriends talking to the papers – you read any of it? Whoa! Murrrrky! Henry's boys are due to give their side soon, I imagine she'll have to go into hiding, or to America.'

'She caused a lot of problems.'

'Don't be too hard on the old b-b-b-b-bird. That afternoon was also a rather horrid one for *yours truly*. I lost miserably at bridge, Bunny'd gone AWOL with your *friend* Lyle and I was facing an Elton John-themed supper, here, all on my own when Yuleka appeared, insisted we eat together and showed great interest in how the peerage system worked. It was jolly sporting of her.'

'Do you imagine leaving her husband to drown on their honeymoon was self-sacrificing?'

'Ah. So you also think she planned to bump him off. Wouldn't put it past her but they say he did nothing for you, his daughter, and that I can't forgive. Better see what the old b-b-b-buggers are doing for din-dins... Oh, must say, your mother's a bit of a looker, what? I see where you get it from now, not from *him*.' He winks, tapping his nose. 'Smashing legs. Do put a g-g-g-good word in, would you?' He looks at my drink and, with an imaginary glass in his hand, toasts, '*Santé*, dear girl.'

87

The fire-engine-red sun lowers itself behind the palm trees left rugged by the storm's assault. I drink to Henry. By the time I've finished my glass, I hear shoes slapping against the marble floors.

'There she is!' cries Mum, hugging me. 'There's someone I want you to meet – meet properly, I mean.' She turns to the man who'd been walking alongside her. 'This is Stella Tyler, my daughter, and this is Mr Bradshaw, Marcus. Marcus is Henry's solicitor and he knows *everything*!'

Mr Bradshaw, the man I'd met earlier with Yuleka, has discarded his jacket and unbuttoned his shirt.

'I'm sorry for your loss. Your mother and I go back a long way. Henry and I worked together when she was a mere slip of a girl – and still is!' he says, looking over her approvingly. 'I have to leave for London now with,' he lowers his head and winces, 'Mrs Hardwick, but I just wanted to wish you a speedy recovery. You've spent some time here with Henry over the last week, Stella, you can only imagine what a tumultuous state his affairs are in, really quite a mess and–'

'Apparently, Yuleka's been claiming sickness benefit for the last three years while working as a pole dancer – the social security department are after her – and that's just for starters,' interrupts Mum.

'The case that Henry was involved in concerning Yuleka Hardwick, well, it could throw up questions of perjury and some quite serious allegations. There's much to sort out.' Bradshaw shakes his head and continues humbly. 'I shall leave you both now and hope that we meet again under happier circumstances. Enjoy your last few days, and get better soon, young lady.' He turns to Mum. 'Florence, so wonderful to see you again. We shall be in touch.' He holds her in his stare until she blushes. 'Goodbye,' he says, and leaves the room.

'I was his secretary all those years ago! Oh, darling, you look terrible. Guess what? My team came second in the volleyball! I've been chosen to play again tomorrow. And Ferdi has invited me to dinner. I'll bring you back a doggy bag.' She squeezes me against her.

'Mum, are you all right, I mean, about Henry…?'

'I am, my Stella, I am. Isn't it strange how years and years can pass and nothing happens and then – suddenly – all the buses come at once!' She looks up at the first stars. 'I'm sad, yes, but I'm released. It's like I was living in a chrysalis and now–'

'You're a butterfly?'

'A red admiral – why not? I realise now that Henry wasn't strong enough to believe in me, Stella. Don't make the same mistake with Joseph. Things are going to change for you too, darling, I mean it… we're going to be mother and daughter butterflies! Have a good night's rest and I'll see you in the morning.'

'Have you been taking my codeine?'

'Cheeky!' she says, flicking her leg up behind her.

'G'night. Don't spread those wings too far, Mum!'

The swimming pool lights come on, changing through all the colours of the rainbow.

88

Later that night while dozing in front of a film, I hear tapping against my window, then see Peter's face trying to peer through my shutters.

I put my dressing gown on and open the door. He stands there, a bunch of flowers in his hands.

'How's the invalid?'

'I'm letting you in because I know you'll pester me all night if I don't. Not because you're invited.'

Peter pushes the flowers at me, walks straight to my mini-bar where he takes out two miniature whiskies and pours them into a toothbrush mug. I see him look at my indigo-patterned legs. He shuts his eyes and takes large gulps before nodding at the flowers in my arms.

'Flowers. Always sweeter picked from someone else's garden, right?'

'But they're from my balcony, you prat. At least put them in a vase for me.'

'Sure.' He drops them on the counter, sighs deeply. 'What happened when you saw me... and Bunny... on the boat. That was really embarrassing.'

'Peter, I was in the storm for two hours before someone got around to making an emergency call. My father died out there. Your little love tryst,' I swallow, 'wasn't a priority.'

'I get that. I just want to explain.'

'Save it.'

'I left you and Henry alone to give you your moment with him, I thought I was *helping* you.' He ignores my 'huh'. 'Come on, no one thought there'd be a storm like that! How was I to know you weren't on one of the boats coming back? How was I to know you'd be so stupid as to stay in a cave at a time like that?'

'Because when you got to the mainland, Henry and I weren't with you. Ah, but you don't think of anyone else but yourself.'

'You're right, I know but... yeah, you're right.' We both shrug. 'See, Stella, when I dropped Bunny off at her hotel, she made a great scene outside the entrance, refused to go in. It was kinda awkward. She was... y'know.' He lifts his hand to his mouth in a drinking motion. 'So she came back here. She *swore* she'd sent her chauffeur to get a boat across to you. And anyways, we thought Yuleka would be getting Henry back but apparently she was cuddling up to Roy. She likes the idea of a title now. Point is, neither of them did anything. I'll never forgive them!'

'Peter, you just didn't care.'

'We'd had too much to drink, and then...' He slides his gaze down to his drink, purses his lips.

'I thought you weren't into *that* kind of thing...'

'What *kind* of thing?'

'Sex.'

'It's not as simple as that.'

'I could have died, and you waited until the last minute to help me. I thought we were friends at least.'

'Come on, you survived!'

'*Henry* didn't.'

He sits down and asks as earnestly as he can fake, 'How do you feel about that?'

'Excuse me if I pass on the chance to trauma-bond with you.'

'They said it was his heart.'

'Flowers are not enough. Peter, please. Just go.'

'Stella, I'm not trying to excuse myself, I know what I did was...' He leans forward, putting his head in his hands. 'When I heard the thunder and lightning, I started to have flashbacks of the war, the PTSD thing kicked in. Memories of the bullets and the–'

I cut in, 'Have you actually been in any war?'

He has tears in his eyes as he goes on. 'The guns, the faces of wounded children, the–' He looks up at me. 'Huh?'

'You are not a war reporter.'

'I'm not a… what?'

'You're a compulsive liar.'

'Ottoline.' Peter kneels by my feet. 'A lot of my work is undercover, Stella. Top secret stuff. She doesn't know anything about espionage!'

I laugh despite the pain in my ribs.

'Listen to yourself! You've lied about everything since I met you. You left me in that cave without bothering to get help but what hurts is that you told Bunny about Henry being my father. That was really cheap, even for you.'

I lean against the door to the terrace.

'No, please, let me tell you something true,' Peter says seriously from inside my room. 'I'm a complete asshole. Did I ever tell you I was a complete asshole?' He picks up the flowers and starts munching on the stems. 'These are gross by the way.' He spits out bits of plant. 'Okay. Okay. I *was* in Sarajevo. It's just that the fighting had ended by the time I arrived so I helped organise a big outdoor rave… but I was *there*.' He peers into his drink. 'I *could* have been a war journalist. I *met* one once. He said I had all the right qualities for it. We were going to meet in Afghanistan but then there was this party in Ibiza and I missed the plane to Kabul. I've been deep-sea diving in the Red Sea, that's very close to the Left Bank… and…' He pokes at the ice cubes in his drink. 'We're kinda in the same boat you and me, Stella, my dad didn't want to know me either. The difference is, your dad never really knew you, so you can't take it personally. My parents were okay when I was growing up, but now they're not satisfied with the *finished* product.'

'But they support you, financially?'

'A kind of limbo amount of money. Enough so that working

isn't worth it but not enough to start up something different. I did a brief spell in one of my dad's companies but I couldn't do it, going in there, *every day*? So I follow Bunny around and she looks after me. That's the deal.'

'Oh, Peter, really?'

'What's a boy to do?' I limp back to my bathroom cupboard and take some painkillers to assassinate my headache.

'Got anything interesting?'

'I'm not sharing my analgesics with you.'

'I wouldn't either.' Peter pours himself another bottle from my mini-bar. 'You hate me. I get it. But I hope you can remember the good stuff. It was nice, huh? When we were on the beach, that first night you were here? I was happy. For the first time since... I don't know when. Why is everything always good in the beginning and so shit at the end?'

We stroll to the end of the terrace facing the quiet, black sea, laid out under the night sky like newly pressed tar.

'Bunny, y'know, she just dragged it out of me – the stuff about your dad.'

'Imagine how you'd bear up under torture if you can't even keep a secret from Lady Templeton-Crest?'

'Yup, I'm a fraud.' Peter groans mournfully. 'But I can't live any other way.' He lets the last few drops of his drink roll down his throat. 'You know, Stella, if I were you, I'd go after Henry's estate. I know a guy, he could–'

'I'm not you.'

'Lucky you.' Peter tries to take my hand, but I move it away from him. 'It's your last day tomorrow, can we spend it together?'

'No.'

'You're the one person I've met in my life who hasn't disappointed me.'

There is silence while he genuinely thinks I might find something positive to say about him.

'See you around,' he says. This time he doesn't bounce over the wall, he moves around it and through the gate onto his side.

'Just one thing,' I call over. 'I guess I should thank you for getting the rescue team – you took your time but it saved my life.'

'Stella.' He clamps his hands on either side of the fence and leans against it with the weight of a defeated man. 'I wish I could take the credit, sweetheart, but I don't know who alerted the police. It wasn't *me.*'

'Not you? So who got the rescue boat? They said a man called, someone who'd been on the island…'

'The police asked questions the next day, but that was the one thing they couldn't ascertain. Who'd called? Apparently the guy never left his name – why not want to get credit for saving you and your mom? Might have even got money or an award. Weird.'

89

Days after Henry's death, a healing calm permeates the hotel. The funereal plants are upgraded to mauves and discreet pinks. Guests, whose faces have become familiar to me, whisper goodbyes before their taxis crunch the gravel like soft applause as they make their way home. New guests are ushered in with luggage, pockets full of tipping change and a thirst for the complimentary rum punches. They've all heard the story of the barrister who died on his honeymoon to a con artist and boat trips to the island where it all happened are booking up fast.

My mum, however, does not slow down. This has been her first holiday in thirty years apart from mini-breaks to the English coast when I was a kid. It is wonderful to see her so happy and winning the trophy in the Miss Paradise Beach Club competition and get yet another room upgrade. While I spend my time reading and dozing, she goes sightseeing and kitesurfing. She also spends a lot of time with Ferdi when he isn't working – they are up to something, something which involves me not going on any social media or watching TV.

'Stella, we're on holiday. Contact with the outside world is strictly forbidden.'

The day before I am due to leave, I'm in a deep sleep in my hotel room when the telephone rings. I snake my dead, aching limbs up the bed and knock the phone my way, grapple with it and croak, 'Yeah?'

'Stella, zat you?'

'Yes.'

'It's Ottoline. Did I wake you up?'

'Yes… I…' I'd answered before I could even discern whether I was dead or alive, let alone 'up' and my lips are so dry it is hard to move my mouth.

'What time is it?'

'It's twelve o'clock.'

'*Today*?' My bruised brain had been sliding in a dark, warm marsh for over twelve hours.

'Sorry, who is this?'

'Ottoline! I met you on Johnny's boat.' I struggle to sit up. 'Fuck, Stella! I'm so sorry! Johnny and I feel terrible! You know you were on the local news? Johnny wants to know if there's anything he can do? You know, it wasn't his fault... I mean, he had no idea that–'

'Ottoline, I chose to stay on the island. And so did Henry.'

She takes a deep breath in as I sip from the glass of water by my bed. 'There might be an inquest.'

'Tell Johnny not to worry.'

I wonder again about the man I'd seen with Henry just before he died.

'It must have been a fucking nightmare.'

Neither of us can think what to add: where do you go from near-death experiences? Ottoline has the answer: lunch.

'Anyway, I rang because I'm on my way to *the* event of the year – I can't say a word about it as I'm sworn to secrecy – but I don't want to go on my own – come with me?'

'An event? I don't know if I can face it.'

'I'll pick you up at the hotel gates in an hour.'

I wonder where Ferdi is before remembering that it is his day off which is why I'd slept in so long. I miss him as I shuffle around the room, stiff from the pain in my limbs. I fold back the shutters and look out onto my terrace.

Another stunning view of the sea framed by flowers of every colour and the solid blue block of sky. For the last few days, I've hardly left my bed because my bones hurt too much but it is my last day in Barbados and I am going to make the best of it.

Before getting ready I go into my mum's room, where she is holding two dresses in front of her mirror.

'Lamb or mutton?'

'I'm vegetarian.'

She throws the two dresses down.

'It's a big day–' and then she clasps her hands over her mouth.

'Why? Why is it a *big* day?'

'Oh, nothing. Nothing. I just want you to look nice. Nothing wrong with looking nice is there, pumpkin?'

She springs up to hug me.

'What's going on, Mum? Tell me!'

'Nothing!' But her smile is almost lifting her off her feet. 'Please make sure you look really, really drop-dead gorgeous.'

'I've been asked to lunch, do you want to come too?'

'I can't. I'm busy.' She checks behind her for visible panty line. 'Stella, please be sure to leave a note with reception to say where you'll be today. We need to be in regular contact. It's extremely important.'

'Okay. But I don't understand why you're being so mysterious.'

'All will be revealed.'

90

Ottoline is waiting for me at the entrance of the hotel, lying back in the seat of a turquoise, open-top American car, sunning herself like a sleek cat. She mouths the words to Katy Perry's 'Roar' behind her designer sunglasses, her swish 50s-style ponytail bouncing down her back. She jumps up and leans over the door to give me a hug.

'God, you've fucking been through it!'

'Do I look a mess?'

'No, absolutely *stunningo*. Drowning suits you!' She waits until I'm settled in the car before asking, 'So, did he totally break your heart?' The engine starts.

'Who?'

'Peter! Why, were there others?'

'No! It was just a holiday flirtation, that's all.'

'Well, something must have happened because he's disappeared.'

'Nothing to do with me.'

'How come he left you in the storm? We assumed you guys were together.'

'A misunderstanding.'

I don't know why I bother to defend Peter, but somehow I've a sense that he's worse off than I am at the moment.

Ottoline raises her eyebrow. 'Was it something to do with Lady Templeton-Crest?'

I shrug.

'You know all about Peter and rich women, don't you?'

'I did a crash course. Ferdi, who looks after me at the hotel, he calls her a *skettel*.'

'What's that?'

'Bajan for a "wicked woman".'

'And what about a wicked *man*?'

'A "Mr Lyle"?'

'Touché!' Ottoline laughs as she swerves round a corner. I can breathe better now she's finished wringing any information she needed out of me. 'Don't imagine he's having an easy time of it, poor lamb. Hanging around the rich when you don't have the money for the bus fare home is just about the most demeaning occupation possible. I should know.'

We've driven away from the lush coast, lined with some of Barbados's biggest hotels and are now moving through a shanty town passing families all dressed up in their Sunday best making their way towards a tumbled-down old colonial church. My waves to the children are returned with beaming smiles. We drive on but instead of the flowers I'd been living with, all is brown and dry, ramshackle, and dusty. Ottoline gestures at the makeshift homes.

'This is what they don't show you in the holiday brochures. Y'know Barbados is one of the most densely populated areas in the world. We could've taken another route but it's interesting to see, isn't it?' Ottoline slows down for us to pass through the shacks that people live in. A few heads turn wearily towards us, dull eyes look over the car. She waves at the children; most wave back listlessly, apart from two who run alongside us trying to flag us down.

There is a line of bodies lying along a half-built-up or half-knocked-down wall, wrapped in cloth and newspapers. They look like discarded post bags until I see a dark leg moving to scratch the other leg, or a finger coming up to swat a fly. As the car passes the edge of the village there are still more bodies, some drinking in groups, smoking and watching the road. Ottoline slows the car while she bends down to change the music on her iPhone.

My attention is drawn to one villager lying on a sun lounger with a makeshift mattress made from the same cushions I have in my room at the hotel. They also have a blanket rather than rags for covering, in fact, it is the blanket I recognise before the face. The same ones I have in my cupboard at the hotel. Then I see the sleeper's face. It is Ferdi.

'I burnt my tits sunbathing yesterday and it's…' Ottoline wriggles in her seat. She puts her foot down on the accelerator, shouting over the music.

I turn round to see him once more as we drive away. The bundle hasn't moved. So that's where Ferdi is on his day off.

As we drive away from the lines of huts, I hope we've disappeared unseen from his world. I am humbled and horrified to have witnessed the reality of Ferdi's life. I can't tally the man I know with this environment, that little plot of earth from where he gathered his smile and his dreams before bringing someone their breakfast in bed in a hotel featured in *Lifestyles of the Rich and Famous*.

Leaving the village, we return to the coastal route and breath in the fresh sea air as the car speeds along, passing colourfully-painted houses, mango groves and ruined sugar plantations. We begin driving up a hill towards a large white colonial house amid acres of lush gardens and lines of tall palm trees.

'So, tell me about this lunch, what's the great mystery?'

'It's not *just* a lunch – it's a *wedding*! Yes, Stella, I'm inviting you to the wedding of the decade. Actually, the wedding of the century! Joseph West and Sylvia Amery's wedding! Aaarrrh!' She squeals, bobbing up and down in her seat.

'You know Joseph?'

'No! Never met him but Rebecca Hobson, his agent, is my best friend – well, friend. We were at nursery school together before she got expelled. Anyway, watch this.' She slows the car down and presses 'redial' on her phone.

'Hello? Paul – Ottoline – I've got the info you wanted. It's *La Belle Rêve*, Dorian's Mangrove at 15:00 hours. Cheers.' She clicks her phone shut. Looks to me. 'Aren't you totally over-excited! It's all been kept under wraps – all the press know is what's been leaked by a "close friend" of the couple...'

'They have a close friend?'

'Yes... me!'

'So why would you tell the press... if ...?'

'Well, of course they *want* the press to know! It's how it's done! The cat and mouse stuff with the tabloids just builds the hype more! Get it? But there's also something else going on. Rebecca said something is going to happen today which has never happened before. That's what all the secrecy's about but only Sylvia and Joseph know. I can't wait! It's going to be so cool. And we're going to be there!'

91

As Ottoline chats, we drive closer and closer to Joseph – Joseph and his future bride.

The wilderness turns from yellow to green, from dry to verdant, from towering rushes to manicured lawns and meticulous flower beds.

Ottoline slows down at the top of the drive with marble columns and iron gates, above which reads *La Belle Rêve.*

'We're here!'

She presses the intercom and sings out her name. A camera-eye tracks us and the gates swing open. We continue driving until Ottoline stalls the car six metres in front of a *Gone-with-the-Wind* mansion. We park next to a red Lamborghini and Ottoline jumps out of the car, leaving me still trying to absorb the shock.

'Here, take my hand.' Ottoline opens my door and I tumble out onto the driveway. 'Oh my God! I just can't wait for today to happen! Beautiful, isn't it? God knows what it cost to rent but apparently the magazine exclusive is paying for it all – that's why it's all top secret because if anyone else publishes a photo, the deal's off!' She turns to see me lagging. 'Come on! We'll get you a strong drink.'

'But look at me, I'm not dressed properly or…'

'Don't worry. They've got an outfit for you. *We're going to be the bridesmaids!*' she squeals.

'Bridesmaid? Again?'

'Hurry up. They only had a week to organise this thing. Apparently Sylvia doesn't have any girlfriends – no one dares let her near their boyfriends or dads, so Rebecca wanted to make sure there were at least a few single girls in tight dresses to hold flowers and wink at the boys. I said I'd love to, I thought you would too. Chillax, babes, no one can see your bruises.'

So far I've survived reading about the love of my life's engagement in the paper, losing my job, confronting my real father, his death, finding myself on holiday with my mum – surely I can get through my ex-boyfriend's wedding?

Ottoline hikes up the steps while fastening the car keys in her little designer bag. Inside, we follow what sounds like canned laughter to the garden where a crowd of about fifty people sit around the swimming pool next to a large white marquee covered in white flowers.

A deep breath. A smile. A few hours to keep it together.

'Hello, beautiful people!' Ottoline sings as she waves her arms in the air, flashing her débutante smile and nearly tripping over a man watering the Elizabethan roses. She turns back and waits for me. 'Oh, Stella, if you're worried you haven't bought them a present, don't – I added your name to mine.'

92

I'd only ever seen Rebecca in photographs of Joseph where she appeared in the background, usually in a black dress with ghostly skin and eyes in a deep squint from the flashing of cameras. In the flesh she is different. She has wild sandy hair that falls haphazardly around her head, Tibetan-terrier style. She has a large, red face and a considered smile that is strangely prepossessing. Her handshake is firm and resolute. She emits a confidence that is firmly grounded in her huge paddle-like feet and deep voice. As she looks at me, I catch sight of Joseph walking around the far edge of the pool talking to a small group of bathers.

Ottoline steps back to introduce me to our hostess.

'So this is Stella. Hi, Rebecca.'

Rebecca grabs my hand and booms, 'So you must be the girl who nearly drowned this week. Nick darling, this is the "storm girl"!' She clicks her fingers at a passing waiter. 'Two daiquiris pronto!' She looks at me a little longer than you would a stranger – she must realise I was the Stella who'd been with Joseph for the last five years, but I can't tell. 'Unless you'd rather have champagne, as you can see, we've got crates of the stuff.'

'Becks, what's the big secret?' Ottoline asks her friend.

'You'll soon find out. What's happening today will blow your little minds!'

Nick shakes my hand while Rebecca points at me.

'We heard you could have been killed and look at you! As good as new – apart from… and… and…' She lifts up my hand to see the scratches and bruises on my arms. 'And here she is, coming out to celebrate a wedding. What a trooper! D'you need an agent? Haha.' Rebecca puts a drink in my hands. 'Come, let's chill out until the photographers get here.' She aims a microphone attached to a headset to her mouth and calls out to a platinum-blond man who is aligning rows of flowers down the garden. 'Hey, Florian, let's have more gardenias by the entrance!' She looks over to me as she sips her drink. 'Florian's come all the way from Monaco to do the flowers, such a sweetie – *love* the plinths, hon, let's have more! More! More! On *both* sides of the congregation! And trail the ivy right to the ground... that's it!' She continues ordering people around over the microphone. 'Joe! Joe! Ottie's here with the drowned girl! Come say hello then you have *got* to get ready!'

Ottoline clings to my arm. 'Oh God, there he is! That's Joseph! Isn't he just scrumptious?'

Joseph, who is balancing along the edge of the pool, waves at me.

'Joe, I'm ringing the Tom Ford people now. I think we should close the deal. Okay?'

'Can you wangle just a bit more merch out of them, boss?'

Before making the call, Rebecca looks up at Ottoline and mouths, 'Where's Peter?'

Ottoline throws her arms up in the air. 'Fuck knows. I suspect he'll get in touch when he needs bailing out of some crisis or another.' Ottoline gives me a reassuring look as she pops a watermelon slice in her mouth.

Joseph plays with the waterfall that flows into the pool with a group of achingly muscular and tanned men his age who hang around waiting to follow whatever Joseph does next. In a line of dogs at the trough, Joseph would eat first, the others – the sub-dominants – would wait behind until he'd finished.

Joseph kicks a ball across the lawn but it hits a tree and ricochets into the pool. One of the sunbathers is woken up by the splash. It is Sylvia.

'Joe! Do you…?' She raises her eyebrows. Her eyes are so blue and her skin, her body, her whole being so physically perfect, even more beautiful in real life than the photos I'd scrolled through.

'You were in the way!' says Joseph.

'Just we're trying to sleep, huh?' Her perfect lips curl into a smile, a wisp of blonde hair falls from the bundle she's pinned to the top of her head. It falls across her cheek, she lifts it, arching her back slightly. Then Joe kicks the ball again into the pool – she glares at him. 'That's it, Joseph, that's enough. I'm adding that to the prenup – not to kick balls near me!'

'Well don't you let your dogs sleep on my pillow!'

'Creep!'

'Party-pooper.'

She sticks her middle finger up at him. Joseph checks to see that I've witnessed this exchange.

Rebecca, who's been busy with the chef, stands in front of me again. 'Stella, have you met the others, this is Cristobel, my little sister; Max, of *Fallen Angels*, remember? Alex Tindell, hairdresser to the stars. If you girls ask nicely he just might give you a styling. Sylvia Amery, our blushing bride. She's over there. Sylvia, bridesmaids are here. And not too much sun! She's with her friend Blizzard, you ever heard her music? No, me neither, but we're all invited to Mykonos for her show. Whatever you do, *don't* wake her up. Friends from London over there, Emilia Fortescue, Deputy Editor of *Hot Gossip* – and…' She continues running through the names of celebrities coming later, which makes Ottoline jump up and down with excitement. 'Margaux, update.'

Margaux is sweating copiously in a fluorescent-yellow plastic dress. She stands in front of Rebecca and proclaims: 'One hundred and forty-eight minutes.'

'Fuck!' shouts Rebecca and Ottoline.

More flowers arrive in a van that nearly drives into the marquee.

'Joseph, are you going to say hello to your bridesmaids?'

93

Joseph slopes up to the bar next to me and drums on the counter.

'Virgin mojito. Hi, Stella,' is all he says.

I hoped that over the last few months I'd been inoculated against the effect Joseph has on me, but I haven't. Still, I manage to muster, 'Congratulations.'

I turn to Rebecca. 'We already know each other.'

'Yes, the dog walker.'

With Joseph and I both in front of her, she lowers her phone and lifts her sunglasses above her hairline so we are forced to look back into her wizened black eyes, frayed with lines of stress, sleeplessness and probiotic drinks.

'Okay. Right.' Rebecca Hobson squares up to me as though we've just collided cars on a busy junction. 'Stella, I want you to understand something *very* important. Joseph, you too, listen up. This is Joseph and Sylvia's big day. It's an *important* day. A nothing-can-go-wrong day, y'know? We've been organising this for like for *ever*. So, no surprises – like… *nothing goes wrong*. Is that clear? Stella, go with this right till the very end. Don't react until it's all over, do you understand?' Joseph looks at me. I shrug, feeling far too old to be told off, especially for something I haven't even done. 'Do you understand?'

'Look, I shouldn't be here. I'm going to call a taxi–'

'We *need* you here, Stella. Just promise me you won't react until it's all over.' She taps frantically at her temples and empties out her lungs in one long exhalation. Then, 'Joe. Remember. Everything must go as planned. Get me?' She walks out to where the lawn starts, claps her hands in the air and adjusts the microphone. 'Okay, Sylvia! Listen up. Everyone! Joseph, please, listen. Stella,' she says, waving me over, 'this involves you too.'

Margaux manages to walk over to us, her heels piercing the grass every step.

'Listen up, everybody. This is how it goes. Sylvia? You listening? After the ceremony, a private plane will take you both to St Bart's. Tomorrow morning you are to stroll arm in arm through the market. That afternoon the press will see you at the Old Colonial Hotel smooching on the beach. Sylvia, when Paula comes she'll fit you with a few bikinis. After that, evening, Johnny's boat – are we organised for that, Ottoline? Good. Telephoto lens sort of thing, but we need a few more faces and bodies on deck. Okay? Sylvia, go easy on the tanning: we don't want crispy bacon. It's going to hit the media Saturday through Monday. Right? And don't forget to keep flashing the rings tonight – get it in all the pics. We've got to get them back to Tiffany's by Tuesday. Over to Margaux.'

Margaux takes a mini-step up to the mic and goes over the plans once again.

I start to get what she is saying. I mean, really *get* it.

Joseph walks past me dropping some ice into my drink.

'This wedding, it's just… all staged? Just for *publicity*?'

Joseph raises his eyebrows at me. 'I was trying to tell you all along.' There is regret in his voice. And bitterness. After all we'd been through, I'd not believed it when he insisted the romance with Sylvia had been orchestrated by his agent – and now I am hearing her machinations, right down to what underwear they wear.

Rebecca clicks her fingers for our attention again.

'All clear, Joseph?'

'Over and out.' He makes sure I am watching and listening when he makes a show of walking up to Rebecca and dropping something in her lap. 'Keep that will you,' he asks, 'I'm going for a swim.'

'It better be the last because Justin's waiting to do your hair,'

Rebecca says as Joseph starts to walk away. Then he turns, looks at me, and moves his head over in the direction of the swimming pool.

Rebecca opens out her hands to see what he's entrusted her with. It is the compass I'd given him.

'Ah, sweet,' sighs Rebecca.

'What's that?' asks Ottoline, looking up from a magazine she is flicking through.

'The compass he wears around his neck. He'd sworn never to take off.'

'Bless,' says Victoria, a blonde, puffy girl. She peers up at the compass's face for a while before saying, 'It's stuck.'

Joseph winks at me as he swings a towel over his shoulder.

'I'm going for a quick dip too.'

Joseph hangs back for me to join him but as I turn, Rebecca calls out, 'No! It's not all right! We want to hear everything about you and Peter! Stella, tell us all about him! Peter… Ah!' gasps Rebecca. 'Ah yes! Did you know, Joe, Stella's the love interest of Barbados? She's the reason why Peter Lyle's been so elusive all week. We'd heard about his mystery woman. Aha! Stella, who's not only conquered the ocean, but Lyle's heart!'

One girl, who's been hanging upside down in a tree since we arrived, somersaults down and pines, 'So you're the one who caused him to leave the island! What did you do to him?'

'I thought he didn't have a heart, Becca.' Another girl whose name I'd already forgotten whines.

'You've got to tell us about it – right from the first snog!' insists Rebecca as she catches my wrist and tries to drag me back to the table. I look over at Joseph just as a man in a black polo neck thrusts another drink in my hands. I see the shock in Joseph's eyes. Rebecca's phone rings again. 'Joe, pass my ciggies… just there. Hang on a sec–'

Joseph starts walking away, slowly, as if in physical pain.

'No, no… Joseph!' I call, but he is picking up speed and in seconds he'll be out of earshot.

I say as loudly as I can, 'Don't believe the rumours! Peter and I, we were just friends!'

'Not what *I* heard!' Rebecca laughs while listening to someone on the phone.

Rebecca's little sister raises her head and looks at me quizzically.

'Do you mean you're going out with Peter, *American* Peter?'

'No, I said, I'm not!'

'Course she is! Who could resist?' adds Rebecca. 'Harvey!' she says down the phone.

I am losing sight of Joseph.

'Oh he's gorgeous, I'm so *jelly*!' exclaims Cristobel, pounding the grass.

'Stella, do tell us… is he the most amazing lover? Is he… Isn't he?' She laughs loudly. 'Becca, can you imagine, Peter a total *nul au lit*!'

Rebecca looks up from the phone. 'Yah, I can!'

Nick comes to my rescue. 'You girls are just terrible! Stella nearly died a few days ago and all you want to know about is her sex life!'

I break from the group and start running after Joseph.

Behind me I hear Rebecca asking, 'Margaux! Where's Margaux? She's supposed to– Stella! Ottoline! The bridesmaids' dresses! Stella, where are you off to?'

94

Desperate to explain myself to Joseph, it isn't long before I've ran past the length of the mansion's sprinkler system and am thrashing through dry, spiky grass. I call his name until I make myself hoarse. Catching my breath, I can hear helicopters in the distance, a gospel choir getting in tune, amplifiers being set up and the distinctive sound of champagne corks popping.

Is he not going to turn up for his own wedding?

I stop for breath and hear a branch snap behind me.

'Joe?'

Rebecca holds out the compass. 'You might need this?'

'I'm looking for Joe. I need to speak to him.'

'He's probably in the RumBah. He drinks there.' She tosses me the compass.

'But first, we need to get a few things straight.'

'Peter and I, it wasn't like that – you made it sound as though it was because you wanted Joe to think… *You* arranged all that to make it look like… Why?'

'Hey, maybe it's better for both of you if you just get on with your lives. Face it, you could hold Joseph back.'

'What gives you the right to meddle with other people's private lives?'

'Er, my work. It's how we do things. You thought he was shafting Sylvia.'

'I read his Twitter updates.'

'I *pay* someone to write those – *everyone* knows that.'

'Why? What *are* you doing? How can you blame me for not knowing Joseph wasn't with Sylvia when you'd convinced everyone else?'

'Excuse me, I said we're here for *a* wedding. I said wait till the end. I never said Joseph and Sylvia were–'

'What kind of person are you, Rebecca?'

'An agent.'

'Isn't interfering with your clients' love lives a little outside your job description?'

'Look, it's what I do. I *manage* people. Listen, Joe needs to appreciate that girlfriends, money, careers – they come and they go. Don't think I don't care about his feelings, I do, but right now, he's hot, he's bankable, he's fit – but people have to be talking about him. That's how it works.'

'I know how important Joseph's career is to you. But can't you just stick to that?'

'When I was at university I was diagnosed with a blood cancer,' she says.

'I'm sorry, that must have been awful.'

'Awful, yes. I had to rethink my whole life. When I was told I couldn't have kids and it could come back any time, I left university to set up my own company. I love my job and the people I work with. I want the best for the talent I represent and I don't want to see them moping around after some girl who can't really cope with her boyfriend's success. Someone who'd run off with the first guy she meets. Joseph loves you, Stella, he's miserable without you but excuse me if I take the opportunity to show him you can lose everything in a minute. Every day has to count. This is the time to be out there, in the world, not walking dogs together and filling up supermarket trolleys. He can do all that when he's old and fat and teaching drama in some local school.' She wafts away a fly. 'So why don't you back off and give him the chance to be the best star he can be?'

'But I *could* cope with his success. That's why we worked so well together – we let each other do what we loved, we didn't judge or restrict. Of course I hated all the stuff about him and his co-stars but… I wasn't a threat to his career.'

'Thing is, Joseph's just one of many young men I have on my

books. He's not better looking, he's not more talented or driven, what makes him different is that people want to buy into the package – the life they believe he's having – and part of that lifestyle is that he's always dating gorgeous women, especially Sylvia Amery, and in forty minutes it's going to get even more exciting when–'

'Rewrite the next part: he stays with the woman he loves and who loves him.'

I turn from her and hurry through the trees back to the house, hearing her behind me. 'Stella! You've got it all wrong – *again*!'

95

'Have you seen him?' screeches Ottoline, slaloming between the caterers and guests.

'No. I couldn't find him.'

'Everyone's here.' We sit down to give me a minute to catch my breath. 'His brother's a bit of all right, isn't he? What are we going to do? Sylvia keeps asking where he is.'

'Maybe he doesn't want to marry Sylvia…' I whisper as an orchestra tunes up.

'Who?' she says, turning to me.

'What d'you mean "who"? *Joseph!*'

'Huh? Who said Joseph was getting married?' She looks at me, bewildered.

'Oh my God, Stella! You mean, you still *don't know* "The Big Secret"!'

'What big secret?'

'Rebecca just gave us all the debrief! Oh my God, it's *so* cool! The Joseph-Sylvia thing: it's not real! It's all made up – a decoy!'

'A decoy? For what?'

'This is all for Sylvia and Blizzard – they're the ones getting married!'

'Sylvia and… not *Joseph*?'

'No! This is Rebecca's *pièce de résistance* – the big Hollywood *gay* wedding!

Joseph's the best man and he's giving her away! *If* we can find him!' Ottoline pulls me up by my elbow as she gets me up to speed. 'Sylvia really wants him to be here,' she says, panting. 'Joseph was the person who helped her "come out". This is all because of him! But Rebecca said, he got upset and…' The sound of helicopters and a gospel choir rehearsing drown out her words.

'Stella! Come on! We've got to get ready – we're the fucking bridesmaids!' I follow Ottoline through the mansion to the main bedroom where Sylvia's make-up artist sits in front of her, perplexed over how to add to an already-perfect face.

The new information whizzes around my brain. Rebecca had alluded to this not necessarily being Joseph's wedding, and it *isn't*. He isn't in love with Sylvia, he'd *never* been.

'More bridesmaids!' Sylvia laughs, as two women dressed as Las Vegas showgirls add another layer of tropical flowers to her hair.

'Have they found him?' asks an actress who starred in a BBC period drama my mum used to love.

'No. Still looking,' says a man wearing a tribal headdress, drawing on an e-cigarette – the same man who played the drums at Henry and Yuleka's wedding.

'He's been so down lately, since he broke up with his girl,' says Sylvia, sipping at her champagne glass. 'Isn't it always the way that just when you find success with one part of your life, another turns shit. Well, there goes my career! Oh, hey, Ottoline and...? Your dresses are waiting for you – you guys better hurry! Oh, there's my baby...' She coos as room service comes in with a little dog dressed all in white satin with a veil pinned down by a diamond tiara.

'That dog flew all the way in from LA?' I ask.

'Uh-huh.' Sylvia nods at me. 'She's a therapy dog, aren't you, baby? Aren't you?'

'Come on, ladies!' The make-up artist claps. Seeing a bathroom free, I jump into a waterfall-shower to wash away all the grass, the dirt and the tension from that afternoon.

When I come out, I hear voices from the garden, still calling for Joseph.

'We'll find him, don't panic!' yells a woman as she tears down the staircase. 'Don't panic! Jesus! Find him!'

We slip on the simple satin dresses and add the flowers to our hair while a make-up lady comes at us with her mascara brush. While she is dabbing my lips with gloss, Sylvia appears.

'Stella,' she says, dropping to her knees.

'You look just… so… beautiful!' I say, and really mean it.

Sylvia closes her eyes, dips her head down and looks back up at me. She puts her hand over my wrist. 'I know you – you're *Stella*! Joe showed me photos of you. I didn't click until… and you're here!' Her laugh tinkles around the room. 'Oh my God! You are *Stella*. You're *Stella*. Wow! I am *so* happy to meet you!'

'If only I'd met you six months ago!'

'I know – can you imagine the way I felt? Blizzard's been mad as hell with all the stories but at least we were together. I always said to Joe, straighten it out, just go to her and tell her, but all this long-distance gossip, so many different people telling you all kinds of things – and then you vanished! What you must think… about me… and…' She takes my hands in her soft little fingers. 'Joseph's my *best* friend. He wasn't ever my… y'know? I don't do cock. You believe me, don't you?'

'I do *now*, but then, he wasn't there and everyone was saying you were in love and I had to protect myself.'

'We live in a crazy, crazy world.' Sylvia sighs, her complexion like candle wax. 'It was a big deal to come out about Blizzard. I was terrified. Then Rebecca had the idea of making a really great story – it was only at the last minute that Joseph agreed to this wedding idea, he wanted it here in Barbados. We swore each other to secrecy. Rebecca made him promise not to say anything to *anyone* but Joe was just so worried about you.' A diamond-shaped tear teeters on her eyelid. She waves away someone trying to brush her hair. 'He was heartbroken when you guys split, he wanted to do something really dramatic and special to win you over and prove to you that he's never been, like, even remotely interested in anyone else.'

Margaux bursts through the door. 'Let's go! Are the bridesmaids ready?'

'It'll be *you* next, Stella,' Sylvia says as she turns and hurries down the staircase.

96

As we gather, waiting for Sylvia to appear, Ottoline takes my hand. 'You could have told me you were Joseph West's bloody girlfriend!'

The orchestra strikes up playing overtures from Broadway musicals, people sing or hum tunes they know until a cheer breaks out when Blizzard appears at the top of the aisle dressed in an aluminium suit with a giant white carnation in the pocket. The string section is interrupted by a rap version of 'Here Comes the Bride' blaring over the speakers.

A flight of doves are released into the air as Joseph steps through an arch made entirely of flowers. For a moment I think of Henry and how close we might have come to him being part of my life. Joseph puts out his arm and leads Sylvia through. She stands next to him wearing a dress made entirely of white rose petals.

Joseph wears a dark suit, white shirt and is, predictably, irresistible. The two of them look at each other and laugh conspiratorially then try to look as solemn as they can, but they can't suppress their smiles. There are explosions of 'Ooohs' and 'Aaahs' in the crowd when Sylvia's dog trots up in her diamonds and veil.

Margaux gestures at us to follow behind Sylvia and Joseph until they stop next to Blizzard. Joseph gives Sylvia a kiss on the cheek and joins her hand with Blizzard's. The priest, a Caribbean woman in layers of multicoloured skirts and a beaming smile, welcomes them onto the centre stage.

Joseph moves to the side and stands beside a woman who claps wildly. I peer at her and see it is my mother, in pink with large hibiscus flowers in her hair. Joe holds his fingers clasped together, looking thoughtfully into his palms.

'Fucktastic!' whoops Ottoline.

When the service is over, we are free to move around the garden and congratulate the couple. Joseph smiles at everyone, but I can tell he is distracted, distant. I hang back until he is free of the crowds around him.

I find Mum dipping a crayfish tail in mayonnaise.

'This could have been your wedding, Stella. What a balls-up you've made of your life.' A petal around her left ear is drooping onto her cheek.

'Can you pour me a glass?'

She pushes a champagne flute into my hand while watching Sylvia and Blizzard slow dance.

'I can't believe it. Joseph had wanted to show you how it all worked – the manipulation, the string-pulling, the drama of it all! He wanted to surprise you, make you see that Sylvia's not at all for him. He wanted to come out in public about his feelings for you, but instead, he finds out that you were the one going off with some other man. You didn't even tell me!' She puts up a hand in protest. 'Don't, Stella. I have to go and comfort someone who's feeling very bereft – and that's *Joseph* if you haven't worked it out.'

'Stella, my dear, I've been trying desperately to get in touch with you!' booms Johnny, with Kimberly smiling by his side. 'I just want to say how really sorry and responsible I feel about what happened. The captain of my boat should have made sure everyone was safe – I have already set up an enquiry and...'

'Sorry? Oh that. It was nothing to do with you, don't worry...'

All that Mum said runs through my head.

His apologies continue until Ottoline cuts in. 'If you want a lift, Stella, I'm leaving now.' She glares at Johnny.

'See you ladies later at the party,' says Johnny as they glide back into the crowd.

Ottoline looks tearful so I ask her if she is all right. She isn't.

'Someone told me that Johnny and Kimberley spent the afternoon looking at engagement rings. Sorry, I just can't take it–'

'I'll come with you.'

'You don't want to talk to Joe?'

'Yes, I want to talk to him, but not here, now, with all of this going on.'

97

Ottoline spins the car to a stop at the hotel entrance and takes a deep breath.

'Look, it's not my business but if I stood a chance with Joseph West, I wouldn't hang around.' She puts a stern hand on my shoulder. 'You didn't even speak to him at the wedding. What could he be thinking? I mean, now that you know the truth about him, you've heard everybody saying how much he loves you, what's keeping you from telling him there was nothing between you and Peter?'

'He and Sylvia came up with this elaborate drama, which involved keeping me in the dark – didn't they think how this would impact me?'

'It didn't work out, they fucked up but the important thing is that he loves you and he wanted to make it right. Work it out, babe, and don't listen to Rebecca – love's more important than silly careers – she's never had a boyfriend in her life, and it's made her so cynical. But the truth is, she was planning this gay marriage thing with Sylvia and it was Joseph who suggested doing it in Barbados because he knew you'd be here. He was bloody miserable before today. Meanwhile...' Ottoline unravels a list of the *World's 50 Richest Men* from her handbag, 'this one...' she points at a picture of a small, fat bald man grinning over a bow-tie, 'is coming to the dinner tonight. He owns seven houses, just got divorced from his fourth wife. Nice smile, eh? When he closes his mouth.'

We promise to keep in touch when we are back in London and as she speeds away with a wave, I turn into the hotel for my last night in Barbados.

The receptionist hands me my keys and holds up a newspaper cutting about the rescue for me to sign. Other staff come to see my bruises and ask if I'd actually seen the dead lawyer's body. Then they all want to talk about Sylvia's gay wedding – an excruciating twenty minutes.

The pool has been lit up like an aquamarine gem where the first stars hang over the palm trees. No Peter, no Templeton-Crests, no Yuleka.

No Henry.

Ferdi. I shut my eyes, trying to push out my last picture of him wrapped up on the dusty pavement under a makeshift home. But each time, the image of him nestled into the rubbish comes back to me.

I pass Peter's room on tiptoes as if afraid to wake a ghost. There is no light under the door, no sound, nothing; it is empty, waiting for the next tourist to occupy his bed, see the same view and fill his wardrobe with their clothes. I give him a mental wave goodbye and thank-you for the late-night drinking and moonlight swims.

98

'Miss Stella! Miss Stella!'

Ferdi speeds towards me down the corridor – bends his knees and slides over the polished floor for about two and half metres until he comes to a balletic pose.

'Good eh? We call it floor-surfing. We have competitions when the guests aren't around.' He holds my wrists with urgency. 'Miss Stella, I've been looking for you everywhere!'

'Oh, Ferdi, I can't take any more surprises.'

'I've got *good* news! There's a *man* to see you, ma'am.'

'But it's your day off – what are you doing here?'

'Day off, yes, that's why I'm in mufti, but the island has been abuzz with the wedding – your mother told me all about it. *All* about it. The party will go on all night but *he*'s waiting in the library.'

'*He*'ll have to wait.'

'To *wait*? Do you–'

'Yes, Ferdi. I've got to do something first.'

'But… but… but he *really* wants to see you.'

All this time, Ferdi is nudging me towards the library. I turn towards my room when Ferdi touches my arm, insisting, 'But you don't know *who* he is!'

'I've an idea, Ferdi. Tell him I'll be there in a minute.'

'It's *Joseph West*, ma'am!'

'I thought so.'

'I asked him to wait for you in the library – he wanted somewhere "private". He's drinking a tequila sunrise.' By now, Ferdi is almost dragging me.

'Ferdi, I have to do something first – it involves you.'

'Me?'

I walk into my room looking back to ensure Ferdi is following.

'Oh, ma'am. He's so charming. We talked about his films and his career. I even told him I thought he was wonderful in *The Pearl-Fed Woman*. He was amazed I knew the film and that I'd guessed who the killer was in the first ten minutes.'

I walk over to my writing desk, find a page of the hotel's headed notepaper, and jot down a few lines for Joseph, fold it over and put it in an envelope.

'That's my favourite one too,' I say, distractedly, as he lists the films that he'd enjoyed Joseph in.

'I'll wait here for a reply.'

I hand the letter to Ferdi who is baffled by my leisurely approach to having a movie star waiting for me.

'This is *totally* Jane Austen!'

A few minutes later Ferdi rushes back in.

'This is all very exciting, Miss Stella.' He stops to catch his breath. 'He said, "Tell her, I will see to her request, as long as she agrees to have dinner with me tonight".'

'You might like to know what I wrote, Ferdi?'

He bounces on his heels, shaking his head.

'I said that I would see him on *one* condition. The condition is that he reads your script or whatever you can show him tonight, and, if he likes it, he will help you with it. It's not a promise of anything but–'

'Oh, ma'am!' His lips are quivering. 'Oh! Oh! Oh!' he cries, twirling around in front of me. 'Oh!' His arms close around me. I laugh at his happiness, both of us filled with so much hope, both of us on the precipice of believing in luck.

'He loves you, Miss Stella, I could see it in his smile. I never wanted to say but I knew there was someone you were missing all the time, and when you were in the hospital, my first thought was of that person, and that they might never know the love they were losing. And then – your mother told me everything – and now! Joseph West and my Miss Stella! Go to him, don't waste another minute, there's still a little bit of sunset left.'

99

Joseph is sitting in the English rose garden that the library leads out to, still wearing the suit from that afternoon but the shirt is untucked, smudged with mud, the jacket is crumpled and his chin carries a five o'clock shadow. His eyes are tired, deep in thought. My heart stops for a few seconds at the sight of him.

Joseph puts out his hand. 'I'm Joseph.'

'*Everyone* knows who *you* are.'

'No one knows me as well as you.'

Joseph has a way of dropping his head to one side, looking up at you so that you see the corner of his smile before you get to the full kilowattage. It's devastating.

He hands me a tequila sunrise.

'Cheers.' The last rays of sun illuminate my drink. Crimson. Red. Orange. Yellow. The setting sun, the warmth of the alcohol, and sitting next to each other with the roses nodding in the evening breeze, leaves us depleted, sated. We rest our heads against each other.

'I feel,' says Joseph, 'I feel as if we've arrived on dry land after months and months of being shipwrecked.'

'Are we safe now, Joe?'

'Oh yes, my Sparkles. And this new land is going to be even better than anything we ever imagined.'

'I've got so much to tell you – and you've got a lot of explaining to do.'

Before Joseph can speak, two men stand by my side, looking at Joe.

'Excuse me, but we're great fans. Any chance of a photo? Sorry to interrupt. It would mean so much – oh, and great about the nomination. Rooting for you, mate.'

Joseph poses with the two guys while I take the photo but when they leave, more people begin to wander into the bar waiting for their chance to speak to Joseph.

'Shall we get out of here?'

'Come on, lean on me.' I rest against him as we walk out of the hotel and onto the moonlit sands. 'I still can't believe you were in the sea during that storm. I didn't know you were such a good swimmer.'

'I didn't either, until I started drowning. That's also a metaphor by the way.'

'Gotcha.' Another kiss before Joe holds my face and asks, 'Can we just… cut. Cut, cut, cut everything and start again. Take two?'

'Definitely. I've learnt so much since that day I gave up on us. I can't expect you to understand this, but I felt that I didn't deserve you, and then when it came time to building a life together, I got scared and then with all the stories, that just confirmed my fears. I wasn't sure I had the foundations with so many pieces missing. But I can go forward now, I can face anything if we're together.'

'But, Sparks, I made massive mistakes too. I took for granted that you would just be there by my side and go along with all the fantasy and craziness of what I do. It must have been so difficult – and hurtful – to read all that stuff. I should have spoken out and made it clear, but I was also caught in the whirlwind of attention and ambition. Forgive me?'

I bring my lips to his and we stay like that, the sea rolling in and out around us.

'Okay, so, here goes.'

He carries me to shallow waters and drops down on one knee, grapples around in his suit trousers and pulls out a ring box.

'Stella. Take this – it was the best the hotel shop had – Ferdi arranged it at quick notice–'

He opens the box and slides the ring over my finger.

'Did she say yes?' asks my mother, galloping over the sands from the hotel bar, her dress bunched in one hand, Ferdi trying to keep up with her.

'Of course I did!'

PART SEVEN

HOME

100

Bulging black bin bags of cloud weigh over the city. The streetlights are still on after last night, and they'll continue to stay on throughout the day. Raindrops ping onto the skylight, breaking up into thousands of mercurial pellets rolling above our heads. Joseph moves his hand over my hips and I'm warmed through, his mouth brushes my neck, tickling my ears. I roll on top of him, moving my lips over the roundness of his shoulders, his hands press into my back. We wiggle our toes together, groan at the same time, break into a giggle. And as we're about to make a kiss landing for each other's mouths, his phone goes off.

'Yeah?' Joseph listens while lightly stroking my back. 'Hold on a minute.'

He puts the phone down and roars in frustration, grabs my waist, rolls me over and in twenty seconds covers my body with kisses before picking up his mobile.

'Okay, ready.' Joe talks while I lie there, under his hands, neither of us able to look away from each other. 'Okay. Well if they want to send the script over I'll look… uh-huh… I'd consider that too. But if… hmm? Okay.'

Rebecca. She's calling from a film set in Bulgaria. It's going to take a while.

I slide out from under his hard, ripped stomach. It's almost unbearable to leave him, but as he taps my bottom and winks, the parting isn't so bad: we both know without saying that next month we'll be on our honeymoon, and we'll have three weeks together alone – no telephones, photo shoots, premieres, no interviews, just us.

I make my way to the bathroom with Elvis pattering behind. As I'm washing my face, Joseph peers in.

'The car's here.'

'Already?'

'I'm late.'

'Coffee?'

'I can't. The traffic's terrible apparently.' He holds up two shirts.

'Purple.'

'What are you up to today?'

'Getting married, Joseph, is a full-time job.'

'And you get to sleep with your boss,' he says, nudging in next to me and squirting toothpaste onto his brush.

'But I'm the boss, right?'

'But of course,' he says, giving me a minty kiss.

'Sorry to interrupt, little lovebirds,' Kira, Joseph's – and now *my* – personal assistant, sings as she carries in her MacBook Air all set to synchronise our diaries.

'I brought a morning muffin, skinny latte and an Americano for Joseph as he should be dashing out right–'

'Now!' he says, passing me and looking at Kira's calendar on the screen. 'We've nothing on for tonight, have we?' He takes the coffee while putting his other arm through his coat sleeve.

'No, just the run-through for Saturday night's chat show at five in the studio. Do you want me to book somewhere?'

'I'd really like to stay in, torture myself with Stella's cooking – better still, get Mimo's to deliver. I'll check in later, Sparks.'

Another kiss and he's out.

While Joe leaves to make the world swoon, Kira and I go over ideas for publicising my animal rescue adoption centre which Kamilla and I are setting up for next spring.

As Kira makes a better job of organising my life without me, I nip into the bathroom for a shower. The last of the bruising has faded and I can move without my cracked rib hurting. I run the water, watch it fall, put a hand in to gauge its temperature. The torrent of splashing takes me back to the storm. Waves pulling me backwards and forwards into the sea, slamming me over the rocks – but then I catch sight of my ring and I'm home again.

101

'Love that jumper!' effuses Kira, waving a pair of scissors in one hand and a tube of glue in the other. 'Have you got a moment to go over the guest list?'

'Sure.' I wonder how to break it to her that there are even more people coming to the wedding. Every day names are added to the list which already covers six spreadsheets.

'Okay. A quick recap,' she says, reminding me why Joseph calls her our very own Miss Moneypenny. She leads me to the kitchen table. 'I know you and Joseph are "visual learners" so I've made a 3-D model of the church, the house, the marquee. See? Look, here are all the guests!' She looks at me while I take in this miniature world she's created for us. 'We can arrange them all around the table like... this!' She hops them around the different tables. She's taken pictures of most of the people from Facebook or magazines and stuck them on little bodies.

'There's Kamilla! Chas, oh, my mum... Rebecca, and who's that... Sylvia! And Blizzard!' In front of me is the full cast of my life lined up in cardboard cut-outs. 'Kira!' I laugh. 'This is fantastic, thank you!' She peers at me over the model wedding like Winston Churchill about to explain a military operation.

'The big question,' she muses, 'is how to *group* the tables?'

I look at the cut-outs of Joseph and me.

'Leave it with us. Just make sure Ottoline has a place on the top table between two very handsome men. And that Abigail, who was once our social worker and who saved our lives at one time, is right in the centre of it all too.'

The buzzer goes. It's my taxi to take me to my last dress fitting. 'Coming down,' Kira calls into the intercom.

Half an hour later, I'm still sitting in the car moving slower than the pedestrians swishing through the rain.

My phone vibrates. It's Joseph.

'I'm just going into a meeting. Miss you.'

'Miss you too. Let me know if you have any thoughts about where to sit your aunt Bernice.'

'Aunt Bernie – the dog table. See you tonight.'

I sit back and look out at the curtains of rain. An email appears from an estate agent who thinks they've found the perfect house for us in the country. We've been looking for a holiday home but also somewhere to house rescue animals while we find them appropriate homes. It's good news and I want to pass it on to Kamilla, but I'm still waiting to hear if her IVF has taken.

Text alert:

> Am in the area this afternoon – shall I drive your van round? All love, Tash xxx

Tash knows she's not invited to the wedding, that she'll never be, but she continues haranguing me in the hope that I'll forget we were never friends.

I tap back:

> Keep it.

And then I think back to the last time I saw Tash and search in my wallet for the dry cleaner's ticket. After my dress fitting, I guess I should pick up all the stuff I left there, or at least pay for it.

The dry cleaner's assistant sighs at the ticket as she dumps batch after batch of clothes out onto the counter. When everything in my name is balancing on the counter, she needs to stop to catch her breath and the flow of sweat running down her face.

'We didn't think you'd be coming back. T-shirts. Socks. Jeans… See, some strange people think we're a storage option. Legally we have to keep it for three months. You can see, we've not much space as it is. Anyway you're here.'

'I'm here.' I wave my credit card at her, and a twenty-pound note.

She slides the card machine towards me. Watching me, intent on spotting a scam.

'You'll need help – have you got a car?'

'I'll get a taxi.'

'Right.'

After I've paid, I sense we're not done. Another woman parts a curtain of men's jackets and waddles over to us. She checks the ticket, looks back at me. 'I was here the day you came in – February, wasn't it?'

'Yes.' I prepare myself for yet another announcement of the establishment's rules and obligations concerning left items.

'Huh. It was February. A Sunday. I work on a Sunday. For my sins.' She makes an unsuccessful attempt to close her arms around her middle. 'After you left, this fancy car – grey Aston Martin – pulled up. You couldn't miss it. Woman came in. Asked lots of questions. About *you*.'

'Me?'

'You. What your name was. What you'd dropped off. When you was coming back. Well, I didn't see why I couldn't give the information to her, but it didn't feel right… data protection and all. So I said I'd not tell her. Not that we knew anything anyways. Just your name and that you were paying upon collection. For this lot. Then she asked us, if *she* told *us* your name, could we confirm it. "All right", I goes.' She looks down, reading off something. '"Stella Tyler." I said, "Aye, that's the correct name".' She looks back at me. I nod to move the story on. 'Then she wanted to know when you were going to pick your stuff up. How was I to know?

So I said, "We haven't made any arrangement, she has up to three months", as you see.' We both look at the notice again. 'So she wanted paper. A pen. Charlene had to buy her envelopes. The lady gave her a large tip. Nice. Then she wrote summit. *This*.' She lowers herself under the counter and pulls out an envelope with my name on it. 'She said to give it to you when you came to pick up your stuff. So here it is.'

She hands me the envelope.

Once I'm settled in the taxi flanked by mountains of dry cleaning wrapped in plastic film, I take out the envelope.

102

Caroline Hardwick buzzes me in. I stand in the hall, surrounded by paintings of men with ruddy cheeks, frilled collars and glistening eyes looking at me disapprovingly from dark canvases and heavy gold frames. Meet the relatives.

The house is grand but feels as though someone left in a hurry several centuries ago. Despite its careful cream colour scheme and expensive old wooden furniture, it's falling apart. The single hall light buzzes and there's no heating. Mould spores reproduce along the skirting boards and sepia-coloured grease tarnishes the chandeliers and picture frames. Dust balls scud across the floors.

While I'm fighting the urge to push up my sleeves and wipe down the surfaces, Caroline comes up from the basement.

We stand on her landing looking at each other.

She's a slight woman in a pale-yellow cashmere cardigan over a light jumper of the same colour, a row of pearls like baby teeth border the collar.

'Aren't you pretty,' she says flatly. 'Prettier than in the papers.'

I follow her further into the hallway. This would be just the sort of house my mother would have broken into, it has the prerequisite high ceilings, central sweeping staircase and original fireplaces.

Caroline fumbles with a little lamp on the floor. She flicks it on then wraps her arms around her body as if she were a newborn chick.

'It wasn't easy, tracking you down: you were always so quickly on the move – outwitting the tabloid press, I suppose. Must say, we've had our share of media interest too. Nightmare. Well, I told you on the phone.' She puts her hand on my shoulder, one, then the other. 'It was *brave* and *kind* of you to come. Would you like a drink of something?'

'Tea? If that's...' I take care to walk around the pile of takeaway pizza boxes waiting for removal, '...no problem.'

We walk down the stairs into the kitchen, which takes up the whole lower ground floor and smells of blocked drains. Patio doors open out onto a largish London garden with an unmown lawn. The plants are overgrown, burgeoning out of their terracotta pots and splitting off into mutated versions of themselves up and down the cracked walls. The only halogen spotlight in the kitchen that works is directed to an overflowing bin.

Caroline dithers over the cupboards, tapping her fingers as if composing a piano concerto.

'Let's see, let's see... I have to do all these things myself now,' she laughs and looks round at me, 'what sort of tea would you like?'

'Oh, anything. Builder's tea would do fine.'

'I don't know if we have that...' She opens a cupboard, stares blankly at the piles of unspecific grains and liquids oozing from containers. 'It's a long time since we had any workmen in, you can probably tell,' she mutters. 'They probably drank it, probably all they did.'

Caroline moves on to a Victoriana tin box wrapped in colourful paper that must have been given to her many years ago. She screws up her eyes and holds it up to read the label as if she were scrutinising a piece of jewellery passed on from someone she distrusts. She reads it out, 'Tea from the Hill Club, Nuwara Eliya, Sri Lanka... best before 1992... what you do think? Does tea *expire*?'

'It looks fine.'

She wrinkles her nose. 'Milk and sugar?'

Normally yes, but I say no to spare her another expedition to her cupboards. She lays our teas out on a tray which I carry upstairs to the sitting room.

103

'Do you smoke?'

'No,' I answer. She looks down, bites her lower lip in disappointment. 'Well, on occasion.'

'I've taken up smoking, do you mind? I know how fascist young people can be – and I'm all for it, saving rainforests, caring for one's body and organic everything. Thing is, when your husband leaves you with nothing after twenty years of marriage and then drops dead on his honeymoon, one can't help but question what really is dangerous in the world, you know. Would you make this an "occasion" and join me?'

'Sure.'

She pushes a high-backed tapestry chair over to an old armoire, climbs on to it and grapples over the top and brings down a leather bag. With her back to me, bottom in the air, she fishes out a packet of cigarettes and a lighter. She then flicks the bag on top of the cupboard before stepping down, straightening up her skirt. She sits down, breathes out long and hard.

'So you got my note from those women at the dry cleaners. How funny.'

'You were in the grey Aston Martin. I'd seen you following me, but you weren't the only one.'

'Not a very discreet car for spying. I've never been a car person – just had the Land Rover for the country house and a little electric thing for nipping around London. When I found out Henry was having an affair and that divorce was on the horizon, I went to the nearest showroom and bought the most expensive thing on the forecourt.' She looks around the room and takes in a deep breath. 'Only good decision I've ever made.' She bites a nail. 'I only ever wished your mother happiness despite the… incidents. And all the letters and phone calls, and the nocturnal visits. I lived in fear of her leaping out at me from the pantry or behind the shower curtain. Bit of a drama at the time but a long time ago.' She waves her cigarette back and forth as though seeing the years dissolving like smoke.

We drink tea, and I wonder how deep we are to plunge. 'Henry's death must have been a terrible shock for you all.'

'*Henry* was a terrible shock to us all. What a sorry, sorry tale. We don't know whether or not to do a funeral. Is he mine to mourn? The children's? She cremated him out there – *she* did! Where's the protocol in these situations?'

I can't answer her questions, only add more of my own. 'Did Henry ever speak about me?'

'No.'

'Did he tell you he had a child?'

'No. Not him. Your mother did. Incessantly. She wrote to me just after we'd got engaged. Very *kind* of her. Told me about their affair and her baby – enclosed photos, copies of letters, the little cards from his favourite flower shop. Of course, I should have left him. It was clear he had feelings for her but I was young and scared, ashamed, I only had him to listen to. And when you love someone you want to believe them.' She twirls the cigarette in the air and looks through the smoke.

'He never wanted to see me, or–'

'Well what could we have done with this baby? Have it over for weekends? Christmases? Send it to school with Tom and Barnaby? How could we *explain* it? Henry's father would have had a heart attack – or worse, cut us off!' She plays with the cigarette packet. 'Henry'd tried everything to persuade the girl, your mother–'

'Florence.'

'Florence. You know we've talked? She's quite a character. We're even planning a spa weekend together. She's the only person who understands what's going on. Anyway, at the time, she couldn't have been under any illusions about his intentions. She *chose* to have it.'

'I am the "it", Mrs Hardwick.'

'I know… I know. Sorry. This must be very difficult for you. Oh dear. I've been through so much lately that I have become quite numb. I forget, I'm not nice to be around anymore, I've not only lost every penny, home, friends but also my dignity, integrity. It makes you mean.' She wriggles in her seat as if trying to dislodge a bubble of indigestion. 'All this *anger*.'

I remember the disappointment on my mother's face when my birthdays came and there was no card, or when I graduated and Robert, her boss, was there in place of my father. I look over at a silver-framed photo of Henry dressed in a blonde wig and suspenders at some legal fundraising event.

'Internet's a marvellous thing. I found you in less than a minute. I suppose having a celebrity boyfriend makes it even easier – sorry, fiancé. Congratulations, hope you make a better job of marriage than I did.' Caroline shudders. 'It's a shame that it's too late for you to meet him.'

'I did meet him, didn't mum say?'

The crease in between her eyebrows deepens. 'You met Henry?'

'I was the last person to see him alive.'

104

I text Joseph to say I'll be home later while Caroline brings up some of her late husband's vintage wine from the cellar. She starts a little fire, sits back and says, 'Right, from the start!'

I tell Caroline my life story. She presses for details. She gulps, gasps, slaps her thighs and lights another 'ciggy' for us both. I have never had such an appreciative audience. She knows all the characters: Roy and Bunny Templeton-Crest, Peter even. I finish with the scene where Yuleka burst into my hotel room accusing me of ruining her honeymoon.

'Ah. So you've had first-hand experience of my nemesis!' She puts a hand over her mouth to stop herself laughing or crying or something. 'If ever I deserved a punishment, I damn well got it! The house is up for grabs, all our friends are too embarrassed to call, my children loathe me, I'm selling the last of my shares to pay for the only tutorial college which'll take Barnaby, can you believe, and I'm up at six every morning to work as a private secretary to one of my old school friends?'

'Why would *you* deserve punishment?'

She drops to her knees, shuffles over to me and puts her hands to her face gathering the strength to speak.

'I've had a secret for a long time, telling you that secret was the first thing I wanted to do when I was free from Henry. It's why I've been following you around.'

'What is it?'

'The letters, cards, drawings… things you sent Henry over the years… he never received them.'

'But I sent them to him.'

She drops to one side, relief emptying out of her.

'I intercepted them.'

'But they were sent to his office…'

Her voice becomes a whisper. 'His personal secretary was his old house matron from Eton. When her husband died, she fell on hard times and it was my idea he took her on – she was absolutely bloody useless but she was devoted, just so grateful for the job. She'd have done anything for us, particularly for me. She knew about you and she guarded "the secret" – destroyed everything you and your mother sent. The day you came to Henry's office, do you remember?' Of course I remember. 'He didn't know you were there – never found out. *She* called me. I panicked, told her to send you back. I thought it was blackmail and it was cruel. Henry may have done the same, who knows.' She readjusts her seating position, crawls over to the photograph of Henry and stares at his face. 'I suppose there are some things he isn't entirely to blame for. I didn't want the shame, the complication, the *living evidence* that he'd betrayed me. He didn't know you tried to get in touch. I'm very, very sorry.'

Her words act like a spotlight awakening dark, hidden pain.

'You've every right to be angry. I got in touch with you to tell you this, and to say if there's anything I can do to make it up to you.'

It doesn't take long to answer.

'I want his name on my birth certificate. Do the boys know about me?'

'They do. *Now*. But it's all been shattering for them. Their father's affair, the divorce, the death, and then learning they have a sister they never met. Barnaby's the worst affected. You saw how I have to hide all my belongings around the house: if it isn't nailed down, he steals it. He's taken everything. All my jewellery, the family silver, even my bloody nail scissors. Everything.'

'Why?' I ask.

'Clubs. Drugs. Revenge. Resentment. He hates us all.'

'And what about your other son?'

'Tom? He's in the City, got a lovely girl. Tom will be all right.'

A clock somewhere in the house chimes. I stand up and put my coat on. Caroline moves towards me, clutching my arm. 'I'm terribly, terribly sorry, Stella, we should have done something for you. I've many regrets in my life, but this weighs the heaviest.'

I tug at the Hardwick front door until it opens into the cold night air.

Dear Daddy,

I'm watching the autumn sun setting over the rooftops of my university town – yes! Here I am: my first night as a law student. Mum and Robert drove me down, we had lunch on the way – I was too nervous to eat – Mum cried, awkward! I'm sharing a room with Bo, who's very posh, she went to Roedean girls' boarding school and is studying classics though she doesn't know why. Luckily she's okay about me having Lancelot and Guinevere, my guinea pigs, although she did ask if we were going to eat them at some point. That's public-school humour, right?

Everyone's in the bar or going out for meals but I thought I'd get a head start on our readings before crashing. Kamilla had a party for me last night which ended just as Mum and Robert were loading the car to drive me here!

So far the other students seem friendly, some of them invited me to see a play tomorrow starring a boy called Joseph West who all the girls are already in love with. All they seem to think about is sex and getting drunk, no one wants to talk about jury reform or Guantanamo Bay.

Love, Stella xxx

Before turning up the road to Sloane Square Tube, I look back along the river at the tall, red tower block I grew up in. Mum's probably getting ready for bed now, I could walk over and tell her about this afternoon but I'm too churned up.

I fight with the buttons on my coat. Caroline had made me invisible to my father. That's a story I could tell myself to exonerate Henry because I'm still trying to protect him – why? Because he's half of me? Because he's not here, and they are? Because I still can't let go of the idea that Daddy is waiting in the wings to step up and love me? The weight of my coat falls from me. Do I still feel not good enough for him? My jumper's too tight. Outrage pounds through me. That house, those mollycoddled boys, her pearls… the way she talked about my mother, called me 'it'. I rest my head against a lamp-post in front of the Thames as my fists tighten in fury.

'Stop!' There are arms clasped around my chest. 'Stop! Don't do it!' Someone grabs me. Tightly. Weighing themselves against me. I try to break free but he is strong, breathing against me. I don't move for long enough that he begins to release his grip.

This isn't a random mugging. I've seen this man before.

The man in the red socks: at Henry's wedding in Holland Park. In Barbados – at the Wedding of a Thousand Dreams. At the scuba-diving school… and when I was in the cave, sinking beneath the water level, struggling for breath, he was on the motorbike – he left Henry to die.

'Are you going to kill me too?' I ask when I get some air in my lungs.

'I'm trying to stop you from killing yourself!' he shouts, tightening his grip again.

'You think…?' I see the serious look in his eyes. 'You think

I'm going to jump?' He releases me, stands back to look at me, when I laugh. 'I was looking for my Oyster card!'

He slaps his forehead, grinning.

'I'm Tom. Your half-brother.'

'You were with Henry when he died.'

'I just wanted to talk to him. Like you wanted to talk to him.' He stares at me, willing me to believe him. 'You know he wouldn't take our phone calls, open our letters, agree to even see us – his *own* children!'

'Sounds about right,' I say, rolling my eyes.

'Yeah, you'd know.' He looks up at the charcoal night. 'All we'd ever done was to try to get his approval, his attention. We longed for his affection and then, at the end of it all, he said he was ashamed of us because we couldn't stand on our own two feet! He said he was going to give everything – everything! – to Yuleka because "*she* was the only person who'd ever loved him"!' He holds out his hands to emphasise his point. I have the same mannerism. 'So I went to Barbados to confront him, to make him see the mistake he was making but more than that, what a fucking liar he was! Mum told us about you – that all along we had a sister we never knew about. On top of everything! The two of them... All our lives, my brother and I were used as props to make a deceitful man, his miserable wife and his loveless marriage look socially acceptable. I went to Barbados to get him to face the truth. I didn't push him – I didn't! He slipped when he turned his back on me...'

Tom looks out at the traffic but we both see the same thing. Henry falling, Tom standing over him.

'But I let him fall.' He sniffs, looks across at the power station. 'Come on, you must have hated him too.' He waits for me now. He's pale, he has dark rings under his eyes and his pupils are dilated with fear.

And now my turn: 'He told my mother he was always coming

back for her, for us. We never heard a thing from him.' I look into Tom's face. 'From the age of seven I used to write to Henry, even went to his office to plead for help, but I was turned away. Henry, Caroline – even Henry's secretary – kept me out.' I realise I'm shouting. I catch my breath while we look at each other, gathering information. I want him to understand what it felt like for me to be on the outside.

Tom drops his arms to his side and speaks gently. 'Please, Stella, don't imagine we were getting the love and happiness you didn't have. And he broke my mother's heart over and over again. I didn't mean to cause his death, but it was kind of fitting that he died turning away from his family.'

Leaning against the river's barrier, I look up at the streetlights.

'So it was you who called the rescue police?'

'Yes. And I came back, watched you, made sure you were all right.'

'You bought me those flowers and the card, didn't you?'

'I wanted to talk to you, my *sister*, but I didn't know if you knew about us or if you wanted to. And then your mum turned up!'

'It was an eventful holiday.'

'That man, Peter Lyle, he used to look into your room when you were changing.'

'What?'

'I didn't intend to follow you but as we were on the same mission, sometimes we crossed over... remember that crazy wedding? The speech when Henry was called a wombat! This is going to sound really lame but if there's anyone I could have chosen to be my sister, it'd be you.'

We turn our backs to the Thames and walk in silence up to Sloane Square Underground station. At the gates, before going through the barrier, I say goodbye to Tom.

'Stella, look, I shan't say "let's get together soon" or anything like that – I know you probably have a lot of mixed feelings about us. We're a pretty shabby bunch. My brother and I, we're in a lot of turmoil and Mummy's totally bats... but we'd like to get to know you... *if* ever, *when*ever, *how*ever you'd like to. I don't know how one usually does these things, but...?' He stops trying to find the words for feelings so complex to express. 'Bye, Stella.' He wraps his arms around me. We stay like that for a long time, connected, warm: brother and sister.

107

'Don't Elvis and Cha-Cha make a beautiful page and bridesmaid?' asks my mother, adjusting the lace on their collars.

'They're like Romeo and Juliet...' says Simon, tears in his eyes.

'Apart from the double suicide fiasco, right?' asks Mum with a wink. 'Sure there aren't too many flowers?'

'No such thing as too many flowers or too much love, darling,' says Florian, feeding another canna lily into my bouquet.

'Stella, the car's waiting!' Kira calls up the stairs. 'Joseph wants to know what you're doing.'

'Tell him I'm on the phone to the Samaritans.'

Mum slaps my hand. 'Listen, Ferdi's got something to tell you.'

Ferdi hands me my bride's bouquet. 'The library at the Paradise Beach Club is, from today, going to be known as the Wests' Library!' He smiles his Ferdi smile. 'Isn't that wonderful news?'

'Fabulous!'

'And they want you and Joseph to stay there sometime next year to inaugurate it. They'll pay all your costs.'

'We'd love to, Ferdi.'

'And you look like a princess. Princess in a *good* way.'

'Thank you and you look pretty snazzy too, Ferdi.'

Simon raises his arms at me. 'Don't keep us waiting too long or Cha-Cha will need another piss.'

Ferdi gives my mum a long kiss on the lips and whispers, 'See you at the church.' He winks at me. 'Good luck, Miss Stella!'

The two of them take a run up Mrs West's landing and slide until they reach the stairs. Mum looks back at me. 'You wouldn't think I'm nearly fifty, would you?' She waves Ferdi off and returns to me.

Simon and Ferdi canter down the central stairs with Florian to join the rest in the courtyard where the cars are leaving.

'This is it!' says my mother. 'Hurry up, Stella, before he changes his mind!'

'Thanks,' I say, flicking the powder puff in her direction. We look out of the window to see the cars leaving for the church.

'Darling,' her eyes well up, 'I'm so proud of you! Today you're laying down the foundations of a new life together, a *family*!' She stops a tear rolling down her cheek. 'I mustn't cry and ruin my winged eyeliner, but pink champagne makes one so emotional. Where's Ferdi?' she asks, looking out of the window for him. 'Oh there he is.' She watches him getting into a waiting Mercedes. 'Isn't he handsome? Do you think I'm a cradle snatcher?'

'You make each other very happy, so why not?'

'But... nearly fifty.'

'You keep saying!'

My phone beeps. A text from Kamilla saying that everyone's in the church and *Stella, there's a woman here with a rabbit? Is that okay?* I reassure her Happy is very welcome. Just as I finish, I'm interrupted by the sound of footsteps on the stairs outside. We look at each other as we hear a light tap at the door.

'Yes?'

Two young men stand at the entrance. They look at me, then at Florence.

'Come in. Tom, Barnaby.' I kiss each one, being careful not to crumple my dress. 'This is my mother.' The three of them look at each other not knowing what to say. Tom breaks the awkwardness, shakes Mum's hand. I notice that he's holding an A4 white envelope.

'Sorry to interrupt, we wanted to give you this before you got married. It's from all of us.'

Barnaby brings out a jewellery box from his pocket and opens it. Inside is a diamond necklace with a ruby at its centre.

'Oh my word!' says Mum.

'It's beautiful! Tom, Barnaby…'

Barnaby helps me put on the necklace. 'My mother wanted you to have it. It belonged to Granny Hardwick. We felt it was right to give it to you today.'

Tom holds out the white envelope.

'Something else. It might be important… for the registrar.' I put my hand out to take it but Tom hands it to Mum. 'It's for *you* really.'

Mum stares at the boys, taking in everything about them. She draws the envelope from Tom's fingers.

'We better get going,' says Tom, backing up to the door. 'You look ravishing – and you too, Stella!'

Mum blushes at them before looking uncertainly at the envelope.

I give a last wave, turn to Mum. I can tell that she likes them, and it's not because of them, it's because of her: she's changed. When they close the door, Mum says, 'Henry was just like that, at that age.' She wipes away a tear.

'They really want to make things right by us.'

'I can see that – those diamonds are real. It's a good start!' she says, touching the necklace.

'An heirloom, eh?' I hold the envelope out to her. 'Open it.'

Her hands are shaking. She tears the top of the envelope and pulls out a type-written piece of paper.

The waiting car downstairs beeps twice in a chirpy get-a-move-on way.

'It's my birth certificate.' Not that I needed to tell her. Florence holds it in her hands and reads the words, 'Father: Henry

Hardwick. No more "unknown".' She shrugs her shoulders and puts the document back in the envelope.

'Are you happy now? Caroline and Henry's lawyer, Bradshaw, they got it changed. It's official.'

'Look at the time!' she says, adjusting her neckline. 'Time to leave now. Got everything?' Mum steps into her shoes, avoiding eye contact.

'Aren't you happy?'

'Of course I'm happy, it's your big day!'

'No, about this.' I hold up the certificate. 'Remember, from the first time I ever saw my birth certificate with "Father: Unknown" on it, it'd been my ambition to change that. And here it is. Look!'

'I've seen it, love. It's just a bit of paper,' she says, fanning her face with the envelope. 'Why would that make me happy?'

'You always said it was *all* you *ever* wanted – for him to be named on the birth certificate. Aren't you pleased?'

'I didn't want it for *me*, it was for *you*.'

108

Mum takes out a gardenia from a vase of flowers on my dressing table and settles it behind my ear.

'Stella, darling. Don't look disappointed. What makes me happy is that you've grown up into a kind, intelligent and very wise young woman despite everything.' She looks back at the flower in my hair. 'I thought I wanted Henry, but I didn't really know him at all. And Henry, bless his soul, he didn't know himself any better either, all testosterone, fear and pride – and I wasted so many years waiting for him.' She smooths out the pleats in my dress. 'Oh, I nearly forgot. Joseph wanted me to give you this.' She goes into her handbag and takes out a package.

The compass I bought Joseph in Camden Market falls out. There is a little note attached from Joseph:

> *My sparkling light, I got this fixed. It's no longer stuck. You can now go in any direction you want, but I hope you always travel West. Very nearly your husband, Joe xxx*

The gardenia my mother gave me is so cool, gentle against my cheek compared with the weight of the diamonds around my neck. Mum talks fast on her mobile to the vicar about an escaped rabbit in the church. She's also left to defend a dog who's lifted his leg against the pulpit. Kira comes up the stairs to help carry the train of my dress. This isn't really a beginning, just another point of the circle, but a good place to end the story which started a year ago, sitting on the Underground, on my way to work, seconds away from believing everything was over, when it had only just begun. Stop now: this is the point when everything is right.

THE END

ALSO BY RUBY SOAMES

<u>Seven Days to Tell You</u>

~ A gripping and unpredictable psychological suspense full of twists

ACKNOWLEDGEMENTS

After Deborah Paxford read the first draft of this novel, she said it felt like 'a holiday' which is exactly what I wanted my readers to experience. I am always so grateful for her constant encouragement and support. Thanks also to Claire McAlpine for her incisive comments and Robert Marcus for his expertise in grammar, syntax and language. I'm also indebted to Pamela Screve, Harriet Macaree and Suzanne Stannard for their intelligent and honest comments of this book. And, of course, special thanks to Jon Bryant for slaying the clichés and axing the adjectives, cups of tea, two great kids and for putting up with me all these years.

This second edition is all thanks to Betsy Reavley and the fantastic team at Bloodhound Books, especially Associate Editor Abbie Rutherford for her creative and painstaking work and Tara Lyons, Editorial and Production Manager.

ABOUT THE AUTHOR

Ruby Soames was born in London and studied literature and theology at Bristol University before doing an MA in Creative Writing at Manchester Metropolitan University and an MSc in Psychology at the University of Liverpool. She now teaches in France with her two children and travel-writer husband. Her first novel, *Seven Days to Tell You*, was published as a result of the Hookline Novel Competition but has been re-published this year by Bloodhound Books. She has written three novels, published short stories and a selection of newspaper articles.

For more information about the author, visit: www.rubysoames.com

A NOTE FROM THE PUBLISHER

Thank you for reading this book. If you enjoyed it please do consider leaving a review on Amazon to help others find it too.

We hate typos. All of our books have been rigorously edited and proofread, but sometimes mistakes do slip through. If you have spotted a typo, please do let us know and we can get it amended within hours.

info@bloodhoundbooks.com

Milton Keynes UK
Ingram Content Group UK Ltd.
UKHW021321030424
440552UK00012B/76

9 781916 978645